VALENTINA SALAZAR
is NOT a monster hunter

Also by Zoraida Córdova

Middle Grade
The Way to Rio Luna

Young Adult
The Vicious Deep trilogy
The Vicious Deep
The Savage Blue
The Vast and Brutal Sea

The Brooklyn Brujas series
Labyrinth Lost
Bruja Born
Wayward Witch

The Hollow Crown dulogy
Incendiary
Illusionary

Star Wars: Galaxy's Edge: A Crash of Fate

Adult
The Inheritance of Orquídea Divina

VALENTINA SALAZAR

is NOT a monster hunter

ZORAIDA CÓRDOVA

Scholastic Press
New York

Library of Congress Cataloging-in-Publication Data available

ISBN 978-1-338-71271-1

10 9 8 7 6 5 4 3 2 1   22 23 24 25 26

Printed in the U.S.A.   37
First edition, June 2022

Book design by Keirsten Geise

For Dhonielle Clayton, who believed in this story first

The Real, True, Honest-to-Goodness Confession of Valentina Alexander Salazar, Junior Monster Protector

This is the real, true, honest-to-goodness confession of Valentina Alexander Salazar and the worst summer ever.

Confession #1: Monsters are real. I'm probably not supposed to tell you that, but in order for me to explain the rest of my story, I have to make that clear. I repeat: Monsters are real.

Ever gone camping and felt like someone was watching you? Ever catch sight of a strange creature out the corner of your eye? Ever walked down a street and seen something dash into the sewers? Chupacabras, Bigfoot, the Jersey Devil, the Loch Ness monster—I'm sure you've heard of the most famous ones, but there are so many more creatures that you didn't know were out there.

Now, I know some people might think that such beings *couldn't* possibly exist. But they do. I've seen them. Deep down, I bet you believe me, unlike most grown-ups. Like my daddy always said, "Just because it's in your imagination doesn't mean it's any less real."

That brings me to confession #2: My family and I are monster protectors.

Or we used to be. You see, there was a big accident a few months back and we had to stop. But before the accident, we drove all over the country searching for magical beings to save. If you're wondering why these creatures need saving, then you, my friend, are asking the right questions. After all, aren't monsters just fangs and claws and nightmares? Some of them are, and I'm not going to lie—this job isn't for the faint of heart. You've got to understand, not all monsters are, well, *monstrous*. Some creatures look scary, but they're just misunderstood or scared or lost. That's where we come in. We find them and we help get them back home.

Don't ever confuse us with the no-good, smelly, jerkface monster hunters. No way. You see, the Salazars (that's my family) come from a long line of monster hunters. For hundreds of years, they roamed the planet and tracked down creatures who slipped into our world. *Killed* them. *Blip! Slash! Splat!* Even if a monster wasn't hurting anyone and took a wrong turn into our sorry earthly realm, the hunters had one rule: Slay the beasts.

My dad was different. He wanted to help, and so, he broke off from his family tree and became the first ever Salazar to save creatures instead of hurt them.

Then he met my mom, and she joined the family business. Then came my eldest sister, Andromeda, then Lola, then Rome, and they saved the best for last—me.

I shouldn't be telling you this, but I need to clear my name after everything that's happened. Anyway, like I said, there was an accident involving my dad and just like that—*snap*—he was gone.

And finally, I present confession #3: This is the worst summer of my whole eleven-and-a-half-year-old life. Things started to go downhill when I tried to steal the van.

Wait, no. Things *really* went downhill when I was blamed for starting the fire.

Hold on. That's not right either.

I should back up some more, so you really see *my* side of the story.

So here it goes. Let me tell you what happened.

The Salazars of Missing Mountain, New York

My peculiar life can be divided into two sections: the Before and the After.

In the Before Times, my dad was alive, and we lived on the road. We were homeschooled. Mom taught us math with an old abacus made of turquoise beads, and Dad taught us astronomy by staring at the stars while cowboy camping (that's when you sleep outside without a tent around a firepit in just a sleeping bag). Mom taught us Spanish since it was her first language. Even Dad sat in on those lessons because he said he had many talents except the ability to roll his *R*s. Dad would teach us book stuff and the history of the places we drove through even though we never stayed in one place very long.

In the Before Times, our home was the Scourge—a

1965 Ford Falcon camper van that still looked brand-new because of how often we polished the surf-green exterior. We'd accumulated a hundred stickers that almost completely covered the back bumper. Dad drove and Mom navigated. Andie and Lola kept the gear trunk organized. Rome and I researched the creatures we tracked.

In the Before Times, we'd have long stretches when there were no cases, no beasties to find or weird occurrences to investigate. That's when we'd stay in towns for a few weeks and buy real groceries and Dad would teach us to play acoustic guitar and Lola would play fútbol and I'd watch all the movies we could rent.

The Before Times were the best times.

After Dad—after the accident, things changed. There was a funeral that felt pretty hazy. Sometimes a bad thing happens and in the moment, you feel terrible, but then when you try to remember it, you can't. You forget details.

All I remembered was that we packed into the Scourge, Mom got behind the wheel, and she drove. She didn't stop until we were in a quiet little town called Missing Mountain in upstate New York. Mom parked in front of the oldest, most haunted-looking house at the dead end of a street and said, "We're home!"

Being without Dad changed us.

In the After Times, there were no more guitar lessons or cowboy camping. There was no more highway karaoke or research or finding cases. There was a lot of crying and sadness. We stopped tracking and helping lost monsters. The great Salazar protectors became a bunch of NOBODIES.

In the After Times, Mom put all our tools, Dad's journals, and her favorite blue leather jacket in the garage. And the Scourge? Our beautiful, trusty camper van began to collect rust and dust in the garage. It was *criminal*. Mom even secured one of those boots on the front wheel of the van, the kind cars get when they're towed.

In the After Times, there were no more Salazars on the road protecting wild monsters. Instead, we were landlocked *and* had to go to school for the first time ever instead of being homeschooled. My mom joined the PTA! Lola and Rome were too busy to have family dinners, and when we did, they were filled with the kind of silence that sounds like radio static.

Safe to say, I wished I could go back to the Before Times.

✦✦

The first day of the Worst Summer Ever started off pretty much like every other miserable day in Missing Mountain.

I woke up to the creaking of floorboards. Oh, the house isn't actually haunted or anything. Sure, the lights always flicker and there's an attic full of bats, smelly old trunks, and cobwebs. But still, no ghosts (I've checked). However, there *were* cookie crumbs on the pillow beside me, and they were *not* mine. Honest.

I cleaned up the dusting of cookies, stepped into my fuzzy slippers and bathrobe, and made my way down to the kitchen, where I found the source of all the noise. Lola was already ready for school and cooking breakfast. I checked the trusty grandfather clock in the living room and there were still forty minutes left before we had to leave for school. In the Before Times, Lola was always the most organized, making sure the Scourge was tidy and our gear never failed in the field. But in the After Times, Lola invented a whole new level of organized. She joined the literary society, the baking club, and the cheerleading squad, *and* still managed to have the best grade-point average in her whole entire grade.

There she was, frying eggs and bacon in her KEEP CALM AND BAKE ON apron. Her green-and-white cheerleading uniform was ironed, and her long black hair was plaited in two long French braids.

"You know it's the last day of school, right?" I asked,

opening the fridge and taking out the milk jug. "You can wear regular clothes since there's nothing to cheer about."

Lola handed me my favorite unicorn-shaped coffee mug. Its horn was chipped, but that just gave it character. During our travels, I'd always wanted to meet a unicorn, but out of all the magical beasts we'd returned to the realm of Finisterra, we never came across one of those.

"Did you know," Lola said, folding her arms over her chest, "that you've woken up on the wrong side of the bed for two hundred and forty days and counting?"

Why did people say that? "Waking up on the wrong side of the bed." As if there was a *correct* side of the bed to wake up on. I let loose a long sigh and filled my mug with milk, then two tablespoons of chunky brown sugar, and added a little bit of coffee. My dad used to say that he had café con leche like this straight out of the bottle when he was a baby. It made Mom roll her eyes.

"And for your information, I'm cheering *for* the last day of school," Lola said as she flipped my eggs in the pan, then caught the two slices of toast that shot out from the glitchy toaster.

Everything in the house was a hand-me-down from

our great-aunt, who hadn't changed a single thing since a hundred years ago—or whenever 1959 was.

My sister set my breakfast in front of me and kissed the top of my head. That "wrong side of the bed" feeling completely went away as I salivated over my food. Lola was good at lots of things—school, martial arts, spotting the difference between a chupacabra and a chupavaca, fixing the wiry guts of car engines—but she was *excellent* at making breakfast. She put all her heart into it so we'd be fueled up for the day.

"Fine," I mumbled. I didn't want to upset her before I asked my big favor.

Rome walked into the kitchen and grunted a "good morning." Rome's thirteen, and lately that's how he communicates. He walks around with these big headphones he got at the thrift store. They make him look like a DJ. His horrible heavy-metal music screeches from them. Mom warned him he's going to damage his eardrums, but when she's not around, he cranks up the volume.

Lola didn't tell *him* that he woke up on the wrong side of the bed, but I just sprinkled salt on my eggs and dove in. I needed them in the best possible mood.

Rome swiped his favorite mug, one that had a picture of the Galactic Knight (our favorite movie villain) on it, and filled it to the brim with black coffee. I wrinkled my nose as he sat. How could he drink it without any sugar?

Lola slid his plate in front of him and he muttered, "Thanks."

Rome assembled his breakfast into a bacon, egg, and cheese sandwich and ate it in three bites. He scrolled on his phone, real serious like. His dark brows were smooshed together and created a little crease between them like Dad used to have. Except Rome's smoothed out. Dad's was permanent.

While Lola resumed making breakfast with one hand and reading a book in the other, I decided to go for it.

"I was thinking," I said. "Since it's the last day of school . . . can we go to the lake?"

Rome glanced from me to Lola. She made a "hmm" sound, which was interrupted by a closet door opening and shutting. You could hear a mouse creeping in the house, that's how thin the walls were. Every day was the same, though, and I knew what would come next. The shower curtains parting. The water running through the pipes of the old house. I pointed toward the front door just as the bell rang. We didn't get up to answer because it was just Ms. McCall, Mom's friend from work, letting us know she was waiting outside and Mom was about to be late. Again.

"Well?" I repeated, waving my strip of bacon in front of Rome's face. "Can we? Pretty please?"

Rome leaned over and snatched the crispy morsel between his teeth.

"Hey!" I stared at my empty fist where my beautiful, last piece of bacon had been.

Rome chuckled, probably for the first time that week, maybe month. It was kind of a relief. In the Before Times, Rome was always laughing and joking around with Dad. He liked to collect facts about the towns we were in, and he was helping me choose my very first journal, like the kind Dad used to write down everything he discovered. I'm a *junior* monster protector, and that would have been my first step in becoming a full-fledged, bona fide Salazar protector. But then all the bad things happened and we ended up in Missing Mountain and I never got to complete my training.

Lola laughed and said, "You know better than to put bacon in front of a Salazar, Tiny."

"I told you not to call me Tiny anymore," I grumbled.

"Why do you want to go by the lake?" Rome asked. His hazel eyes narrowed with suspicion.

I drank a big sip of my café con leche. "Uh, I don't know. Maybe because it's the last day of school and there's nothing else to do in this place? This house is dark and we need exercise and the sunny vitamin—"

"Vitamin D?" Lola corrected me.

"Exactly."

Rome and Lola exchanged a *look*. The kind of look older siblings give each other when they think the younger sibling is being unreasonable. From up above we heard the squeak of the water turning off and Mom's wet footsteps rushing into her room. The doorbell rang again, this time twice, and the sound of Mom's blow-dryer went off.

Lola walked across the kitchen, her slippered feet slapping against the ugly orange linoleum floors. My heart raced as she opened the top cabinet above the refrigerator. She'd found my hiding spot, which was partially filled with tea sets. It should have been the perfect hiding spot because Salazars don't drink tea.

"Wait—" I started to say.

Lola's manicured fingers wrapped around a newspaper tucked behind delicate porcelain teacups. She dropped last week's issue of the *Missing Mountain Gazette* in front of me, the headline circled with my yellow highlighter. It read: HONEY HILL LAKE MONSTER SIGHTED BY DAY HIKERS. The margins were covered with notes in my messy handwriting. *Connected to the Lake Champlain monster? Could have swum from Lake George. Get Lola and Rome to take me to the lake.*

"It's not what it looks like," I said defensively.

Lola caught another blast from the toaster, arching over like a killer ballerina. She arranged the toast on a plate for Mom, then cracked two more eggs so hard she broke the yolks. "*Pro tip*, Tiny—"

"Don't call me Tiny," I hissed.

Lola continued, "If you're going to try to trick us into taking you to the lake, don't write out your master plan."

"I never said tricked. I said *get*."

Rome took off his headphones, so I knew it was serious. He practically slept with those things on. They were like his own private helmet shielding him against the world. Even against us.

"When you leave out your true intention, it's still a trick," he said. "It's a lie by omission. Don't lie to us, Val."

I picked at the chipped unicorn horn on my mug. "How am I supposed to get you to spend time with me if the truth doesn't work?"

"We spend time together," Lola said.

"No, we don't." I bit the inside of my bottom lip. Why was telling them how I felt so difficult? "I've counted. We've gone to the park twice. Once to watch you run a marathon and once because I got detention to volunteer at the Missing Mountain pet adoption day."

Rome picked his headphones back up, the screeching banshee shredding the silence between us. He didn't put them back on but made a sound of frustration. "We're together every day."

I rolled my eyes. "Breakfast doesn't count."

Lola sucked in a breath, like I'd kicked her in the shin. She glanced at our plates and then the pans that popped with bacon and eggs. "Then I guess you'll all be eating cereal for the rest of the summer."

I winced and wished I could take it back. Lola did work hard to feed us every morning. "I'm sorry. I didn't mean that. I'm just—" My breakfast roiled in my stomach. But I knew I had to be brave and tell them how I felt. It was the only way to make them understand. "Ever since Dad—you know—you're all different. Lola's always too *busy* to be home except in the morning, and Rome's always in his bat cave. Andie left us. Mom's always at work, and when she does come home early, she's too tired to do anything but take a bath and go to sleep. I just thought that maybe if we had a case, like in the Before Times, things could go back to normal."

They blinked. It's like I hadn't said anything at all because the door rang again. Lola turned back to whisk the eggs, added more grounds and water to the coffee maker, and shoved two new slices of toast into the angry toaster. Rome drained his mug but stared at the wall. The door rang again, a few times in a row, and Lola shouted, "Mom! Ms. McCall is waiting!"

"I'll be right out!" Mom hollered.

"Forget it." I shoved my way out of my seat.

"Val," Lola said. She sighed, and her shoulders were bunched up like she was holding a really heavy backpack. She dropped the latest issue of the *Missing Mountain Gazette* on top of the old one. She'd already done today's crossword puzzle. Was she showing me that she had more time to do the crossword than for me? I scanned the rest of the page, then saw it. Next to that was a tiny article, easy to miss. HONEY HILL LAKE MONSTER DEBUNKED. "The hikers fell for the senior prank."

"Oh." I don't know why, but I felt my eyes burn. I blinked super fast as I took my plate to the sink and washed it clean.

"I know you wanted this monster to be real," Lola said softly. "But even if it was, it's not an excuse to trick us. Besides, that's not our problem anymore. You can't keep doing this. You can't keep looking for monsters when there aren't any."

I looked to Rome for some support, but his face was scrunched up with that little frown between his brows. All he said was "We promised when we moved here that we were done with that—*stuff.*"

How could Rome call our life's work *stuff*? Like it was the tricycle we all outgrew or the camping gear we hadn't touched for eight months.

"*I* didn't." My voice felt small and tight.

At that moment the front door opened and Ms. McCall's tense voice called out, "Hello?"

Rome put his headphones back on, and Lola poured Mom's coffee into a silver travel mug, then filled a second one, which she offered to Ms. McCall. After several months of the same routine, Lola had timed it down to the moment when Ms. McCall stepped into the kitchen. She thanked my sister and took a quick sip.

"Sorry for barging in," Mom's friend said, as usual. Her green eyes darted around the kitchen like she was waiting for a zombie to appear or something. She always looked nervous coming here, and I wondered if she was secretly hoping to find out if the rumors about the Salazars being "witches" and "occult chicken worshippers" were true. She took a sip of the coffee and sighed like she was getting a video game power boost.

Lola turned on the sweet smile she reserved for teachers and adults. "Mom's getting ready."

"Good stuff," Ms. McCall said, and I could swear her eye twitched. "Another ten minutes and we're going to be late."

Ms. McCall worked with Mom at some fashion magazine in Manhattan. Her silky black clothes looked out of place in our kitchen, with the terrariums hanging from the windows, orange wallpaper, and pictures of Great-Aunt Hercilia's cats, which were buried in the backyard pet cemetery. I caught Rome staring at her, and his cheeks turned pink. He got up and offered her his seat, then quickly washed his dish.

"Thanks, sweetheart," she said, and rested her purse on her lap. "I used to wear that same uniform, Lola. Go Grizzlies!"

Lola repeated the chant and finally sat down to eat. She glanced at her watch, then nervously eyed the kitchen entrance. Mom was always running late, but that day she seemed unusually flustered. "It's so funny that they'd choose a grizzly as the mascot. There aren't even grizzlies in the neighborhood."

"Funny isn't the word I'd use," I muttered. "This place is called Missing Mountain and there isn't even a mountain. Like, how does a mountain go missing?"

"That's part of the charm, dear."

"What charm?" Everyone who lived in Missing

Mountain called it charming, but what was I missing? Lola glared at me. I knew we weren't supposed to be rude in front of guests, so I kept quiet.

Ms. McCall grinned but ignored me and pointed to Lola's wrist. "What a beautiful piece. Is it vintage?"

Lola chuckled nervously. The watch was more than vintage and it did more than tell the time, not that we could tell Ms. McCall that. "Sort of. It's a family heirloom."

"Like Valentina's signet ring," Ms. McCall said.

I snatched my hand away before she could try to inspect the family ring on my middle finger.

"Exactly," Lola said.

I wanted to tell Lola that *she* was lying by omission to Ms. McCall's face, and how was that any different from me trying to get them to take me to the lake? I get it. Fine, I shouldn't have tried to trick them, but it was my last resort. And anyway, I wasn't going to do any monster-related tracking or research, honest. We could rent a canoe and while we were there I could investigate the claim. That was all. Mom always said that multitasking was a skill.

Speaking of Mom, Ms. McCall was drumming her fingers anxiously on the table and checking her phone when Mom darted into the hall. Even all those months later, I still wasn't used to seeing her in business work clothes. She wore a navy-blue pantsuit, delicate pearl earrings, and a tiny ruby on a thin gold chain. That necklace was the only thing about the Before Times that was the same. Dad had given it to her, and she never took it off. Her black hair was swept into a low bun, and two wavy strands framed her face. She didn't wear any makeup, except for mascara, which made her long lashes look like spider legs. Her honey brown skin was smooth, but I noticed the dark circles under her eyes, like she hadn't slept at all. Again.

I missed what I thought of as the Before Times Mom, with her blue leather jacket and vintage shirts. The mom who could recite poems from memory and break down a campsite in less than five minutes. My mind couldn't make the Before and After fit.

"Lauren!" Mom said, hurrying into the kitchen. She kissed Rome on his forehead, and he rolled his eyes. Then Lola, then me, and finally she squeezed Ms. McCall into a hug. "I'm so sorry I'm late. It's been a *day*."

I wanted to point out that she'd been giving the same excuse for eight months' worth of days, but I decided to be good.

Ms. McCall wasted no time in hurrying them out the door. Mom called out a final "Be good! See you at dinner!"

In the Before Times, Mom did work, but she was an "environmental law consultant" and she did it over the phone and in her pajamas. In the After Times, she wore fancy suits and made sure her magazine didn't get sued.

I guess everyone in my family was different now, even my sister Andromeda. You might have noticed that she wasn't in the house. You see, a few months ago, Andie ran away to go live with our uncle and the hunters. Mom kept saying that Andie needed time. But it had been eight months since Dad's funeral, and she hadn't come back. Things weren't how they used to be, but they also weren't getting any better, in my opinion, even though no one seemed to ask for my opinion.

Lola handed her dish to Rome and he washed it. That was the rule. Whoever cooked didn't have to clean up. My sister turned to me and raised her brow. I was still sipping on my coffee and pouting as I reread the *Gazette* article about the prank.

"What?" I slathered honey and jam on a piece of toast.

"You just ate," Lola said. "And you have ten minutes to get ready or you're walking to school with your nemesis."

"Fine. I'll be ready in *two* seconds," I assured her.

"But what about the lake? If the monster is a hoax, then you won't have to worry about me looking for a mission."

"I don't know, Val—"

"*Please.* Pretty please. I won't bother you for the rest of the summer. You can go back to whatever you do that doesn't include me."

"That's not—" Lola started, but she stopped and stared at Rome and me. For a split second, her eyes filled with sadness, but she tried to play it off. What did Lola have to be sad about? Her life in Missing Mountain was perfect. Then she finally relented and said, "*If* we make it to school on time, we'll go to the lake after."

I raised fists of victory in the air. "Yes!"

Rome held up his finger, looking more like Mom than he ever had before. "Just for canoeing."

"And corn dogs and sundaes," I added. "All that canoeing works up an appetite."

Lola sighed and held out her hand for me to shake. "Deal."

I ran upstairs, taking the steps three at a time. I left the slice of honey toast on my dresser, then hurried to our shared bathroom. I put on a shower cap and took a fast shower, then brushed my teeth. I used Lola's lotion, the kind that smelled like peaches and flowers, even though she wrote DO NOT TOUCH on it with black marker. It's not my fault that it smelled so good. Plus, I was kind of mad at her for discovering my original plan.

When I returned to my room, the toast was gone. Only crumbs were left behind.

But I wasn't worried about that. I was too excited that we were going to the lake after school. I yanked on my favorite T-shirt. It was from a gift shop in Missoula, Montana, and it said I BELIEVE in neon-green letters and had spaceships and moons and stars and rainbows on it. I hopped into my jeans, smelled the socks on the ground, and found two mismatched ones that didn't stink.

"We're heading out the door!" Lola shouted, then sneezed loudly. "Ticktock!"

I snatched my backpack from my bed and slid down the banister. I landed in front of the shoe rack and tugged on my sneakers.

"Burp!" said a little high-pitched voice. It wasn't Lola or Rome and it definitely wasn't me, honest.

"*Excuse* you." Lola laughed, pulling on her backpack.

"Sorry." I chuckled, taking the blame.

We filed out the door. Lola locked up, and I let go of the breath caught in my chest. I leapt down the porch steps and landed in the tall, unkept grass in front of our house. I could feel something—someone—moving in my backpack.

Lola might have found out one of my secrets by uncovering my hiding spot, but I had another one. A secret my family couldn't find out about. *Ever.* A secret that broke one of the first rules of the Salazar handbook.

You know how I said that my family protects monsters? Well, that's mostly true. We find them, save them, and help them get back to their realm—Finisterra.

Confession #4: I kept one.

3

Valentina Salazar Breaks All the Rules

I should have known things were going to go down-hill from there when the first people I saw on the way to school were Maritza Vega and her friends. They were dressed in brand-new matching purple outfits. When she saw me, Maritza trained her stare on my messy hair, then my sneakers, and rolled her blue eyes.

Here's the thing about Maritza. She likes to talk about people really loudly, to make sure everyone hears the mean things she says. I didn't really see the point. Why not just say something to someone's face?

"Surprise, surprise," Maritza said. "Another bargain bin cartoon T-shirt."

"How is she even related to Lola, who's, like, the coolest human ever?" Harmony asked.

"And Rome," Sunny said, and made a little sighing

noise, like a balloon that let out all its air at once. "He's *so* dreamy."

I did what Mom told me to do. *Be the bigger person. Ignore them!* I tugged on the straps of my backpack and felt movement within—and a tiny little growl.

"Let me at 'em!" said the high-pitched voice coming from my backpack.

"Shhh," I hissed, and walked faster. But not as fast as Lola and Rome, who were vanishing down the street.

I tried to catch up with them, but they had longer legs and didn't even wait for me. *Typical.* Besides, when we turned the corner, Lola's cheerleading squad absorbed her into their hive, and Rome blended in with the other angry kids sporting big headphones dressed in all black. It gave Maritza and her friends time to catch up to me right at the steps to the school. It was even too late for me to blend into the groups of Missing Mountain kids trying to make the first bell.

"Who is she always whispering to?" Harmony Holiday asked.

"Didn't you know?" Sunny Ramnarine said. "Ghosts are *real.*"

"I believe." Maritza made her voice all funny, and when I turned around to look at her, she was holding her index fingers on top of her head like antennas.

In the Before Times, I never had to deal with bullies at school because we didn't have to go to real school. Since ignoring them wasn't working, I turned around and confronted them, just like Rome said. Although Rome used different words that forced him to add his entire allowance to the swear jar.

"I do believe," I told them.

If Lola and Rome had waited for me, this never would have happened. Though, if they were with me, they wouldn't approve of me talking about monsters to regular kids. Another rule of being a Salazar protector was secrecy. But these girls already thought I was weird. I figured I'd just lean into my best quality.

The trio of girls stopped. They glanced around, but the kids just parted around us and went inside the building. I hopped up on the bottom step and leaned against the railing.

"If you knew everything I do, you wouldn't get out of bed. You'd go to sleep every night with a flashlight under your pillow because there are monsters out there, real ones that are waiting to bite your toes and fingers off. There are creatures that used to be part of another world, but they're stuck here and can't get home. They hide in forests and in lakes. They can see you when you're not looking. Some of them are sweet and friendly. Others . . . well, consider yourself lucky that you don't believe."

For a moment I saw a flash of fear in their eyes. But then I realized they weren't looking at me. They were looking past me. Slowly, I glanced over my shoulder to find Principal Connolly. Before him, I'd never had a principal, so I don't know what they're like at other schools. But Principal Connolly always looked like he'd just watched a pigeon fly into his office and poop in his sugar-free Cream of Wheat. He had thinning curly hair the color of dead grass. His eyes were always scrunched up, like the sun was in his face. I don't think I'd ever seen him without his arms crossed over his chest. You know what I mean. When grown-ups get real mad and they cross their arms and tap one of their feet to let you know you're about to get in trouble. That's what Principal Connolly was doing.

"Good morning, Principal Connolly," Maritza and her friends said in voices as sweet as pancake syrup.

Principal Connolly's face softened just a tiny bit. "Good morning, girls. Shouldn't you be in homeroom?"

They snickered as they ran up the steps. I started to follow them, but the principal shuffled sideways like a crab and blocked my path. His nostrils flared, and because he was standing so high above me, I could see all the hairs and boogers in there. I felt a movement in my backpack and reached back and tapped it.

"*You,*" Principal Connolly said, like he was the big bad wolf trying to blow a house down.

"Me," I said. "Uhh—good morning. I was just heading to class."

He took a deep breath. I could smell the chive cream cheese he'd had for breakfast as he exhaled. I didn't move. I'd seen monsters in the wild and I knew not to provoke them.

"*Miss* Salazar, what did we say about bothering the other students with your overactive imagination?"

My mouth went all dry and nerves made my fingers restless. I shrugged. "Not to do it?"

"That is correct." Principal Connolly pinched the bridge of his nose.

Jeez. All I did was write one little essay for world history about how unicorns must have existed in Scotland since they're the literal national animal, and then when Ms. Younger made me read it out loud, everyone started saying that I still had imaginary friends and believed in aliens and stuff. I mean, they weren't far from the truth, but I wasn't going to correct them and expose our secret life as monster protectors. *Ex*–monster protectors.

"I've tried to be patient, Miss Salazar," he continued.

For someone who really wanted me to get to class, Principal Connolly sure liked to talk at me a lot. "Your brother and sister are exemplary, well-behaved students. They've been through the same—ordeal— as you and they've excelled in their short time at Missing Mountain School."

I wanted to tell him that I wasn't Rome and I wasn't Lola. I was Valentina Salazar, the one and only. But I'd already been to his office too many times in the eight months we'd been in town. The one thing that sucked about being homeschooled practically my whole life was that when we enrolled in the Missing Mountain school system, there were too many rules and I couldn't always keep track of them.

"I'm sorry, Principal Connolly." I didn't bother to tell him that Maritza, Harmony, and Sunny were making fun of my clothes for almost seven blocks. Who was he going to believe? The three girls in matching new clothes who always smiled and followed the rules, or little ol' me?

"It's the last day of classes, Miss Salazar," he reminded me, as if I wasn't already counting down the hours. "Let's get through the day in one piece, shall we?"

I nodded quickly and hurried inside. My first few months at school I kept getting lost. Even though

Missing Mountain was a small town, the school encompassed grades K through twelve in one big building. It didn't help that every hallway was full of the same beige doors and rusted green lockers. I raced through the corridors, which I was pretty sure was against the "no running" rule. Thankfully, the monitors were too busy looking at their phones to notice me sliding from one hall to the next.

With my heart pumping loudly in my ears, I squeaked to a stop right in front of the door. I was about to step inside when the bell rang.

"Valentina Salazar, you're late," Mrs. De Bernardo said. Her dress was the color of the cold salmon Lola liked to eat on a bagel. She wore a black hat with a net that half covered her eyes and matched her lipstick color.

"Principal—"

But she wouldn't let me finish. She made a "harrumph" sound and let me pass. Everyone was already at their desks. I didn't try to explain to her that it wasn't my fault. I'd broken rule #1 (*students must be in their seats in time for the morning announcements and after lunch and recess break*) lots of times. What was one more?

I made my way to my desk in the back of the room against the windows. I unzipped my backpack and a tiny purple hand with sharp black claws poked out. I pulled the backpack shut and slammed my palms on the desk. The noise was so loud that everyone turned to look at me.

"Notebooks out," Mrs. De Bernardo said, sounding like one of those mechanical dolls with low batteries. "Today is a free-writing period. Pass forward last night's assignment."

"Uh-oh," I whispered. I had my journal, which was rule #2 (*students must always be prepared with appropriate supplies and completed homework*). But I didn't have the second part. Last night I'd been too excited to sleep. I kept thinking about the Honey Hill Lake monster. A fat load of good that did me.

All around me, there was a flurry of paper. I spread open my journal. The little purple hand extended my favorite pink gel pen, and I tore out a paper from the back. I hated tearing out the beautiful paper, but I couldn't end school with a bad grade. Not another one, at least.

Since I was all the way in the back of the class, I had a few moments before it was my turn to hand in "last night's" assignment. I wrote my name, Valentina Salazar. The date, June twenty-fifth. The teacher, Mrs. De Bernardo. Class, 6-203. Then I jotted down what I planned on doing for the summer. I kept it short because we didn't have any plans. We were supposed to stay in boring old Missing Mountain with nothing to do but go to the Dairy Princess and watch the grass grow.

Harmony, who sat in front of me, turned around and snatched the paper from my hands. "Nice try."

My pen dragged and left the last word unfinished. I winced as I watched my paper get handed down from Harmony to Sunny to Maritza in the front row. They held my piece of paper like it was covered in cat pee. When it reached Mrs. De Bernardo, she made a grumbling sound and muttered something that sounded like "Just a few more hours, Beatrice, and then you're on the bus to Atlantic City. Just a few more hours."

As the morning announcements came on the loudspeakers, I relaxed a little bit. I turned to the last entry in my journal and wrote *DEBUNKED*. I'd have to cut out the newspaper clipping and add it to the Honey Hill Lake monster theory. Sure, I admit, that's what I was busy doing last night instead of my homework.

In the Before Times, Mom and Dad *never* gave us homework. Now, how was I expected to go from zero homework to having to read a book AND do math AND learn all the formations of clouds in the same day?

At least the free-writing period gave me a chance to reread my other failed cases. That particular journal belonged to my dad. He ordered handmade ones with the family motto stamped on the front cover. *Protector. Valiant. Heart.* Salazars were protectors. Salazars were valiant. Salazars had heart. After Dad's accident, the journal was supposed to get locked up in the garage with all his other things. I couldn't stand the thought of it just sitting there, collecting dust, or getting eaten by whatever mice lived in Great-Aunt Hercilia's garage, so I took it. He would have wanted me to have it, I know it. That way, it was like I was always carrying a little piece of him even though he was—you know.

The family journals are filled with sketches, newspaper clippings, theories, stories. We write down everything that we know about a case. For instance, during my first week of school, I thought that there was an abelita nesting in Maritza Vega's head. Abelitas are a rare kind of bee from the other realm. Their pink fuzz can give you terrible hives. Even though they look cute and fuzzy, their sting could paralyze a person and leave them for dead. What if Maritza was deathly allergic? So, I broke rule #4 (*students must keep their hands and feet to themselves*). I tried to grab the pink ball sitting right on Maritza's head.

It turned out to be a fuzzy scrunchie.

I apologized for pulling on her hair, but she's hated me ever since and has convinced all her friends to hate me, too. I can't blame her, I suppose. I'd be mad if someone pulled my hair. It's not like I could explain myself either.

So, abelita sighting—DEBUNKED.

I turned page after page of what the school counselor called "Incidents" and I liked to call "Misunderstandings." I realized that all my Missing Mountain cases had been debunked.

Abominable snowman—DEBUNKED. *And* I got detention for breaking rule #5 (*students must be respectful of their classmates, teachers, and school property*).

The howling rat-lizard—DEBUNKED. Turned out I unscrewed a ceiling tile and let loose a colony of regular old rats. I didn't get detention for that because Mom said the school had a health code violation, so, we called it even.

None of my cases had panned out. I know. I *know* what Lola and Rome said. We're retired. Out of the game. *Not* protectors. But that's the thing. How can you be one thing one day, and then stop being it the next?

I slammed my journal shut so I wouldn't have to stare at all my failures. Big mistake, because that's when Harmony decided to turn around. Sunny and Maritza got out of their seats (which was against the rules, but Mrs. De Bernardo conveniently wasn't paying attention to *them*, was she?).

"Settle a bet for us, will you, Valentina?" Maritza said. She sat on the edge of Jerry Jacob's desk, but he was asleep and drooling on his notebook and didn't seem to mind.

"What bet?" I asked. I needed to be careful. I smelled a trap.

Sunny glanced down at her lap and bit her bottom lip. She whispered something too low for me to hear.

"I can't hear you," I said, though I think I could, and my stomach squeezed painfully because I knew it was going to be awful.

"She asked," Harmony said, her muddy brown eyes crinkled at the corners as she twirled one blonde curl, "if you are adopted."

Harmony and Maritza snickered. Other kids listening in did, too, turning their heads and waiting to see what I would say. Jerry kept on drooling. Mrs. De Bernardo flipped the page of her novel.

"Well?" Maritza demanded. "I mean, there has to be an explanation for why you're so weird. I think you're adopted. Sunny and Harmony think you're the milkman's daughter."

Milkman? We didn't even know anyone who sold

milk. I clutched my journal. The journal that was supposed to be my father's. My father, who told me every day that I was unique like a star and reminded me that being different was a good thing. My dad, who wasn't here now to remind me of that anymore.

I bit down on my tongue. I felt a shuffle in my backpack and rested my hands there to quell the creature inside.

Look, if you're used to dealing with mean kids at school, you know that sometimes they say things just to get you so mad your blood boils. I was thinking of something to say back, like how they were insulting kids who were adopted just to pick on *me*. Why is it that when you really need it, you can't think of a comeback? Then later, in the shower or while you're brushing your teeth, the perfect retort just springs in your brain noodles. But all I wanted was for the day to be over and to be paddling across the green waters of Honey Hill Lake with my siblings. Then I remembered—if I got in trouble, I wouldn't get to go to the lake. I needed to be on my bestest, most boring behavior, and the only way to do that was to get far away from the Trio of Terror that was Maritza, Harmony, and Sunny.

So I didn't give them the satisfaction of a reply. I snatched my journal and pack.

I hurried to the front of the room and stood right by Mrs. De Bernardo's desk. She flipped a page. Her eyeliner reminded me of bat wings. She exhaled like she was tired. "What *is* it, Valentina?"

"Can I go to the bathroom? Please?"

I fidgeted some more so she wouldn't have to ask me why I didn't go before I left the house that morning. Daddy always said, "When nature calls, you've gotta answer."

She didn't take her eyes off her page, but she handed me the hall pass. I hurried out the door and went to the third-floor bathroom, the one that's been under construction since before I moved to Missing Mountain, so no one is ever there.

I know I'm not supposed to lie, but I didn't say that I needed to "use" the bathroom. Just that I had to go there.

I locked myself in one of the stalls and sat on the toilet seat. I unzipped my backpack and a purple blur flew right out.

Rule #6 says, *Students cannot bring pets to school*. But technically, *technically*, Brixie wasn't a pet. She's my friend. Remember when I said that I kept a creature I wasn't supposed to? That's her.

Brixie was not supposed to be in our realm. Right before my dad's last mission, we went to investigate a nest of pesky colibrix that were destroying straw-berry farms and orchards in California. Colibrix are ancient beings—they're like a cross between a fairy and a hummingbird. They once roamed flowering valleys in South America, but after magic left our earth, most of their kind went along with it. Those that remained found their way to odd corners of the American continents.

I didn't like thinking about the last time I ever saw my dad, but that was the same day we found the nest of colibrix. Only, we were too late. A group of no-good hunters got there before we could, and they'd killed Brixie's family. I was the one who found her, injured and scared, in the hollow of a tree. She was still a fledgling, about three inches tall, with a long, pointed nose. Her hair was made of soft purple and blue feath-ers that matched her wings. Her hands and feet had long black talons that looked sharper than they were.

I kept her safe in my pencil case and made a little nest out of cotton balls and twigs. After everything she'd been through, I didn't have the heart to send her back to Finisterra. Dad told us that Finisterra meant "the world's end." It might have been the end for humans, because it was a land without people or building or roads. But it was home to beasts and monsters. A land where magical beings roamed. I bet you've never heard of it, but it's there, in a realm that's almost impossible to get to. Almost.

Picture our world as, let's say, half of a burger bun. Now picture Finisterra as the other half of that burger bun. Now imagine a single slice of Swiss cheese. That slice is the only thing keeping our worlds separated. Finisterra is huge, just like our world. The part of the world where Dad's family is from—they call it Finisterra. But there are other names in other languages and in other parts of the globe.

Creatures like Brixie find those holes in the Swiss cheese and they wind up here. But not all creatures are as sweet as my friend. I worried for her. What if a blood-sucking chupavaca got her? What if she wasn't strong enough to defend herself? So, without my family ever knowing, I kept Brixie my own little secret all those months, feeding her honey toast for breakfast and all the sugary treats she could eat. And she could eat a lot.

At six inches tall, Brixie was small for a colibrix, but her traumatic experience must have stunted her growth the way the school nurse told me coffee would stunt my growth after she threw out the coffee I brought from home.

"What's wrong, Val?" Brixie asked, her wings moving so fast it was like a constant *hummmm*. "This is the cold flush place. I don't likes it here. Nope nope nope."

Brixie could never understand what a "bathroom" was because she bathed in the rain and in flower beds. Toilets terrified her after she dove into one, seeing the pool of blue water in the bowl (thankfully no one had, you know, *used* it). She got a nasty surprise when the water turned out to be bleach and she was sick for a whole week.

"Oh, same old waste-of-time Missing Mountain," I muttered, resting my hands on my cheeks. "I hate it here."

Brixie flew right at my head and clung to my hair. I grabbed her and placed her on my knee. "I know you miss the scrumudge. But you have a new home now. Like I used to have a home in my tree, but now my home is in the pencil case in your closet."

"It's *the Scourge*," I corrected her. I felt guilty complaining about homes when Brixie had lost everything and everyone. I'd lost someone, too, on the same day. "And that's my favorite pencil case. It's from *War of the Galaxies*—"

"Your daddy's favorite movie, I knows it!" Brixie dove into my backpack. "Maybe we can do like

Captain Alonso did in the big battle and throws Marglitza into a solar trash crasher."

I snorted. "It's Maritza. And it's fine. I mean, it's not *fine*. She shouldn't talk to me that way. But I won't have to see her after today. We're going to the lake after school. Don't forget to stay close. I haven't explored it well enough, and I don't know what's out there."

"Okie, sweet Val. I promises." Brixie fished out a silver gum wrapper from my backpack and tied it around her chin like those head scarfs from my mom's favorite old movies. She flew whippet fast out of the stall. "Wait— Did you hear that?"

"Hear what?"

The buzz of her wings bounced off the tiled walls. She puckered her lips together and whistled. "Like that."

We listened, but I only heard the strange metal sound of the pipes. I opened my journal and started a new page and wrote a reminder for myself for next year. *Look into pipes.*

Brixie settled in my pack and began nibbling at a peanut butter and Oreos sandwich I'm pretty sure I left there last week.

"Do you think there are more colibrix like me in Honey Hill Lake?"

I hated to be the one to tell her so, but I shook my head. "Sorry, kid. Missing Mountain is about the most boring place in the universe."

"Rome and Lola seem to like it."

"Don't get me started on Rome and Lola." I rolled my eyes. "Lola's always at some cheer thing and Rome should change his name to Captain Crankmonster."

Brixie handed me a gummy worm, but it was covered in pencil shavings, which she didn't seem to mind. "Everything will be all rights, Val. You tells me that all the time."

I shook off the funky feeling that was starting to creep in. Brixie was right. I *had* given her excellent advice. Things *would* be all right. All I had to do was make it to the end of the school day.

I was about to find out how wrong I truly was.

The Girl Who Cried Werewolf

I somehow made it to lunch and ignored Maritza and her friends, though they really did try to get my attention to insult me some more. Why would I *ever* want more of that? Anyway, lunch was the only period when all the grades dumped the kids out in the courtyard. When I first started school, I thought it would be a chance for me to hang out with Lola and Rome, but within a few weeks, Lola began sitting with her cheer squad and the soccer team that drooled more than raptor-pigs. Rome sometimes hung around with kids from the art club, but he usually sat and sketched in his journal, all alone. I used to think that we could sit alone *together*, but Rome liked his space, and I got used to eating by myself, sneaking treats to Brixie.

I set down my tray and poked my spork at the cold macaroni and cheese. All around me, kids were shouting about their summer vacations—camp, beaches, exotic places like Canada. No one asked me what my plans were. I scrolled through my phone, catching up on messages from my online chat, but even those friends had more to do on the last day of school than me.

I scrolled through the "monster" tag on UniTube for videos. Most of them were spoofs and pranks, or hoaxes from people who claimed they found a "mermaid" that turned out to be a rubber shark stapled to a Barbie doll.

I was halfway through a video of a man who claimed his pool was haunted by the ghost of his goldfish when I heard someone crying. I wasn't trying to eavesdrop, but they were so loud. When I found the source, I was surprised to see Sunny. Something had majorly stressed her out. She was practically hyperventilating. Maritza and Harmony were trying to console her, offering water, and fanning her with their binders. They were close enough to hear, so I focused on them.

"I know what I saw!" Sunny said.

"You've had a long day." Maritza's voice trembled. Something had scared her, too. "The sun's too strong and maybe you were just seeing things."

Sunny's face scrunched up, and she pointed a finger at her friend. I'd never seen her so angry, especially not with Maritza. "You saw it, too! Don't pretend."

Harmony held her hands out. "Let's get Mrs. De Bernardo. She'll know what to do."

"And say what?" Maritza snapped. "That Sunny saw a fire-breathing chipmunk? We'll sound like Weirdo Salazar."

Just then, Maritza looked my way. Our eyes locked, and for the first time ever, my nemesis looked away before I did.

My heart began to race. Fire-breathing chipmunk? I'd never heard of such a thing. I wanted to ask them some questions, but then I stopped. There was *no* way. They were messing with me the way the senior class had pranked the whole town with the fake Honey Hill Lake monster.

But what if they were telling the truth? What if they *had* seen something? A good protector does a thorough investigation. That's what my dad would have said, at least.

"Come on." Maritza dragged her friends away.

I *had* to tell someone. I ran across the yard and found Lola. I wedged my way through the sea of soccer players to get to her.

"Hey, Lola?" I waved at my sister. Her hair was in two long French braids and her big brown eyes blinked at me like she was a cartoon princess. "Can I talk to you?"

Her friends all turned to stare at me. "Alone," I added.

"Give me a minute, okay, Tiny?"

"Don't call me that," I mumbled under my breath.

One of the soccer players even said, "How cute," like I was some sort of puppy that had walked up to them to be petted. "Oh, come on, Lola, you never hang out," another one of them said.

I couldn't believe what I was hearing. *All* Lola did was hang out with her friends instead of me. I knew I couldn't wait for her. I still had one more sibling to turn to.

"Forget it." I stalked away and went across the yard to Rome. He was alone on the long picnic table. On the opposite end were two girls and a boy from his grade who kept glancing over at my brother. I could practically see cartoon hearts bubbling in their eyes.

My brother didn't even look up. He moved his pencil furiously across the page, stopping only to eat chocolate-covered pretzels from a bag. I couldn't quite make out what he was drawing, but I saw teeth and claws. He slammed the thing shut.

"What?" he snapped. When I jumped at the clipped

sound of his voice, he softened. Even the kids moon-
ing after him scattered. "Oh. Val. Sorry. The monitor
kept asking me to turn my music down, and I thought
it was him again."

I set my backpack on the table and told him about
what I'd heard Sunny say. A tiny, taloned hand
reached out from my zipper and stole one of Rome's
chocolate-covered pretzels. He started to look down,
but I waved his attention back to me with concern.

"We're near Bear Mountain, right?" I said. "There
are several creatures rumored to live in the surrounding area."

"Drop it, Val," Rome grumbled.

"But—"

Rome shoved his sketchbook and pencils into
his backpack. He reached for his bag of chocolate-
covered pretzels and frowned because it was now
empty. I was tempted to tell him about Brixie, just to
get a reaction out of him. But he only shook his head.

"We're not supposed to do that stuff anymore. You
promised just a few hours ago."

"But this is different. I didn't go *looking* for anything,"
I explained. "I overheard it. The case came to me."

"There is no case. There is no fire-breathing whatever. Those girls are just trying to mess with you."

"But, Rome—"

Rome's nostrils flared. "Do you remember the last time you went in search of a case? You thought your homeroom teacher was a vampire and you filled her coffee with garlic."

My cheeks burned. I admit, that was a mistake. We didn't even have proof of vampires or humanoid monsters. Though it explained why Mrs. De Bernardo wasn't very nice to me. "This is different."

"It isn't." Rome pointed his finger at my chest like I was a bull's-eye. "What part of *retired* don't you get? There are *hunters* who do this kind of stuff. Right now, you're just the girl who cried werewolf."

His words felt like a punch to my gut. "We don't need any stinking hunters!"

"Look, I miss Dad, too, but looking for monsters where there aren't any—none of this is going to bring him back."

Tears bit at the corners of my eyes. "I *know* that."

"No, you don't. If you did, you wouldn't be hiding newspapers from us or searching the internet for strange occurrences or signs of magical creatures. Don't deny it; you're terrible at clearing your search history. I'm telling you, Val: *Back off.*"

Then Rome sulked away.

What was I supposed to do if Rome and Lola didn't believe me? Didn't even want to listen to me?

All around me there were kids kicking around soccer balls, laughing and trading earbuds to share music; friends dunked their fries in globs of mayo and ketchup. And there I was, all alone even though my sister and brother were less than ten feet away. I hated feeling that way. A painful sensation squeezed in my stomach.

Then I heard it. A shrill sound burst through the air. My backpack was open. Blue and purple feathers dusted the grass like a bread-crumb trail. I felt a scream bubble to my throat because I couldn't believe what I was seeing—a horrible green-and-reddish-brown creature the size of a football was dragging Brixie up the trunk of an old oak tree at the edge of the yard. It climbed the tree like a—chipmunk. Sunny's fire-breathing chipmunk.

I whirled around to find Rome and Lola, but they'd made it perfectly clear they weren't going to believe me, the girl who cried werewolf. If I wanted to save Brixie, I had to do it on my own.

✦✦

As I climbed the tree, I couldn't help but think of what Mom had said earlier.

Be good.

Maybe she was tired of getting notes from my teachers about how I liked to walk around the schoolyard barefoot, or how my "imaginative" stories about monsters scared the other kids, or how I corrected my Spanish teacher's pronunciation of Spanish words. I knew Daddy would never have told me to be good. He'd have told me to be great.

Besides, saving Brixie was the definition of good. I kicked off my sneakers and socks, tied my tangled curls into a long ponytail, and began to climb. The oak tree was supposedly as old as the town of Missing Mountain. I found purchase on the gnarly roots with my bare feet. The many low branches and knots made it an excellent climbing tree, but I couldn't even enjoy it because I felt like I had a million little frogs leaping in my stomach.

"Hey! You're not supposed to be up there!" someone shouted.

When I looked down, a crowd of students and teachers began to form.

"I don't see a sign that says I can't climb the tree," I called back.

"It says so right there!" Maritza Vega pointed out.

I grunted and grabbed another branch like a rung on a ladder. "Then the sign should really be bigger because it's easy to miss!" Then I said lower, just to myself, "Hold on, Brixie, I'm coming."

The voices below got louder. I recognized Lola's

voice shouting my name. I froze in my tracks. My heart was like a conga drum going *tappity tap tap*. I knew I shouldn't, but I looked back again. Amid the sea of faces I found Rome, frowning but watching carefully to make sure I didn't fall. Lola was right behind him.

She shouted, "Valentina Alexander Salazar Quintes, get down from there this instant!"

Lola once said that I was like a sugar glider clinging to the bark with sticky little hands, leaping from branch to branch. They wanted me to be good, just like Mom did. But, you see, I'd made a promise to Brixie to keep her safe. She didn't have anyone to protect her. Even if we weren't on the road, I was still the daughter of Arturo Salazar, the greatest protector in all the realms. I had to make him proud, too.

So I climbed. Sweat beaded down my temples. Brixie's shrill scream made me push faster and higher, grabbing branch after branch until I hoisted myself up on the knot where all the branches met like a crossroads.

"Val!" Brixie shouted. There was blood matting the feathers of her arm and she couldn't fly. "Thank sweetness you're heres!"

"Watch out!"

She was so distracted by me, the fire-breathing

chipmunk leapt at her. I was already moving. I grabbed for Brixie and yanked her back right as slobbering teeth bit down in the air exactly where she had been.

"Stay here," I ordered, and set her in a notch of the branch behind me.

The chipmunk was steaming from its nostrils. Two big fangs were crowded by a row of sharp teeth. This chipmunk was *definitely* not a vegetarian. As it lowered the front of its body, ready to pounce, I noticed the bumpy ridge down its spine, like a crocodile's, running from its head to its tail. It reminded me of the time Rome gave himself a haircut by shaving the sides of his head. There was nothing like this in the pages of my dad's journals—believe me, I'd read them all.

The creature let out a low, keening growl.

"Uh-oh," I croaked. Since the species was unknown, I had no idea what to do.

"Save yourself!" Brixie told me. Her species was known for hoarding sugar and worshipping flowers. It was no surprise that she was huddled under her own wings. "I'm not worth dying overs! Bury me with my Kit Kat bars! But promise you won't eats them."

"No one is dying on my watch," I assured her. Then an image of my dad flashed before my eyes. His last smile when he ran into the woods that terrible, awful day. How was I supposed to have known that it was the last time we'd ever see him? I shook myself out of the memory. "Not again. Besides, I'm a Salazar. Salazars get things done."

I tapped the center of my silver ring. Like Lola's watch, this was a family heirloom handed down to me. At its center were intricate whorls and an engraving of our family coat of arms. Pressing it triggered a mechanism that released a round energy shield made of pulsing green light.

The chipmunk slammed into the green light shield so hard it ricocheted off the branch. I thought it was going to go over, but it was fast. Claws sank into the wood, and it scampered back up for another round, but it looked dazed. It shook its head, smoke still streaming from its nostrils.

I needed to trap it. Not only would it be proof to my family that my hunch was right, but a new species needed to be documented and then sent back to Finisterra. But before I could move, the creature sucked in a breath. I crouched down into a ball, protecting Brixie and my body with my shield. And then there was nothing but hot, scorching flames.

Even though my green force field was protecting me, I shut my eyes and held my breath. The pressure of the shooting flames pushed against my shield. I chanced it and looked. Orange fire streamed out of the chipmunk's wide-open mouth. Then it sputtered, like it had run out of gas. The creature scratched its claws, green foam bubbling from its mouth as more steam billowed from its nostrils.

Down below, the worried cries were getting louder. I had to do something, but I was pinned down. Daddy used to say that a protector has to be cunning and clever because we wouldn't just shoot first and think later like hunters. So I thought about what he'd do in my place, and a plan started to click together in my head.

"How's your wing, Brixie?"

She cradled her arm and moved her shoulder. "I can fly."

"Get out of here. Go to our hiding spot."

"Don't make me goes. Don't make me leaves you."

"I'll be fine," I said, but my arm was trembling as I held up my shield. "I still have a few tricks up my sleeve. Or in my pockets. Now *go!*"

With fat glossy tears in her black eyes, Brixie staggered into flight, then zipped out of the tree line in a purple-and-blue blur. The chipmunk snapped its attention back to her and ran along the branch, chomping at the air. It was the distraction that I needed.

"All right, Val," I said to myself. "It's been a while, but you got this."

I tapped the center of the shield to dissolve the

green light. I dug into my pockets for my shimmering fishing net. You might be thinking—Val, how could a fishing net help you trap a fire-breathing monster? The answer is, it was made of metals. Like most of our gear, Dad had invented it. The net really came in handy when he needed to catch a school of octo-piranhas loose in Lake Champlain. The magnetic ends clicked into place, holding the catch in without hurting it.

As I held the cool metal net in my hands, I remembered what it felt like to train with my family. How my dad taught me to cast it to always trap my mark. Technically, I'd only practiced on soccer balls and Rome. Also, technically, I wasn't supposed to carry it at all. The net was to be locked in the garage with the Scourge and the rest of our gear. Sometimes breaking the rules can save your life. Other times, you just get grounded.

I balanced on the branch and took a breath to steady myself. The chipmunk turned its attention to me again, yipping at the air and shredding the bark with its sharp little claws. I won't lie, I was pretty scared. But I was excited, too. This was going to be my very first catch on my own. And with a new species, too!

But before I could throw the net, a bloodcurdling sound came from nowhere. It felt like dozens of needles were stabbing my eardrums. I clamped my palms over my ears, but that did nothing to stop the shrill noise. I couldn't even scream at the fact that my net slipped from my hands and fell over the branch and down to the ground.

The chipmunk squealed and twisted. I realized—it was in pain. It tried to cover its own little ears. More green saliva frothed at the corners of its mouth, and this time, I knew it was getting ready for another fire show. It took a huge gulp of air and when it opened its mandible, it let out a stream of fire.

I leapt out of the way to another branch, but I miscalculated the jump and I screamed as I slipped. I clung to the branch as hard as I could and dangled over the air like bait. I was pretty good at the monkey bars, but my hands were sweaty. Still, there was no way I could fall. Salazars don't fall from trees or mountains.

Then suddenly, the terrible whistling sound cut out. The chipmunk scurried away faster than I could blink.

"What in the name of the saints?" I asked, hoisting myself back onto the branch.

I didn't even have time to catch my breath. My sister appeared out of the tree branches. There were

56

green leaves stuck in Lola's hair and her cheeks were flushed.

"I could ask you the same question," she said.

I couldn't even be annoyed with her for following me up here. "Did you see the fire-breathing chipmunk? Did you hear the whistle?"

"We had a deal." But before my sister could yell some more, we both sniffed the air. A bitter, dark scent wafted toward us. Smoke. Fire.

"We have to get down," Lola said urgently.

"No kidding," I muttered. I knew when to argue, and this was not one of those times.

Lola extended her arm, and I swung my weight to reach her. I didn't want my big sister to have to come to my rescue, but it beat being stuck in a flaming tree. Lola climbed down the trunk as easily as she had come up. I began to follow suit, but I missed my footing. Salazars were not supposed to fall. But there I was, swinging on the split branch. An unfamiliar fear tugged at the pit of my stomach as the branch snapped under my weight.

"Get out of the way!" I yelled.

It all happened so quickly. I tumbled into Sunny Ramnarine, who knocked into Harmony Holiday, who went headfirst into the monitor's gut. He let his megaphone go and it flew backward. Maritza was just getting out of the way when the thing hit her square in the face.

"Oof," Rome said, wincing.

I wish I could say that was the worst of it. As I stood there, barefoot, with everyone staring at me and the burning oak tree, Principal Connolly ran over. I'd never seen someone so angry. Not even that time my eldest sister, Andie, and my mom had a fight over Andie leaving us to go live with the hunter side of the Salazar family.

Principal Connolly's face was redder than a freshly cooked lobster. He strangled the air with his hairy hands.

"Well," he said, looking from me to Lola to Rome. He didn't even let me say that it was my fault. Spit bubbled at the corners of his mouth. He kind of looked like the fire-breathing chipmunk, but I wasn't about to tell him that. "It seems you're about to set a new Missing Mountain record, *Miss* Salazar. I've never given detention on the last day of school."

"Why start now?" I chuckled nervously. I couldn't help it. He was scarier than the monster I'd just faced. At least with monsters I had protocols. You trap them, you send them back to the realm of Finisterra. People were difficult.

58

"Go on," he said. "You know where it is."

"But it's a half day," I said, panic slipping into my voice. "Our mom won't be home for literally hours."

Principal Connolly's smile was pure evil. "Then I suppose that's another record, isn't it?"

"What record is that?" I asked, though I knew it was a trap. In the distance, the sirens wailed.

"For the longest detention ever given to any student in the history of Missing Mountain."

5

The Only Thing Worse than Being in Detention Is a Visit from Monster Hunters

Detention was in the oldest part of the building. Two foggy windows gave a view of the outside world, while a big old clock was bolted to the wall, ticking and ticking down the seconds we'd have to spend there. I bet it was Principal Connolly's favorite place in the whole school because he punished misunderstood students like me.

Lola and Rome sat in opposite corners of the room, leaving me alone in the back row. They hadn't talked to me since we'd arrived. I already knew what they would say. *That was dangerous, Valentina. How could you, Valentina? You promised, Valentina.* Lola flipped the pages of her book so hard I thought they'd rip, and Rome, well, at least he had his music.

The volunteer fire department finally arrived.

It was the smallest truck I'd ever seen, and there were only two firefighters. They put out the flames quickly, and thankfully no one seemed to be hurt. Except Maritza. And Brixie. And my own personal feelings because everyone was angry with me. I was starting to feel really crummy about everything. I'd only wanted to rescue Brixie and I messed it all up. I couldn't even enjoy the possibility of having discovered a new monster.

Maritza Vega walked past the window. She had a red welt right on her forehead and she stared at me worse than the fire-breathing chipmunk had. Maybe the summer vacation would give her a chance to cool off. Disgruntled parents came to pick up their kids. The only people who seemed happy at the day getting cut short were the teachers, who got in their cars and peeled out of the parking lot, leaving tire marks on the asphalt.

Hunched over my desk, I busied myself sketching the chipmunk creature in my journal. I tried my best to remember its blazing-red eyes. The bumpy reptilian ridge running down its tail. I drew tendrils of smoke coming out of its little nose. Then there were the teeth! Two long incisors, curved like the world's smallest saber-toothed tiger. All in all, I did a really great job. I wanted to show Rome, but he had his

head down, his headphones rattling off a song that sounded like the time I accidentally threw our silverware down the garbage disposal. Lola didn't take her eyes off the book, not for a second. There were still a couple of leaves in Lola's hair and somehow they made her look like a fairy princess instead of a troll, which was how I felt with my hair in disarray and dirt under my nails.

Maybe my old cases had been a bust, but I finally had something real. I had a feeling. I just didn't have anyone to talk to about that feeling. Dad would have been my first choice. What would he have said if he'd seen me climb that tree? Would he have been angry? Would he have cheered? I felt a strange itch under my skin, but no matter how much I scratched, it wouldn't get rid of the sensation.

Forget them, I thought, and returned to my journal.

I jotted down several different names: *Neotamias Inferno*. Firemunk. Val's Worst Enemy. Val's Fire Bane. I wanted the name to be good. Ordinary animals were always being discovered in some remote rain forest or deep sea. Same goes for monsters, though new finds are rare, according to my dad. I wrote down my report, including all the details I'd rather forget. (You had to be honest when leaving behind your records.)

Then I wrote down questions I didn't have the

answers to: Where had this firemunk come from? Was there a flash portal nearby? A nest? If Missing Mountain was as boring and ordinary as I had thought, how had it wound up there and at *my* school?

My thoughts came so quickly, I broke the tip of my pencil. When I looked up, Lola was still reading, and Rome was still shredding his eardrums. I got up and went to sharpen my pencil, making as much noise as I could. Still, my siblings gave me the silent treatment.

I returned to my seat and sketched until the end-of-day bell finally rang and I felt exhausted from sitting. I mean, I didn't think I could get tired of sitting, but detention proved me wrong.

Lola shut her book and let go of a long sigh as she scrolled through her phone. "Mom's stuck in traffic."

I groaned.

Rome pulled down his headphones and glanced around. "I say we sneak out and walk home. We've already been here for three hours thanks to Valentina."

"I said I was sorry!"

Rome shook his head. "No, actually, you didn't."

My words lodged in my throat. "Fine. I'm sorry."

"Whatever." Rome rolled his head.

"Enough." Lola bit her bottom lip the way she did when she was worried. "We can't go anywhere. We have to set an example for Val."

"When you were my age, you already had your protector mark," I reminded her. "And last year Rome dove into a sewer to rescue a yacu mama clogging up the pipes. All I get is Missing Mountain and detention. What kind of example is that?"

Lola watched me with her big princess eyes. "Is it really so bad here?"

"Yes!" I waved around the room, at the windows. "We don't belong here. We belong out there!"

"You mean setting trees on fire in different cities instead of just Missing Mountain?" Rome asked.

"The fire was not my fault. If you'd just hear me out—"

"All right," Lola said, crossing her legs and resting her hands on her knees.

"Wait, what?" I had been ready to do a lot more groveling.

"You want us to hear you out, then go ahead. Explain, Tiny."

I grimaced at the nickname but didn't complain. They were finally listening to me. I told them everything—about overhearing Harmony, and the firemunk. I still couldn't tell them about Brixie, which made it difficult and left holes in my story. But I covered the basics. "And that's how we ended up in detention."

Lola and Rome stared at me for so long, I looked up at the clock on the wall to make sure time hadn't suddenly frozen.

"I've never heard of a firemunk," Rome finally scoffed. "But that would explain what happened to my chocolate-covered pretzels."

"Sure. Yeah," I held up my drawing for them to see. "I'm telling you this is what I saw. I knocked it away with my shield ring. I almost caught it!"

"What did you see up there?" Rome asked Lola.

Lola tugged at the tip of her chin. "Just Tiny with her shield and the net. We have to talk about you stealing the family gear, by the way."

"*That's* what you want to talk about? I just discovered a new species, and you want to talk about gear?" I couldn't believe my ears. The Before Times Lola and Rome would have freaked with news like that.

"You could have been hurt," Lola said. "You were reckless."

I pointed out that we were completely fine, even though I'd had similar thoughts earlier.

"Help me out here, Rome," Lola said, exasperated.

Rome glanced back and forth between us, and I could see he was torn. He brushed his mop of black waves out of his eyes, but they just flopped right back. "Val has a point. When you were her age, you knocked over a row of motorcycles because one of the hunter kids made fun of your pigtails. That was pretty reckless."

"Not helping." Lola pursed her lips. "Let's say you did discover a new species."

"I did. Just going on the record."

"It's not our life anymore, Ti—Valentina. We aren't protectors. We're just kids." Lola's voice was so strained I thought she might cry.

"Just *forget* it," I grumbled.

That's when we all heard it. The quick click of Mom's heels getting closer and closer. She turned the corner with Principal Connolly, and she did not look pleased. Her face had this tightness around her eyes and lips, like she was forcing herself to seem pleasant when she really wanted to be angry.

Our mother, Susana Quintes Salazar, had walnut-brown skin, thick black hair, and hazel eyes fringed by a hundred lashes, just like Lola and Rome.

"Thank you, Mr. Connolly," Mom said. She came to a stop at the threshold of the detention room. She flashed a smile, but her eyes said, *Wait till you get home*. "This won't happen again next year, I assure you. It's been a difficult transition since my husband's passing."

Passing. I hated when she said that. "Passing" didn't

capture what had truly happened to my father. Dad had been eaten. When the orü puma was done with him, there was only a piece of my dad's ear left. And then the orü puma flew away. That's not passing. That's chomped. Ripped apart. But sure, it was easier to tell Principal Connolly that version of the truth.

I opened my mouth to speak, but my mother put up a single finger like a warning. We did *not* fight in public, and I knew that.

I followed them out of the school. I stared at my feet all the way to the car. Mom's shiny silver car still smelled like plastic and those little green trees that made my nose itch. We weren't even allowed to put stickers on it.

On the car ride home, Mom blasted her old-school music the way she did to "calm herself." Though we barely got through one whole song before we were parked in our driveway. I glanced at my bedroom window, where my guinea pig plushie was sitting at the window (my signal that Brixie had gotten home okay and was hiding).

"Mom," I said, and shut the car door behind me. "Let me explain—"

That's when I noticed that she didn't look the same as when she'd left that morning. Her ballerina bun had turned into a messy top bun. Was that a cobweb in her hair? I'd seen her office and it was tiny and full of ancient cabinets. But it was clean. The worst of it was her eyes. They were red. The mascara was smudged, like she'd rubbed it while wiping away tears. Had I done that? Was she crying because I got in trouble again?

"I'm sorry," I said.

Mom licked her lips and took a deep breath. "It's been a long day for all of us. I want you all cleaned up and ready to help with dinner at exactly six o'clock. Understood?"

We must have all been so surprised that we weren't grounded that we just said "Yes, ma'am" at the same time and then ran inside the house.

Rome went to his bat cave. Mom said she was going to take her after-work bubble bath. Lola left her backpack and shoes at the door, then went down the hall in her matching socks. I thought maybe she'd make one of those chocolate peanut butter protein smoothies she'd been drinking since she joined the cheerleading squad. (They did not taste anything like chocolate or peanut butter.) Instead, she kept going to the end of the hall, where we kept our family altar.

You know how some families have places where they put candles, statues of saints, or photos of relatives long gone? We have something similar. Hunters of the Order of Finisterra use it to give thanks to the founder of our order—Saint Pakari. The legend of Saint Pakari started in Ecuador in the eleventh century. According to my dad, Pakarikuna was a shepherd of magical beasts. He wandered the highlands of the continent with his creatures and guarded the gateway into Finisterra. Over the years, he learned how to use the magic from the other realm to stay young. He watched the lands and people around them change. To protect them, he sealed off the door between our worlds and created the Order of Finisterra, which is still active today.

Even though Dad had left the Order and began his own branch of protectors, he'd kept the tradition of the altar.

Our altar was filled with candles in different colors and heights. You light a candle, say a little prayer for Saint Pakari, and leave something behind. It doesn't have to be anything big. It can be a piece of fruit or candy or flowers. I watched Lola from the stair railing. She left behind a perfect acorn. Then she touched the framed photo of Dad. In it, he's younger, before Andromeda came along. He's looking off to the side and laughing, probably at something Mom said. They were always laughing at something I never understood, and they'd go, "You'll get it when you're older." But Dad won't watch me get older, will he?

I felt angry for no reason. My throat got dry, and my eyes burned a bit. I didn't want Lola to think I was snooping, even though I was, so I went to where I normally spent my time after school.

I'll admit, it was pretty nice having my own room. The house was ginormous. Great-Aunt Hercilia retired here and lived out the rest of her life in Missing Mountain. I walked past a portrait of her and her wife, Francine. They were tall and imposing, and their eyes followed me whenever I walked down the hall. Both women had been hunters in their younger days, but I never knew much else. They'd liked Dad enough that they left him this house, and no one else in the family got a dime. At least, that's what I heard Mom say once.

I walked faster past the portrait and into the garage.

There it was: the Scourge.

Daddy told me that he bought the car with his last dollars when he ran away from home. Over the years, he'd tricked it out. Retrofitted parts to accommodate my mom, then Andromeda, Lola, Rome, and finally, me. Our whole lives fit inside.

Dad had built clever compartments to stow condiments, toiletries, clothes, weapons, books, charging ports, tins of coffee, pillows, blankets. The back seat converted into a small bed at night, and during the day there was a foldable tray where we did every-thing from homework to cleaning our gadgets.

Andromeda had strung up twinkling lights all along the ceiling. Lola's favorite *War of the Galaxies* action figure was still wedged between one of the seat cush-ions. You know the real special plates your mom has? The ones that are "just for guests and special occa-sions"? That's what the Scourge felt like now. Only for display.

I hated seeing it with a rusty boot around the front wheel. I rested my hand on the wheel mounted above the front bumper.

"Today was a disaster," I said. Yes, I spoke to the Scourge. But you have to see things from my point of view. I had no one else to talk to, except for Brixie. At least the Scourge never disagreed with me.

I opened the doors and climbed inside. Even though all six of us lived in there while we were on the road, Mom always managed to make it smell like clean laundry and sunscreen.

I popped the top of the van and crawled into the bed. For the last eight months it's been my own get-away. I strung a charger for my phone. Stashed a bag of snacks that Rome still steals when he goes through his own pile.

"Brixie?" I whisper-hissed.

I pulled back the blanket on my pillow and there she was, curled up around a red lollipop. Now that I knew she wasn't in mortal danger, I plugged in my phone. Like most of my things, it's a hand-me-down. That's the worst part about being the youngest. All your siblings have already worn your clothes or cracked the screen on your phone. At least the things I get from Lola are well taken care of.

Something was bothering me about the encounter with the firemunk. I mean, aside from setting a tree on fire and getting record-breaking detention. Monsters exist all over the world. That's a fact. Some prefer certain climates. Others find their way through flash portals that appear in the Swiss cheese barrier between our world and Finisterra. But flash portals are rare, and they vanish within seconds. What were the chances that the firemunk had come through one of those portals right at my school? And where had that whistle come from? Places as old as Missing Mountain have legends, and Daddy said that all stories start from somewhere. I'd researched our new home and hadn't even found so much as a haunted house. Perhaps I'd missed something. Mom, Lola, and Rome might have been retired, but deep down, I knew I needed to follow my hunch.

An hour later, though, I had nothing. And I mean *nothing*. The only mystery in Missing Mountain was actually about my great-aunt Hercilia Salazar, a reclusive old woman with a house full of bats. I wanted to correct that Missing Mountain blogger that there were only bats in the *attic*, but I didn't see the point of fighting with someone on the internet. Apparently, my deceased relative was a legend in her own way, but that didn't help me with my firemunk dilemma.

Brixie was still snoozing away, waking up only to gnaw on her candy before going back to sleep. She needed her rest since she'd been through a lot.

My last resort was the Cryptid Kids message boards. I posted a new thread with the question *Firemunk 101. Ever heard of a reptilian chipmunk that breathes fire?*

While I waited for responses, I climbed back down the Scourge and opened up the compartment that housed Dad's old journals. I started to flip through them just in case there was something I'd missed. Dad had been born a hunter, but he'd chosen to become a protector. His whole life was written in the pages of these books, and that made them irreplaceable. I was flipping through one when my phone began to light up with dozens of messages from my chat.

MocoLoco88: Firemunk? Sounds rad.

Rainb0wP00p: Wait. V, have you seen the video?

MocoLoco88: My brother's checking to see if it's legit.

Rainb0wP00p: It can't be.

M3rmaidLyf3: But what if it is?

M3rmaidLyf3: Teddy Roanhorse says it's the real thing. His dad tried to hunt one like 100 years ago for the Order but it almost got him.

Rainb0wP00p: V, you okay? I wouldn't want to see it after . . .

M3rmaidLyf3: Yeah. Mega yikes.

MocoLoco88: VAL ZOMG YOUR SCHOOL IS ON THE NEWS RIGHT NOW.

MocoLoco88: Did you really set a historic tree on fire?

MocoLoco88: But back to the video. Did you watch it yet?

MocoLoco88: VALENTINA CALL ME.

I wasn't sure what Iggy was talking about. What video? I plugged in my earphones to click the link, but before I could do anything else, I heard a strange sound in the garage. I registered the thud of heavy boots. We weren't allowed to walk in the house with shoes on, so it wasn't my family. My heart sped up like Brixie's wings as I realized the sound was coming closer. I quickly climbed back up to the pop-up roof and crouched quietly.

The side door of the Scourge squeaked open. Muddy brown boots stomped inside. On the back of his motorcycle jacket was a symbol I knew like the back of my hand. Two swords that crossed like an X. He was a hunter of the Order of Finisterra. Anger sparked in my chest like fireworks. Why in the name of Saint Pakari was he here?

The smell of exhaust filled the van. He wore his helmet, so I couldn't see his face. The man noticed the stack of books, picked one up. He flipped through the pages with his black-gloved hands and then tossed it to the side. I wanted to scream "Get your dirty hunter hands off my dad's journals!" but I knew that if I revealed myself too soon, I wouldn't find out what he wanted. I needed to watch what he'd do next.

He climbed to the front seat and opened the sun visors, then the glove compartment. What was he searching for? I twisted my shield ring around my middle digit. Was the hunter here to steal from us? Whatever he was after, he wasn't going to take it. Not on my watch.

"Where is it?" he growled impatiently.

I gasped, then clapped my hand over my mouth. He swung around and looked directly at me. I knew his face instantly. If he was here, it meant his pack of hunters wasn't far behind.

It was my dad's brother—my uncle Rafael.

6

Awkward Family Reunion

"H-hey, kiddo!" Uncle Raf stuttered. His hazel eyes, just like my dad's, went wide. I could tell he wasn't expecting to get caught, and I felt a little smug that I'd caught him snooping around.

But that smugness went away when he took off his helmet. The resemblance between the Salazar brothers was strong. They shared the same golden tan, long lashes, bushy caterpillar brows, and strong, outward curve of their noses. Uncle Raf was just a little bit shorter, even though he was the eldest. Dad used to say that he loved his brother, even though he had a Napoleon complex, whatever that meant. How could family look so alike but be so different?

In one of Dad's journals from his runaway years, I learned that Uncle Raf was the deciding vote in having my father exiled from the family as punishment for Dad running away to become a protector. I didn't know why my uncle was here or what he was looking for, but I didn't trust him.

"I was just looking for the lady of the house," he said, resting his hands on his hips.

I raised an eyebrow to let him know I didn't believe him. "In the van?"

"No one answered the doorbell." He tucked his helmet under his arm. "Must be glitchy."

I walked past him, leading him back out the garage. That's when I noticed about half a dozen hunters parked in front of our house. Their motorcycles gleamed glossy black and red. Most of them sat around, helmets still on. I tried to pick out my sister Andromeda among them, but in those matching black jeans and leather jackets, they all looked too similar.

"Where you going, kid?" Uncle Raf asked.

"Inside," I said, but first I rang the doorbell over and over and over again. I sucked in a deep breath and shouted, "Mom! Uncle Rafael is here even though he didn't come to Dad's funeral!"

His eye twitched. He clearly didn't care for my tone or choice of words.

I stopped ringing the bell and the pinging noise echoed loudly. "Bell works fine for me."

Uncle Raf was caught in a lie, but he didn't look

78

bothered. His face crinkled with a smile as my mother appeared behind the frosted glass and swung the door open.

"Valentina, what in the world is the matter?" my mom asked, then froze when she noticed Uncle Raf, then the hunters taking up our front yard. She touched her ruby pendant. She always did that when she was nervous or thinking. "Rafael. What an— unexpected—surprise. It's been months. What brings you here? Andromeda—is she all right?"

He eased my mom's panic with a chuckle and tipped his head in the direction of the hunters. I couldn't even tell which one was my sister. "Everything's right as rain."

I made a *hmm* sound.

Uncle Raf looked down at me, and we had a staring contest, like he was waiting for me to rat him out. But I smiled sweetly and waited to see if he'd lie to my mom.

"Garage door was open, so I popped in and found Valentina here reading my brother's old journals."

Mistake! I should have gone first. My mom gave me that tight-lipped smile. She'd already warned me to stay out of the journals, and after today I could feel a new "sit-down" to go over my "behavior." Uncle Raf was good.

"You're always welcome," Mom said, but she used

her polite voice. Like when she thanked Mrs. Jones for her mayonnaise, hot dog, and gummy bear "salad" during Thanksgiving.

Uncle Raf thumbed at the hunters behind him. "We were driving down from the Hundred-Mile Wilderness. I'll spare you the bloody details. But I thought I'd try and have Andie say hello. See how you're all faring."

"We're fine," I said. "Thanks for stopping by! See you never!"

Mom yanked me against her and rested her hands on my shoulders. What was she *doing*? The hunters were *bad news*. "Would you like to stay for dinner? I'm packing for a convention tomorrow, but I'm more than happy to treat everyone to Thai food."

Uncle Raf's smile reminded me of a jack-o'-lantern. He clapped his palm over his heart. "You're a queen, Suzie Q."

My mom tucked a loose strand of hair behind her ear. "Only Arturo calls me that."

Called, I corrected her in my mind. But I didn't say it out loud.

My uncle's face crinkled up, like he was hurt but still wanted to make nice. "Of course. *Susana*." He glanced back and whistled. "Soup's on, squadron. Leave your muddy boots at the door and tuck in your shirts," Uncle Raf commanded his hunters, and he led them inside.

My uncle sauntered in with his hands on his hips. His eyes were like pendulums swinging from wall to wall, inspecting every inch of the house. Sure, I didn't exactly *want* to live in Missing Mountain, but it was still my house, and as the hunters walked inside and started touching the antique vases and angel decorations, I wanted to make sure they didn't break anything.

"Place hasn't changed a bit since the old bat lived here," someone said, gesturing to Great-Aunt Hercilia's portrait.

They laughed, like it was a joke. I rolled my eyes, and I couldn't quite figure out why that bothered me. I'd seen some of the other houses in the neighborhoods with their new, eggshell-colored walls, and central air, and floors that didn't creak and crack. Lola called it retro and vintage, which I understood just meant "old." But it was sort of growing on me, I guess. Besides, Dad used to spend summers with Great-Aunt Hercilia when he was my age, right up until he ran away from the family.

Soon, it was an invasion. In addition to Uncle Raf, there were six hunters, most of them teenagers, and two of them really old, like in their thirties. There was a girl with buzzed hair dyed bright pink. She craned her neck into the living room and picked up a unicorn made of glass from Great-Aunt Hercilia's menagerie. She played with it, ramming the horn into the side of a glass bear.

"Be careful with that," I said, and she stuck her tongue out at me as she set it down.

The rest of the hunters made themselves at home quickly. A boy a bit older than Rome put his smelly feet on the coffee table and wiggled his toes. A young girl beside him elbowed him, and he took them down. Lola came around, handing out drinks.

I grabbed her by her arm and pulled her into the hall. "What are you doing? They are the *enemy*."

Lola shook her head. "There is no enemy, Tiny."

"Don't call me that." I huffed. "Yeah, well, don't you remember that Dad ran away from them for a reason. Why are they even here? I saw—"

"Tiny. Val. Please." Lola rested her hands on my shoulders and looked deep into my eyes. "Maybe Uncle Raf wants to help Andie come home. It's been a long day. Let's just have a nice dinner, okay? You're the one who wanted more family time."

"Yeah, with *us*, not *them*."

But Lola was already returning to the dining room to set the table. Was I living in a nightmare realm? How had we gotten invaded by a squadron of hunters?

Hunters were everything Dad ran away from. Hunters didn't protect anything—they destroyed and obliterated and slayed. They hated everything, and they'd taken my sister Andromeda.

Speaking of Andromeda, when I turned around, there she was. For a moment, I didn't recognize her. In the eight months since I'd last seen my sister, she'd changed into a different person. Her hair was longer, plaited into a long braid that coiled over her shoulder. Her honey tan skin looked strange, like she never saw the sun, and her smudged eyeliner deepened the dark circles under her eyes. In the Before Times, Andromeda—Andie—was bright. Being around her was like spending a warm day under the sun. In the After Times, there was a cloud permanently over her. She stood in the middle of the hallway with her hands in her jacket pockets and shrank away from me, like she didn't want to be there.

"Hey, Val," she said. I'd almost forgotten the sound of her voice, low and slow like syrup.

"Hello, Andromeda," I said. Despite how different she seemed, I still felt an urge to hug her. I was mad at her for leaving us, but she was still my sister. Wasn't she? She'd taught me how to climb on craggy rock outcroppings, and she'd helped me perfect our favorite ramen soups on cold nights. So why did she act like I was a bug in her presence? An icky feeling settled in my stomach, like the time I ate two-year-old Halloween candy and was sick for an afternoon.

I was about to ask her a question. *How are you? Do you miss us? Are you coming home?* But Andromeda's attention went to Mom, who wrapped her arms around her eldest daughter. Andie shrugged her off, and I could see Mom's face try to hide her hurt.

"I'll get the table set," Mom said.

As she left, Rome joined everyone in the living room. He waved and Andie waved back. It was so weird. You would think we all just met.

I dragged my feet into the living room, where the usually large space was beginning to feel like the walls were closing in.

"There's my boy," Uncle Raf said, and held his arms open to Rome for an embrace. He clapped my brother on his back, then held him at a distance, like an inspection. "You look more and more like your old man every day. Come, tell me everything about land-locked life."

"Hey, Andie," the girl with pink hair called out from the couch. "How's your shoulder?"

Andromeda rotated her shoulder a few times, and I noticed she pushed down a pained wince. "Good, Mariluz, thanks."

"Not everyone can make such a big kill from that distance. You were born to be a hunter."

Andromeda's eye skated over me, then Lola. It was like she was looking right through us. Her mouth was set into a serious line. She didn't say anything as the two hunters sitting beside her clapped her on the back. My entire body felt like I was on fire, like I was facing the stream of flames from the firemunk, only this time I couldn't use my ring shield.

"What were you hunting?" I asked.

"Tiny," Lola whispered at my side, but I didn't listen.

I shook off Lola's hand on my shoulder. "No, Andromeda is a hunter now. I want to know what she killed."

Before Andie could answer, the girl with pink hair, Mariluz, pulled a string from under her shirt and held up a yellow canine serrated at the sides. "A nest of zorrivos that was killing off livestock."

I'd only ever seen a drawing of a zorrivo. They were blue foxes with antlers and serrated front teeth. Dad said their teeth allowed them to cut through tree bark, like woodchucks. They were woodland creatures, harmless really.

"I thought you were in the Hundred-Mile Wilderness," I said. "What livestock could they have been killing off? Trees?"

"Why don't you pipe down about things you don't understand, *Tiny Tina*," a boy said. He had a dusting of freckles, like someone had blown dirt on his face. He mussed up my hair, and that's when I reached my hunter limit for a lifetime. I flung myself at him.

"Who're you calling Tiny?" I shouted. I know I'm not supposed to fight to resolve problems, especially not with others. But I was just too mad to think. I felt hands hold me back and realized it was Rome.

"Hey!" Rome said, and stood between me and the hunter kid. "Pick on someone your own size."

"Enough, Manu!" Uncle Raf barked. The hunters all settled down. Except Andie, who seemed to have vanished. "We're guests. And we're family." At that, he looked pointedly at me.

"You don't care about family," I said. Do you ever get so angry you feel like you're not in control of your body? That's what I felt like. It's like I knew I was talking, but I couldn't quite control myself. I was like a soda bottle shaken so fast I had no other choice but to burst. "You took my sister away. You turned your back on my dad."

"Valentina!" Mom and Lola said at the same time.

Uncle Raf waved his hand in the air like I was a candle he'd just snuffed out. "It's all right. I get it. I was ten once."

"I'm eleven and a half," I corrected him.

Uncle Raf's eye twitched again. He licked his canine tooth and narrowed his eyes at me. "Then *act* like it."

Mom rested her hands on my shoulders and gave a light squeeze. "I'm sorry, Rafael. We're all still hurting after Arturo's death."

"We're *all* hurt," Uncle Raf said. He tapped his fist over his heart. "My brother and I had a . . . complicated . . . relationship. But I wouldn't have wished his tragic end on anyone. I should have been there for you all. I thought that bringing Andromeda into the fold would be enough. But I know I should have done more. I swear, I *will* find the beast that killed him. And when I do, I will *destroy* it."

The words made me flinch. Yet when I looked at Rome, he was nodding along. My brother, who nursed an entire liter of moth-kittens back to health after we'd found them abandoned in Redwood National Park. My brother, who liked to heal our cuts and scrapes and sang along with birds on long walks through the trees. Now he was agreeing with our uncle's violent words.

I didn't like the way my family was changing, and I didn't know how to press pause. Make it stop. I didn't know what to do. All I knew was that I couldn't sit there and share my spring rolls with the hunters.

"Dad wouldn't want you to kill for him," I said.

Uncle Raf dragged his thumb and finger along the stubble of his jaw. "Perhaps if my brother hadn't strayed away from the family creed, he'd still be here with you. Instead of—well—you know the rest."

"I don't believe a single thing you're saying. You're a liar. Dad knew you were a liar," I said.

"Valentina!" Mom shot up and stood in front of me. Behind her, Uncle Raf grinned like a wolf. "If you can't behave, then go to your room."

"Fine," I said.

I know "go to your room" is supposed to be a punishment, but sometimes, you just need time alone. I turned around and shoved past the hunter blocking the entrance of the living room. I felt something awful as I trudged up the steps.

When I passed the hall, I noticed someone standing in the guest room. Andie. I mean, Andromeda. That room was supposed to be hers. Mom had even painted it indigo, her favorite color. Rome had painted the whole ceiling into constellations, even the one she was named after. But Andromeda chose to leave us instead.

"You're missing the family reunion," I said, and leaned against the open door.

"Is that what we're calling whatever this is?" Andie

took a deep breath and shook her head. "You'll learn the hard way, Val."

"What do you mean?"

She turned around and her eyes were glassy, like if she blinked once she'd cry. She didn't blink, though. "I mean that everything Dad taught us was wrong. He taught us the Salazar motto was *Protector. Valiant. Heart.* But Uncle Raf showed me the real Salazar creed is *Honor, Strength, Blood.* Dad should have been more scared of what's out there. If he had, he never would have died and left us."

"How can you say that?" My voice broke, and I squeezed my fists at my sides. "I don't even know who you are."

"I'm still me, Val. I'm Andromeda Salazar. I just know the truth. I know that there are monsters in this world, and they shouldn't be here. Dad believed that they needed to be protected. But how do you protect something that could shred you to ribbons? How do you save *people* from the beasts of the world?"

"We save them one by one." I repeated the words Dad used to say. "Not everything that looks like a monster is monstrous. That's what Dad taught us, and deep down I know you believe that."

"You're wrong." Andromeda shrugged, then turned her back on me. "Like I said, you'll learn."

I left her there and ran to my room. I hid with my head under the pillows. It all felt like too much, too fast. After a while, I heard the Thai food delivery at the door, and Lola shouted for me to come down to eat.

I didn't. I stayed in my room. Then I remembered that before the hunters had arrived and made our horrible day even worse, I was talking to my friends on our message boards.

I scrolled back through the chat, which was going too fast to keep up with. I had a hundred missed messages from my cryptid group. Now that I was alone, I could click on the link they insisted I watch.

I hit play. A boy around my age with cherry-red hair appeared on camera. "Hey, y'all, it's Pete! You'll never believe what I just found!" The shaky camera made me dizzy. He ran into a clearing in the green woods with tall, skinny trees. Slats of stone. A cave too small for anyone to walk into, so you had to crawl. "We've been talking to some locals. My pops says there have been sightings of a giant monster wrecking fences and chicken coops for the last few months. But I, Peter Bereza, am on its trail."

He set the camera down low to video himself crouching into the cave.

"I have a bad feeling about this," I whispered.

Who just entered a cave like that without proper

tools? I smacked my hand on my forehead as I watched him come back out covered in dirt and with bits of twig in his hair.

I sat up and held the phone as close to my face as I could. No way. That couldn't be what I thought it was—in Peter Bereza's hands was an egg I recognized immediately. The egg was the size of a volleyball, with shimmering blue-and-green scales flecked with silver. He grinned at the camera. "I've found proof. A real live DRAGON egg. If you doubt me, then don't go anywhere. Watch it hatch right here on my channel, or visit us at Pete's Wondrous Emporium!"

"Bad," I said. I even looked up, like I was expecting to find Lola and Rome there with me. But I was all alone in my room. "This is bad."

I wanted to rush downstairs, but I couldn't. The house was still infested with hunters.

That Peter Bereza kid was dead wrong. He hadn't found a dragon egg. He'd found something rarer—an orü puma egg.

The creature that killed my father.

The Last Salazar Left Standing

I rummaged through my backpack until I found my journal and turned to the first page. When I first rescued the journal from the garage, the first thing I'd drawn was an orü puma. A golden mountain lion with enormous wings and a tail that ended in the coil of a rattlesnake. The beast that killed my father. The monster Uncle Raf had vowed to destroy only minutes before.

I wondered—*would* Dad want to be avenged? Would he want one of the rarest monsters killed? I'd never doubted these things before, but Andromeda seemed to think differently. I was so confused, and I couldn't talk to my family.

Instead, I rewatched the video again and again until reality sank in. An orü puma was out there and it had laid an egg. I couldn't tell where the footage was shot. It could have been a forest anywhere in the country. When I searched Pete's Wondrous Emporium, *three* results came up. What was I going to do? Call Pete and tell him to take the video down? My Cryptid Kids chat had found it, but they spent their days searching for footage like that. I mean, to be in the Cryptid Kids chat, you had to believe in cryptid animals—magical monsters, ancient beasts, the kind of creatures that haven't been proven. Besides, the video only had a few dozen hits. I had nothing to worry about, right?

But I did worry. I waited at my window until the house grew quiet and the hunters began to leave. Outside, I saw Uncle Raf whisper something to Rome and clap him on the back. Then he thanked my mother one more time. He held her hand until my mother pulled it away.

"My crew's anxious to get back on the road," he said, then glanced up at me, like he'd known I was there the whole time. "I'm only a phone call away."

As soon as they started their engines, I ran downstairs into the living room and snatched the guitar from the wall. I wasn't any good at it, but it's the way Dad called official family meetings.

I strummed. The chord sounded awful, out of tune, and I dropped the guitar. It made a tinny *thud* sound, but at least I got their attention.

"What are you doing?" Rome asked. He aimed to take the guitar back, but I held it by the neck.

"Salazar family rules. Whoever holds the guitar has the floor."

"Val—" Mom started. She pinched the bridge of her nose in the way she did when she was getting a headache. Since Dad died, she'd been doing it more and more.

"Let's just listen to her," Lola said, holding her hands in the air like she was taming a wild jackalope. "Uncle Raf surprised all of us, and the hunters are not the politest guests."

"Thank you, Lola," I said smugly.

Rome slouched in the leather armchair, and Mom and Lola sat on an upholstered bench. We could still hear the motorcycles revving in the distance.

I pulled out my phone and queued up the video. My belly felt like a million marbles were rolling around inside.

"I'm sorry about today," I began. I knew that I needed to soften them up to really get their attention. "I shouldn't have climbed up on that tree during school, and I never wanted to get you guys in trouble."

"It's okay, Tiny," Lola said, her lips tugged into a tired smile. I let the nickname slip because I knew when Lola said it, she still saw me as a little kid.

"What is it that you have to tell us, honey?" Mom asked.

For a moment, I couldn't get the words out. What if Rome called me the girl who cried werewolf again? What if it was just like that morning and Lola had already debunked the video like she did the newspaper story? Why was being brave in front of your family so hard? But that's what I had to be. *Protector. Valiant. Heart.* No matter what Andie said, I know what Dad chose to believe.

"Just watch," I said.

I raised my phone screen so that they could all see. The image was paused on that Peter boy holding the shimmering egg. I restarted the video and let them watch. Like mine, their faces morphed from curious to weary to confused to stunned silence as the boy returned from the cave with a shimmering blue-and-silver egg in hand.

"Is that—?" Mom cut herself off before she could finish.

"It's an orü puma egg," Lola stated.

Mom's face was unreadable. She stared at the screen and touched her ruby pendant.

"This isn't a hoax," I said, before anyone got the idea to claim that.

"It's the right scale pattern." Rome took my phone

in his hands. His knuckles were white. "Orü pumas nest in shadowed areas, according to D-Dad's journals. Yeah, it's not a hoax."

"Then you know what we have to do, right?" I asked.

My family stared at me. The grandfather clock against the wall hammered the seconds away.

"We have to go after it," I said. They all started to protest, but I made my voice as strong as I could and talked over them. "Protector. Valiant. Heart! That's *our* family motto. We are protectors of those who can't protect themselves. We are valiant in the face of fear. Our hearts show kindness. That's what being a Salazar is about. Isn't it?"

"Yes, it is," Lola said. "But—"

"But nothing. This Pete kid wants to livestream this egg hatching because he thinks it's a dragon. We know that it's something way dangerous. I know I've been trying to trick you all into a case. But after the firemunk—"

Lola cleared her throat and glanced pointedly at Mom.

"Excuse me, the *what?*" she asked.

I waved my hands like I could clear what I'd just said. "Never mind that, but my point is: This isn't a trick. I'm asking for your help. We can't just sit by and let this thing go viral. Think about what would happen if that thing hatches and the whole world sees. There's a reason we send monsters back to their realm. If people knew what was out there, they wouldn't know how to cope."

Lola worried her bottom lip. "Dad always said humans don't take care of their own planet; what would they do with a magical one?"

I clapped my hands. "Exactly!"

"There are already people who believe in monsters," Rome said.

"Unicorns and lake monsters are not the same," I said with a huff. "People believe in all sorts of things. But what if there was *proof*? This video would give them that proof. We have to protect—"

"We don't *have* to do anything," Rome interrupted me. "The hunters—they've seen the video. They're preparing to go search for the egg."

We all stared at my brother. I thought about the way Uncle Raf had pulled Rome aside to talk to just him. Was that what he was telling him?

"Why would he tell you and not us?" I asked. "Did he tell you, Lola? Mom?"

Mom and Lola shook their heads.

Mom asked, "What did Rafael say to you, querido?"

Rome looked like a cat backed into an alley. He

snatched the guitar from me, and I bit back the curses I wanted to yell at the hunters. "He wanted me to know that they were going to avenge Dad's death."

You know that feeling you get when your foot falls asleep? My whole body felt like that. Numb. I couldn't believe what I was hearing. If I hadn't asked, would Rome have told us?

Rome's frown deepened as he positioned the guitar on his lap and plucked a few strings. When he did it, it sounded like real music. Like a chime in a soft breeze. That was Rome. He was music and tiny animals that chittered for his attention. He wasn't a muddy, jerk-faced hunter. "Uncle Raf also gave me a family heirloom."

Lola scoffed. "What family heirloom?"

Rome reached a hand into his pocket and drew out two flat daggers with intricate whorls on the handles. Even without touching them, I could feel them radiate ancient power. I knew they were made from kaylorium gold, like the inner workings of my shield ring and Lola's watch. "They never miss their targets, and they're supposed to go to the first Salazar son. They were Dad's."

"Why aren't they going to the oldest kid?" Lola shook her head. "That's so sexist. They belong to Andromeda."

"They belong to no one," Mom cut in. "Your father took everything he wanted to take when he left that house. There's a reason he didn't take those daggers. Your father left that life. He made a new one. However, they were a gift, and I can't do anything about that, even if Lola is right. All I can do, Rome, is ask you to put them in the gear trunk until you're old enough to decide if you want to wield them."

"Mom!" Lola and I shouted at the same time.

She held up her warning finger. "My parents did things differently. To them, it was their way or no way. That's why I left for college. I went so far away, a world away. I made a new family and told myself I'd make new rules."

Rome looked older than his thirteen years then. He nodded and left the daggers on the coffee table.

"What about the egg?" I asked, trying to take the guitar back from Rome. He wouldn't budge.

"Uncle Raf thinks its mother might be the same orü puma that—" Rome couldn't even *say* it. "That got Dad. They're that rare. He thinks it flew away to lay its egg. I say, let the hunters deal with it. We're retired."

"Why are you taking his side?" I asked.

"It's not about sides." Rome strummed lightly. "And he's still Dad's brother. He's still our uncle."

"Doesn't act like it," I muttered.

"Val's right," Lola said.

"Can you repeat that?" I grinned. "I just want to hear it again."

Lola rolled her eyes. "Uncle Raf has never visited us. Not even when Dad was alive. I've seen him more in Dad's old pictures than in real life. He came here for something."

I wanted to tell them about how I saw Uncle Raf digging through the Scourge. But what if I was wrong? My family already thought I didn't tell the *whole* truth. It was my own fault. I had to find another way to make them see my point of view.

"Don't blame this on Uncle Rafael," Rome said.

"He gives you one present once, and now you're a fan of *Rafael*?" I asked.

"That's not fair." Rome started to argue and strum the guitar because we were talking out of order.

Mom stood and clapped her hands hard. "Enough! I know how hard this move has been for all of us. But to make this work, we have to let go of our old life. I know that will take time, but I need your help. No more cases in newspapers." She eyed me. *She knew.* "No more videos. I don't like it either, but the hunters will do what the hunters have always done."

"What about us?" I asked, my voice trembling.

"After the incident today, I realized that I haven't done enough for you kids. Valentina has a point. A viral video of a hatching would be terrible. But Rome is also correct. The Hunters of Finisterra will deal with it."

"You mean they'll smash the egg. They'll destroy it." I fisted my hands at my sides. "That's not what Dad taught us. That's not the way of protectors!"

Mom shook her head. "When I come back, things will change. Please, trust me. It will get better."

"What do you mean when you get back?" Lola asked.

Mom tucked her hair behind her ears. "Oh, right. Last-minute conference. That's why I was so late and hit traffic. I'll be back in five days."

"Five days?" the three of us shouted.

"Again?" I emphasized. "How many fashion conferences are there, anyway?"

Mom's features became hard as marble. "As many as it takes. It's important, Valentina."

"Where is it?" Rome asked.

"Los Angeles." Mom stood. "Lola, you're in charge."

Lola was practically preening like a peacock. Rome looked as annoyed as I did. Mom took the guitar and hung it back on the wall. She rested her hand against the strings, and I watched as she shut her eyes, like she was whispering something. A prayer? The line of a song? Daddy said that sometimes, when you really felt it, those two things were one and the same.

Mom went to the kitchen to clean up, and Rome and Lola went to their own rooms. I went to the kitchen and ate whatever the hunter vultures had left behind. Thankfully, Lola had saved me a plate with my name written on a napkin. I was in such a crummy mood that I could barely eat my beloved veggie spring rolls.

As I loaded my empty plate into the dishwasher, Mom came up behind me and gave me a hug. I was still mad that she wanted us to stay put and let the hunters deal with the orü puma egg, but I couldn't help it. My mom's hugs were the best, and I realized just then that it had been days since I'd spent so much time with her.

"Things will get better. I'll make sure of that." When she said that, it sounded like a promise.

I knew that if opened my mouth to talk I would cry. So, I just nodded and went to my room. I had a promise to keep, too. I was still a Salazar, the last one determined to do the right thing. *Protector. Valiant. Heart.* I couldn't let the hunters get to the egg and tarnish my dad's memory.

And if no one else was going to help me, then I would do it myself.

Do Saints Even Like Beef Jerky?

I don't want to brag, but my plan was excellent. At first.

To start my journey, I packed light. I pulled my bright green duffel out from the closet. It smelled a little funky, and I realized it was because I left a wet beach towel in there from when we first moved to Missing Mountain. It would have to do.

I packed a couple of T-shirts, my favorite ripped jeans. They weren't always ripped, but I've scraped my knees a lot. Sturdy lace-up boots. *Lots* of socks and underwear. Hair ties, hairbrush, toothpaste, toothbrush, pillow. The gear was already in the Scourge. I found my *War of the Galaxies* lunch box where I kept every dollar I had ever made. I was rich! I had a hundred and one dollars, which I'd saved up from helping Mrs. Jones bring in her mail and keeping the squirrels from attacking her birds. Then came phone chargers and batteries for a flashlight. Flashlight! I couldn't forget my journal and a fistful of pens. Lastly, I snuck into the kitchen and ransacked the pantry for ginger ale and extra snacks.

While everyone slept, I crept downstairs to our altar. Saint Pakari's statue was a little chipped from life in the Scourge, but I can't remember a time he wasn't around. He had black robes with a rainbow X pattern down the front of his tunic. The shrine had clippings from some of our cases—the time we saved a cattle ranch from an infestation of long-snout carnivorous snails and the time we found a mammoth caribou trapped by regular human poachers. In my heart, I knew we'd done so much good. We couldn't turn back now, no matter what promises we made to stay in Missing Mountain.

Before every case, Dad would leave behind an offering to Saint Pakari to bless our travels. I took note of Lola's acorn and wondered what she'd been thinking when she left it. I opened a bag of Dad's favorite sriracha-flavored beef jerky and left a few pieces and filled the small glass with ginger ale. I didn't even know if saints liked beef jerky, but it was worth a shot. Dad usually left beer or rum, but I'm not allowed to touch the cabinets for Mom's "grown-up juice."

With everything prepped, I climbed into bed.

"Val!" Brixie whispered. She slipped through my bedroom door, like she always did when everyone went to sleep. "It smells like stinky cars all over the place!"

"*Shhh.*" I always had to remind her to keep it down. Her voice was tiny, but when it was quiet in the house, it could carry. "There were hunters from the Order of Finisterra here."

Brixie dove under the covers and trembled. I assured her they were gone. Then I filled her in on the video my friends had sent me. How the hunters would be on the trail, if they weren't already.

"I'm leaving in the morning as soon as everyone is out of the house. Mom is going to a conference. Lola has swimming lessons. Or cheer lessons. She has too many hobbies, really. Rome will probably sleep until noon like every Saturday."

"It's just youse and me, then?" Brixie asked.

I almost felt a little sad at the way she said that. I was just getting used to not seeing Andromeda all the time since she'd chosen to live with the hunters. I hadn't even considered what it would be like to not see Rome and Lola. Then I remembered that they were always too busy for me anyway. They forgot our mission a long time ago. They were ready to be regular, ordinary kids who went to school and pretended the world wasn't magical. But I couldn't do that. I wasn't built that way.

"Yeah, bud. It's just us. I packed you honey sticks."

Her little purple tongue stuck out like a drooling emoji. "Okies. But you have to let me listen to my favoritest music."

I yawned. "Birdcalls *aren't* music."

"Not to your unrefined human ears."

I turned off the light and curled on my side. Brixie's feather-light weight landed on the top of my pillow where she always curled up with me. When she started snoring, I couldn't help but smile. I supposed I wasn't completely alone.

That morning, I was awake before sunrise. My whole body buzzed with adrenaline. Still, when Mom came in to kiss my forehead goodbye before her trip, I pretended to be asleep. I knew Brixie must have run off for her three a.m. snack and fallen asleep in the sugar jar because my mom didn't scream about a tiny colibrix in my room. All she whispered was "I'll make things right. Sweet dreams, querida."

I loved that my mom called me that. Querida. *Dear one. Loved.* Would I still be her querida if I ran away?

She inched out of my room, and I waited until Lola left. I got dressed in the outfit I'd picked out the night before—dark green leggings, my I BELIEVE shirt, and Rome's hand-me-down jean jacket with a fleece lining. You always had to be prepared if it got cold.

With my duffel slung over my shoulder, I crept downstairs with my sneakers in my hand so I wouldn't make any noise on the warped wood. If anyone woke up, the plan would be over. I had to get to that egg. I had to beat the hunters.

I gave one last glance at our altar and hoped I'd left enough beef jerky so Saint Pakari would bless my journey.

I held my breath the whole time but finally made it into the garage, where the Scourge was waiting.

I know what you're thinking. *But, Val, there's a boot on the van's wheel, and you don't even have your license.*

How cute. You've probably never met someone from the Order of Finisterra. Tracking monsters is a family affair, and everyone pitches in. Dad learned how to drive when he was ten. Me, I'm a *little* rusty, but the Scourge has been retrofitted and upgraded with Dad's tech. It's sort of like autopilot, but the car talks to you like a video game. Dad called it the Salazar Training Wheels Program. I wasn't sure what would happen if I got pulled over, but first I needed to get out of Missing Mountain.

As for the boot, we've had so many parking tickets, one of the first things I remember learning was how to use a screwdriver to get a parking boot off a tire. I found a screwdriver and undid the boot on the front wheel. Then I loaded it up in the van (you never know when things like that come in handy) and climbed up on the driver's seat.

I took a moment and grabbed hold of the steering wheel. Even though my parents took turns driving, I always thought it was Dad's seat. He loved to drive. He said one day he was going to drive from continent to continent. I always wondered how he'd get across oceans.

There, in his seat, I rested my hands on the steering wheel, where there was the faintest outline of his handprint in the leather.

"Hey, Dad," I whispered.

"Hey, Val!" Brixie called out.

I screamed.

She popped down from the visor.

I placed a hand on my chest. Hopefully, I hadn't

woken up Rome. Though he slept like a sack of potatoes. "*Don't* scare me like that."

Brixie covered her face with her pointy black claws and made an apologetic sound of "meep." She flew onto the passenger seat. Her wing seemed much better after yesterday.

"Are you ready to roll?" I asked.

"Where's my tunes?"

"Give me a minute." I fished out a rectangular key from my pocket. It was made of copper and silver with tiny microchips on either side. The Scourge isn't a regular camper van. When Dad bought it, he made a ton of upgrades. Dad was a whiz when it came to machines, something Lola (and Andromeda) picked up. The Scourge was tricked out with an ultrasmart computer. Where the normal dashboard would have been was a control panel with a dozen switches and buttons. I pulled up the navigation screen, inserted the key into the ignition, then turned it.

Nothing happened.

"Are we rolling yet?" Brixie asked, flying out of her seat to tap the control panel. I grabbed her hand before she flipped an alarm and woke up the whole of Missing Mountain.

"No touching. I don't even know what all these

buttons do." I tried the key again. "It just needs a second. The Scourge has been out of commission for months."

Then I remembered—there was something that Dad used to say right before we hit the road. I used to think it was just a habit or something, but maybe it was more than that.

I could picture him then. I cleared my throat, turned the key again, and said, "Let's ride!"

The Scourge revved up with its familiar hum. The navigation panel came on with a display of a road map. Green lights flashed as they came to life.

"Yes!" I slapped the wheel. Brixie swooped in the air and, forgetting she was still in the van, plunked her head on the ceiling. She landed back in the passenger seat.

The rest I knew like the back of my hand.

"Scourge?" I asked.

The voice crackled at first but then got stronger. "Valentina Salazar, age eleven and six months. Not authorized to drive."

For a moment, hearing the Scourge's voice was like hearing my dad again. He'd programmed everything using his voice. It was just a little more metallic, like an android from *War of the Galaxies*.

I reminded myself that it wasn't really Dad. It was

a recording filtered through machines. But it would sure be nice to hear his voice, even a little. I took deep gulps of air and said, "Override."

Green lights toggled back and forth, and the panel made tiny beeping and clicking sounds. "Speak override password."

I panicked. I blurted the first thing that came to mind. "Sriracha beef jerky."

"You have to do better than that! Speak override password. Initiation sequence will self-destruct in ten . . . nine . . . eight . . ."

"Self-destruct?" My voice pitched high. I glanced around the Scourge. I *knew* Dad's password. He'd said it over and over, but it had been eight months without him, and without his voice.

"Seven . . . six . . . five . . ."

"Val?" Brixie asked, zipping back and forth in the air before me. The green light of the dash pulsed like an alarm.

"Let me think!"

"Four . . . three . . . two . . ."

"Mis queridos!" It was a wild guess, but that's what he called us. His dear ones. His loved ones.

I held my breath as the Scourge's green lights pulsed again and made a happy beep. "Override successful. Training wheels on."

"Training wheels." Brixie giggled.

"It's just until I can get my permit, okay?" But I wasn't going to complain. I turned on the radio, programmed to our family's playlist. Then I hit the garage remote.

I buckled in, gripped the steering wheel, and said, "Let's ride!"

The Scourge inched forward on my command. It was the best kind of virtual reality because it was *really* happening.

But as the garage door opened and the light flooded my vision, I noticed something was blocking the driveway. Not something. *Someones.*

I slammed the brakes just in time before I ran over Rome and Lola.

9

The Fear Eater of Fort Washington Park

The thing about Lola is that everyone underestimates her. She's so pretty and sweet. She's the best student and a cheerleader. She has a smile that makes you feel better instantly. Since Mom has been so busy, she's the one who takes care of us. But underneath the "Go Grizzlies" cheer and fairy-tale-princess eyes—my sister has the most terrifying angry stare. I mean, when she's angry, her eyes can singe right through your face like lasers. Like in that moment.

"Uh-ohs," Brixie whimpered.

Lola and Rome walked around the van and boarded. I shouted, "Hide!"

Brixie flitted back and forth. She panicked and hid under the passenger seat.

"*What* do you think you're doing?" Lola shouted.

I lifted the handle of the driver's seat and spun

around to face her. I couldn't help the nervous laugh that bubbled up my throat. "What happened to swimming practice?"

Lola pointed at the house. "I was about to leave when I saw your offering on the altar. It's exactly what Dad used to leave before a mission."

Rome peered around the inside of the van. His face was unreadable and serious. I wished I knew what he was feeling. Did he miss it in here? Was he thinking about our last job?

"I thought you were sleeping," I said to him.

"Lola woke me up." His voice was still groggy from sleep. "I thought, there's no way. Val wouldn't run away and do something so dangerous."

"I'm going to search for the orü puma egg in that video," I said, putting as much strength into my words as I could. "It can't hatch for the world to see, and I can't let the hunters get to it first."

"We—"

I cut Lola off. "I know what you're going to say and you're wrong. All of you are wrong. You think that we're just trying to have a normal life, but we can't. It's like we've been oranges our whole lives and now we're trying to be grapes."

"Grapes are delicious, first of all," Lola said. "Second, that's not what we're doing."

I crossed my arms over my chest. "Yes, it is. From the moment you wake up, you're doing something. Getting us to school. Clubs. Overnight cheer camp. It's literally exhausting just watching you. And I don't even think you like doing all of that, but I know the real reason."

Lola pursed her lips. "What's the reason?"

"You're scared that if you stop moving, you're going to remember that you're sad." I pointed to Rome. "And you! Do you realize that this is the longest conversation we've had in months? You're locked away in your room being angry. You were even nice to *Uncle Rafael*."

"For the millionth time, he's our *uncle*." Rome ran his palms down his face and sighed. "That's not an excuse to run away and hijack the van."

"I wasn't trying to run away, but you've left me no choice! Dad wouldn't sit around and let someone reveal proof of the magical! He wouldn't want us to just sit around while the *hunters* find and destroy one of the rarest creatures in all the realms. Even if it's the reason he's gone." I was so heated that as I waved my arms, I hit the navigation panel.

Dad's voice—the Scourge's voice—interrupted me. "Buckle in, everybody. Roadblock on Main Street."

We were quiet for what felt like a million minutes.

Then Lola touched the corner of her eye and said, "You're right."

"I am?" I sat up straight. "I mean, of course I am."

"That's what we were trying to tell you before you so rudely interrupted." Lola and Rome grinned at each other. "We've decided to come with you. After all, Mom did leave *me* in charge," Lola added.

That's when I realized that they'd entered the Scourge with their own duffel bags. My smile was so wide it hurt. I couldn't believe what she was saying. "You are?"

Lola raised her hands, like she could contain my excitement. "With a condition."

I sank back in my seat. "Oh."

"Last night I couldn't sleep. I kept thinking about what you said. How *we* are the ones who have to find the egg and send it back to Finisterra. How things are different. How we're different. Things haven't been easy here. Mom's trying her best. Rome and I haven't spent as much time with you."

"You got that right," I mumbled.

"I'm agreeing with you here, Tiny."

"So does this mean you believe me about the firemunk?"

Lola pursed her lips in hesitation. "Let's just con-centrate on this. When I saw your offering, I knew that we have to solve this case. Not just because the world can't have proof that there's more out there, but because our family needs closure."

"Like a sale?" I asked, confused.

"That's clearance." Rome snorted. "Closure is like closing the door on something. Like when something is over you put a bow on it or leave it behind, but you're not thinking about it all the time. It's over and you're okay with that."

I tapped my chin. I didn't want to have *closure* on being a protector. I wanted things to go back to the way they were. But I knew that this was my only chance to get Lola and Rome on my side, and maybe, just maybe, they'd remember who they were along the way. "Exactly. That's what I'm doing. I'm getting closure."

"Mom is away for five days," Lola said. "We find the egg before the hunters, send it to Finisterra, and then we come home before Mom gets back from her conference. This is our final mission. After that, it's over. Do we have an accord?"

An *accord* was what Dad used to say when he wanted to make a deal with us. Like the time he bought Andie her first leather jacket if she passed her driver's test.

Lola extended her hand.

Rome looked at it like she was holding a bubble-gum cobra (those things were so cute but had a mean bite). But then his cranky face softened, and he gave us that familiar crooked smile.

"The Salazars' last ride," he said.

I placed my hand on top of theirs before they could change their minds. For a moment, it was beginning to feel like old times. Then Lola sneezed and I remembered Brixie was hiding under the passenger seat.

"Shotgun," Rome said.

I couldn't believe it. "I was here first! This was *my* plan!"

Rome laughed. Really, truly laughed. He grabbed a bag of his favorite chocolate-covered pretzels and climbed into the passenger seat. "You snooze, you lose."

But I wasn't snoozing! I got up at the crack of dawn! The thing was, I wasn't even mad at him. I was too happy that we were together. I took up my familiar seat in the back and buckled in.

Lola pushed up the sleeve of her jean jacket and revealed her compass watch, the one Ms. McCall had liked so much. She tapped the wheel on the side, and its case glowed with green light. Like my ring, it was a family heirloom. Dad had gifted it to Lola on her first mission when she was ten. The green holograph projected the shape of a complex whirling compass. There were the directional arrows, like the usual north, south, east, and west, and then there were other arrows. My heart stopped. I couldn't believe I'd forgotten that the other arrows pointed you in the direction of a monster.

The green light gave a faint pulse. Lola tapped the glass case. "It's going bonkers after not being used for ages."

"Yeah," I said, praying to Saint Pakari that Brixie remained hidden under the seat. "Bonkers."

"What's your plan, Capitán?" Rome asked.

I told them about how there were three Pete's Wondrous Emporiums in the country. "But I have a friend in the city who can help. He's a genius and he can narrow the search."

"And where exactly is this friend?" Lola asked.

I buckled in and said, "Washington Heights."

"Next stop, Washington Heights." Lola changed the navigation to her profile to input the address.

And then we were off. We were really doing it! I could barely contain myself. My stomach felt like I had fuzzy abelitas flying around in there. I closed my eyes and felt the movement of the road. Tilted with the sharp turns my sister made. We slowed down on Main Street where the navigation system had predicted traffic. A bunch of kids from school were gathered in front of the diner and the bookstore next door.

Lola stopped at the light. Her friends looked at the Scourge. I bet they were thinking it was the coolest van they'd ever seen. But the windows were tinted, so they couldn't see her driving. I wondered if Lola wished that she was with them, getting lattes at the coffee shop and then browsing the bookstore next door. Lola gave a little shake of her head before she focused on the road, and we kept on going.

✦✦

We didn't stop until we reached Washington Heights a couple of hours later. New York City was loud with honking cars and taxi drivers shouting out their windows. We exited the highway and drove down streets lined with restaurants and coffee shops. A little old man with leathery skin pushed a mango cart. A woman sold towers of shaved ice to kids dressed ready to play basketball.

"Twenty-four bucks just to park?" Rome asked as we pulled into a parking lot across from Fort Washington Park. Lola bit her lower lip. "We're going to need to be better about our budget. But there's no street parking."

I didn't tell her so, but in that moment, I was so

glad that Lola and Rome had caught me. I didn't even know what a budget *was*, let alone how to have one.

"Iggy said he'd be at the Little Red Lighthouse," I explained.

Rome opened up the rear doors and unlocked the gear trunk. "Who is this kid, anyway? Is he from your creepy crawlers chat?"

I rolled my eyes. "It's my Cryptid Kids chat."

"Andie and I never had message boards," Lola added. She'd traded her cheerleader jacket for a deep purple satin bomber that had MONSTER GRRRL stitched on the back. It was from one of those really old Hollywood movies in black and white.

"Yeah, well, Iggy's brother started it a few months ago," I said. "Their parents were muckers."

Muckers were people who worked for the Order of Finisterra. When the hunters tracked and killed magical beasts, they left a mess behind. During the ride down, I'd told them about how Iggy's parents specialized in making sure there wasn't any surveillance footage catching any critters, which had impressed Rome. Secrecy is the only thing hunters and protectors have in common. Daddy always said that people liked the idea of magical beasts, but if they knew the truth? They wouldn't be able to handle it.

"What's he doing at the lighthouse?" Lola asked.

Even at school, she never lost her habit of scanning the perimeter after getting out of the car.

"He said he'd tell us there, but to make sure and bring the Meridian. So, it's definitely monster related."

"Wait." Lola made a T with her hands. "We never agreed to that."

I shrugged. "I did. This is my mission. You two decided to join, remember?" Then I added a tiny "Please" just because it never hurt to be polite.

"The Meridian opens up a portal to Finisterra," Rome said.

"I *know* what it does," I said. "Besides, we're not *giving* him the Meridian. We're just letting him use it."

"Just as long as he knows that people aren't allowed through," Lola reminded me.

I rolled my eyes. "I know the rules. The only thing that goes through the portal is a magical animal. Believe me, while the rest of you have been trying to act *normal* in Missing Mountain, I've still been studying Dad's journals."

I sidestepped Rome to get to the gear trunk. Not everything in there was deadly. There were stunners, nets, tons of rope. And of course, there was the Meridian. You know what I said about the hamburger buns and the Swiss cheese? Those little holes are flash portals and they're super rare, but they're all over the world. Magical animals find their way here from Finisterra through those portals. The thing is that they're one-way doors, and they can't go back even if they wanted to.

But Dad figured out a way to make a portal any-where. He invented a device called the Meridian, using kaylorium gold that ripped a small hole between the realms, just long enough to send the monsters back through.

I opened the hidden latch on the inside lid of the trunk. The Meridian didn't look like much. It was the size of Mom's compact mirror. In fact, that was where he said he got the design. It was made of copper and iridium. Inside there was pure solid kaylorium gold. I cradled the Meridian in my palms. I wondered if Dad knows that even if he's not with us, he's still helping us. I wondered if Lola and Rome were thinking the same thing I was.

I pocketed the Meridian on the inside of my jacket and caught a glimpse of Rome tucking the daggers Uncle Raf had gifted him into his boots. I wasn't sure why it bothered me, but I had this uncomfortable feeling at the back of my neck. I decided to ignore it because Iggy was waiting. I fished out the metal net Rome had rescued after I dropped it from the tree.

"Let's hope that whatever Iggy is dealing with isn't

bigger than a golden retriever," Lola said, and locked the van.

We walked the long path that led from the parking lot to the park. I'd never been to that part of the city before. There was a huge metal bridge directly over the sprawling green. The lighthouse was the color of dry tomatoes with a black iron fence around it. Our feet crunched on the gravel trail. I knew that the plan was my idea but for a few seconds, I kind of felt like I wanted to barf up the chocolate protein bar I'd eaten on the ride down. But in a good way.

It had been months, *eight* months, since we'd been out in the world like this. I missed my mom. I missed my dad. I even missed Andie. But the three of us was a good start.

"That him?" Rome asked, stopping a short distance from where a twelve-year-old boy wearing yellow goggles stood. He wore an oversize Mets T-shirt and cargo pants with a million pockets on them. He held a tablet in the direction of the river where just across you could see New Jersey. A baseball bat was discarded on the ground by his crisp white kicks.

"Iggy!" I jogged toward him.

He whirled around, pushing back his goggles atop brown corkscrew curls. Up close I could see the deep imprints the goggles had left on his brown skin. He peered at me curiously. "Val?"

"Who else would it be?" I asked.

He looked at Rome and Lola from head to toe. "What's the secret word?"

I cupped my hand around his ear and whispered, "1986 World Series champs."

I didn't particularly care about baseball or anything, but Iggy was extra paranoid about security and he chose the password. He said he spoke three languages: English, Spanish, and computer.

"This your brother and sister?" he asked, lifting his chin in greeting.

"Lola, Rome, meet Iggy."

Iggy pointed a finger at Lola. "You look familiar."

"I just have one of those faces." For a split second, I could have sworn that my sister looked nervous. But I told myself she was probably just worried about the mission. She straightened and gestured to the river. "What are you tracking?"

Iggy narrowed his eyes, scrutinizing her the way Mrs. De Bernardo did my homework. "There's something that's been terrorizing the dogs and kids in the park. Cops think it's just bigger kids playing pranks, but I've caught some footage that says otherwise."

Lola surveyed him skeptically. "*You* caught footage?"

Iggy and I exchanged smirks. "Yeah, lady. Don't you know the government has eyes and ears everywhere? You just have to know your way through their digital labyrinths. I can hack almost any server. But I can't make a door to Finisterra."

Even the mention of Finisterra felt different. We'd spent months pretending to be ordinary kids at school, and at home we barely talked. Hearing Iggy say the word made it feel like old times again.

"And you're sure you can get us a location to the egg?" Rome asked. He was not as impressed as I was. He kept looking over his shoulder like he was expecting something to jump out at us in broad daylight.

Iggy pressed his lips together and made a raspberry sound. "You're the one that's been out of the game. I'm just doing Val a favor."

"Where's your b-brother?" Lola asked, tripping on the last word. It was unlike her.

"How do you know I have a brother?" Iggy asked, arching one bushy eyebrow with suspicion.

"*Re*-lax. I told her," I said.

Lola squared her shoulders and regained her composure. "Do you want our help or not? A baseball bat isn't going to do you any good."

126

"I just want to know one thing," Rome said. "If your parents were muckers, why not call the hunters?"

"*Were* muckers. A job didn't go right. Dad got hurt. Mom didn't make it." Iggy looked away and sniffed, but his face remained serious. "No one pays attention to us in this part of the city. My brother and I took up their challenge. We're not muckers anymore, and we hate the hunters for what they did to our family. Still, someone has to look out for the neighborhood if no one else will. We know what's out there. We do what we can, we just don't know how to replicate your dad's tech."

Lola nodded. We all knew the Meridian was Dad's pride and joy. He never even wrote down how he constructed it, only that it had one purpose—to help us do our jobs as protectors.

"What've you got?" I asked. "Is it the same monster you wrote us about?"

Iggy glanced around. "Yup. Notice how it's summer but hardly anyone's around?"

We nodded. Above us cars zoomed over the bridge, and a few civilians walked their dogs on the green and near the river's edge.

"Most people are too scared to come out here for long. Caught wind of it because my neighbor lost her dog out here. Reported it, but they blamed it on her being a little kid and not being careful." Iggy held his tablet against his chest, and we stepped in closer to hear him. "Then she started feeling sick. Missed the last few days of school. When her moms took her to the doctor, they said there's nothing wrong with her and sent her home."

"Let me guess," Lola said. "She's still sick."

"Yup. I hacked into a few hospital records and there are six kids with the same symptoms right in this neighborhood. No one seems to care. So, I've got to do something about it. Even if I can't figure out what it is. The reports of its size aren't consistent." Iggy eyed Lola curiously. "How'd you know she was still sick?"

"It's called a manchani moth," Lola explained. "It starts off small, like a regular moth. It feeds on the hope and sunshine inside others and leaves the victims super weak, like a really bad flu only without the snot and fever. But it turns all that good stuff into fear. Its wings are made of shadows . . . and the screams of innocents. Kids, puppies, probably adults if they're nice."

"You ever seen one?" Iggy asked.

Lola nodded. "Andie and I failed last time, and it almost got Valentina."

"*Me?*"

She tucked one of my stray waves behind my ear. "Back when we lived in Queens for a few months. You were little, which is why you don't remember."

"*I* don't even remember," Rome said.

I hated being too little to remember. I especially hated that our traitor Andromeda had stories about tracking with Lola and Dad that I'd never get to have.

"If it hadn't been for Dad—I don't even want to think about what could have happened. It got too big. I suppose it started eating our screams and fears, too. How long has yours been a problem?"

"Five days or so," Iggy said. He snapped his fingers. "If it grows as it feeds, *that* must be why I haven't been able to pin down a species."

Lola rubbed her arms against the sudden chill in the air. "The bigger it gets, the more it has to feed. They can be harmless when they're small, but sometimes they catch a whiff of too much fear and they keep getting bigger, hungrier."

"The attacks have generally happened in this area at this time. I've got a trap set up." Iggy grinned at me, like he was asking if I was ready.

Lola checked her watch. The sky grew darker and a breeze spun around us. "At this time?"

"Wait a minute," Rome said. "If there's a trap, then that must mean—"

Worms moved in my stomach. There was a part of the plan that I'd left out when I told Rome and Lola about it.

I'd agreed to be Iggy's bait.

Revenge of the Manchani Moth

If you've never seen a manchani moth, consider yourself lucky. Imagine an ordinary moth. Weird and fuzzy, right? Well, now turn its wings into shadows, so dark they look like goth butterflies. When their wings beat, there's a vibration in the air, like a howling wind that pierces your eardrums. I would have thought that Rome would have loved all the racket, but as the creature appeared under the bridge and screamed, he covered his ears with the palms of his hands, too.

Rome was shouting at me. Probably something about how irresponsible it was to be someone's bait. But Iggy needed someone who fit the profile and would attract the moth. That'd be me. I couldn't help it if I was a ray of sunshine.

"Don't worry!" I shouted. "Iggy has a plan!"

Iggy, who was wearing foam earbuds, like the kind

construction workers use, lowered his goggles and readied his tablet. "Gotcha!"

The ground around us turned dark, like a river of ink had spilled at my feet. When it comes to magical creatures, it can be easy for your brain to want to reboot. Rescramble. Your mind is telling you that you're seeing something else. Mom used to say that it was an evolutionary trait humans started developing after magic left this earth thousands of years ago. My mind was telling me that it had just gotten dark suddenly, but I pushed through that feeling and I saw the monster flying right toward us.

After such a long time away from the road, my body reacted all weird. My limbs froze. My heart raced. I blinked hard as the inky shadows turned into wings. Wings so big they sucked out the sunlight. I couldn't help it. I screamed. Lola screamed. Rome screamed. The manchani moth's body was surprisingly humanoid, with a head that might have looked like a young girl's and body covered in gray fuzz. White spots covered its long torso, and entirely black eyes homed on me like a beacon.

Then I realized, it wasn't me the manchani moth was going toward. It was Rome. I whirled around and blocked the creature's path.

"Whatever you do, don't move!" Iggy shouted.

And then lightning cracked all around us. An electric dome closed over our heads. The terrible sound of the moth's wings was gone, and so were its wings. They vanished and the creature fell to the ground with a soft *thud*. For a moment, there was perfect stillness and quiet. I felt my heart racing in my throat and my ears as the dome got closer and closer, shrinking down toward our heads. I held my breath and shut my eyes for what came next.

"Hold on to your butts!" Iggy shouted. He slammed his finger down on his tablet and the thing moved faster! I squeezed my eyes shut and held my breath as the dome passed right through us.

Have you ever been electrocuted? Well, it wasn't like that. But it did feel like the time I plugged in the blender and the socket gave me a tiny shock.

"What *was* that?" Lola's face was pure fury. Tiny hairs were standing up, escaping from her French braid. Then I realized all of us looked like we'd rubbed balloons against our heads.

On the ground, the dome was small enough to cover the moth. Ropes of electricity crisscrossed from four silver cubes on the grass.

"Like?" Iggy asked, standing proudly over the contraption. "It's my dad's invention. He stopped working on it after my mom passed, but I finished it. I need a name, though. Iggy's cubes? Iggy's super dome? I mean, it traps the monsters without hurting them and makes my job a whole lot easier."

"What about hurting *us*?" Rome growled.

Iggy raised his goggles back up. "Creatures from Finisterra have a different body chemistry. It's charged for them. That's why we're fine and it's not. There's only one charge at a time, which I haven't worked out, so we should get moving."

"Did anyone else notice how the moth went for Rome?" Lola asked, crouching to get a better look at Iggy's invention.

Rome scowled. "It didn't. It went for Val. I'm not exactly rainbows and puppies."

I would have agreed with Rome, except that I'd noticed the same thing Lola had. It was certainly strange, but I noticed something else.

"It looks so . . . sad," I said.

"Sad?" Rome snapped. "It was going to *kill* us."

Lola held up her hands. "A little warning next time would be nice."

"Look, I knew if I explained, you'd worry too much, and we had to act fast. Besides, we're fine. I thought you'd be glad I showed initiation." I laughed nervously, but she only sighed, like she was disappointed.

"You mean 'initiative,'" Lola said. "Let's just open up the portal and get this over with."

It wasn't exactly how I'd thought our first case together would go, but I was hopeful that we'd get in sync in no time.

"My pleasure." I removed the Meridian from my jacket pocket. The copper base was cool in my palm. I'd seen my family do this hundreds of times, but I couldn't help the thrill that ran through me.

"I've never actually seen this," Iggy said, readjusting his goggles. "How do you maintain the polarity between realms to not create a black hole? Wait a sec—can we get trapped inside?"

I noticed how he took several steps back. I mean, if a portal opened up in front of me, I'd be afraid of getting sucked in. I shook my head. "The person who could answer your question isn't here to answer it. And technically you could get trapped if you lost the Meridian. But we're not allowed into Finisterra. That was Dad's main rule."

"Only the animals go in," Lola added.

"Bummer," Iggy said. "I could use a vacation."

"No one's going anywhere if we don't get the manchani moth back," Rome said sharply.

I cradled the Meridian on my palm. The outside

of the compact device had delicate lines engraved all over, like the Nazca Lines in Peru. A brilliant sun was emblazoned in gold on the cover. I pressed the latch and opened it. I was prepared for what would happen next. I'd press down on the kaylorium gold core within, and it would create a great energy surge. The surge would only last for a few minutes, and I readied myself to drop the Meridian and then step back.

Except that didn't happen, because when I opened the compact, there was nothing inside. The core was missing. Gone. Vanished. Completely and totally not there. Without the kaylorium piece, there was no portal.

Lola sucked in a breath. Rome said a word he'd need to put a dollar in the swear jar for when we got home.

"What's wrong?" Iggy looked at us with confusion.

"It won't work," I said. I could barely speak.

And the moth was rousing from its stupor. It pushed itself up on long gray fingers. It screeched and stood on shaky legs. The sound that came from its mouth was unlike anything I'd ever heard. It was like someone was using a cheese grater against metal. Shadows stretched again, and this time the creature moved too fast for us to act.

Shadows elongated, spreading up along the lighthouse and the iron veins that held up the bridge. Its wings were growing back as it fed on our sunshine. Lola and Iggy wobbled, but Rome fell to his knees fast. It was affecting him worst of all. But me? I fought through it. I couldn't make sense of it. Rome was always brooding and hiding in his bat cave with his angry rock music.

Then it hit me. They said that the manchani moth fed off innocents. Their light and hope and all the good stuff. But had anyone ever asked why? Deep beneath the shrieking sound of its cries, there was something there. I'd already seen it—sadness. Why else would it steal the light from others? It didn't have any sunshine of its own.

Now there were four of us and one of it. The manchani moth was alone and outnumbered, like when Maritza and her friends surrounded me in the empty school halls and I had no one to help me escape. When that happened, I was just more myself. If they thought I was weird, I'd just be weirder.

Perhaps the manchani moth needed something similar. It needed to know that it was okay to be sad sometimes.

And I knew just what to do.

"Rome!" I shouted. "Put your song on speaker. Blast it at the highest volume!"

"Which one?"

"The screechy one! Just do it!"

Thank Saint Pakari, he listened. The manchani moth's wings were almost fully re-formed. While my brother fumbled with his phone, I leapt on the moth and grabbed it around its knees. My weight dragged it back to the ground. We crashed along the shoreline.

Then Rome's caterwauling heavy metal boomed. Guitars and drums and vocal cords screamed one long, horrifying note. Slowly, the moth rocked back and forth like it was dancing along to the tune. It turned its ink-black eyes and then it started to cry.

"It's all right," I told it. "It's all right."

The moth released a long wail. It shuddered as it shrank. Suddenly, a warm sensation started from the middle of my chest. It spread. I couldn't put my finger on it, but I knew I was doing the right thing. This! This was what being a protector was supposed to feel like.

"You neutralized it," Iggy marveled. "How?"

But I never got to answer.

Rome lifted his pant leg and withdrew a dagger from his boot. He looked down at the weapon and then at the manchani moth. Just then, my brother reminded me of someone else. Uncle Raf—so sure that every monster was a danger to the world and needed to be put down. I'd been so worried about us becoming boring old civilians I hadn't even realized a bigger problem. Was Rome turning into a hunter?

"Rome—"

Before I could beg my brother to put down the dagger, an arrow whistled through the air. I shut my eyes, but I heard the *thud* of a bull's-eye. I forced myself to look just in time as shimmering fuzz exploded into the air. I wasn't sure what happened until I realized the moth was breaking apart. Its shadow wings and body disintegrated like when I blew on the head of a dandelion flower.

The arrow fell to the ground. Lola picked it up and blew away the shimmering residue. I spun in the direction the shot had come from. I caught a flash of black leather from up on high where the leg of the bridge towered over us. The archer was gone in the blink of an eye, but I knew—it was a hunter from the Order of Finisterra.

The Scourge Gets an Upgrade

We hurried back to the Scourge. No one spoke. Even Iggy, who'd been excited to see the van up close, was quiet. On the way to Iggy's building, Lola white-knuckled the steering wheel and focused on the road like it was the highest level of the *Road Crash* video game.

"Turn right here," Iggy said.

Lola made a sharp turn from Riverside Drive. Cars honked at us for crossing two lanes, but in seconds we were up the parking lot ramp. We drove in circles up, up, up. I lost count until we got to the top level, where there were only a few cars that looked like they'd been parked and left to rust. Lola's watch pulsed with green light and beeped.

"What is wrong with this thing?" Lola asked, tapping the screen off.

I couldn't help but look at the passenger seat, where

(I hoped) Brixie was still hiding. Iggy knew all about Brixie, and he gave me a look that said, *You are in so much trouble.* But still he came to my rescue.

"Probably residual energy from the manchani moth." Iggy cleared his throat awkwardly. "I—uh— let's go get an update from Ozzy on the location of Pete's Emporium."

At that, Lola's face changed. She bit her bottom lip and stumbled on her words. "We should stay here. We're all filthy from the park, and we'll get your apartment dirty. We wouldn't want to bother your dad."

"Dad's working the late shift at the hospital," Iggy said, and scrunched up his face. "And not to worry. We're not going down to the apartment."

Lola relaxed. What was up with her?

Iggy thumbed in the direction of the doors. "Besides, Ozzy's right here."

There was a knock on the Scourge, and I couldn't help but jump. We'd just seen a creature get blown up to smithereens and I was on edge, okay?

Lola waved her hands in the air like she was trying to stop him, but Iggy went ahead and unlocked the side door.

There stood a tall boy who looked like someone had stretched Iggy and added a bunch of muscles. Ozzy was Lola's age, sixteen or seventeen. He was in a soccer jersey and shorts that showed off claw-mark scars on his thighs. He had two little dimples on his cheeks, like when I stuck my finger in the fresh bread dough Lola sometimes made.

Speaking of Lola, she wasn't even looking at him. Was she nervous? Did Lola like a *boy*?

"What's up, guys? Hey, Lola." Ozzy smiled wide, then gasped like he'd remembered he'd left the stove on. Or the fact that he already seemed to know Lola's name. "I mean—hey, sister of Iggy's friend whom I've never met before this second."

Rome went, "Huh?"

"Wait." Iggy snapped his fingers. "*That's* why you looked familiar!"

Ozzy grabbed his brother and tried to clap his mouth over Iggy's words. But Iggy was spry, and he ducked out of his brother's grasp. We spilled out of the van and onto the parking lot.

I turned from Lola to Ozzy and said, "I'm confused. Do you two *know* each other?"

Lola looked uncomfortable. "Sort of."

"Is 'sort of' code for 'definitely'?" Rome asked.

Iggy pointed at my sister. "I *knew* she looked like the girl on your phone background. No wonder you never let me go on tracking missions with you."

Rome and I looked to Lola. Tracking missions? I couldn't believe it. My own sister!

"You've been tracking?" Rome asked her, his voice pitched low. I couldn't quite tell if he was disappointed that he hadn't been asked or angry that she'd kept a huger secret from us. I was a little bit of both.

Lola let go of a long breath, then seemed to relax, like she'd been holding something really heavy and now the weight was a bit lighter. She took a seat on the floor of the van and dangled her feet between the open doors.

"Yeah," she said, turning to the cityscape in the distance. "I've been going on missions with Ozzy and some other muckers."

"Since *when*?" Rome and I asked at the same time. I hated when we talked at the same time.

Ozzy's shy smile returned. "Oh, since last year. Way better than cheer camp, right, Lola?"

Lola's deadly stare returned. "You're not helping, Oz."

"Is he, like, your boyfriend?" I asked.

Lola said, "No," at the same time Ozzy said, "Yes."

"Burn," Izzy chuckled.

"Great," I said. "That's just great. You tell *me* that I can't lie. You tell *me* that I can't look for cases and you've been doing the same this whole time! You're a hieroglyph!"

They all stared at me curiously for a moment before Rome whispered, "I think she means 'hypocrite.'"

"I know exactly what I mean," I huffed. I made an L with my arms. "Give me an *L*. Give me a *Y*. Give me an *R*. Give me an *E*. What does *that* spell, Lola?"

"If you're going to cheer, then at least learn how to spell, Tiny," Lola said.

Rome raised his brows. "Yeah, we're going to study as soon as we're home."

"Forget it, *liar*," I continued.

Lola glanced up at the heavy clouds, like she was waiting for some help from Saint Pakari . . . or from Dad. Part of me didn't want to hear an excuse, but another part of me wanted to know every detail of what she'd done. Had she seen any monsters we'd never heard of? She opened her mouth to talk, but then her watch beeped again. This time, she didn't ignore it. And she definitely noticed the way I sucked in a breath. "There's something here."

I shook my head. "No, there isn't."

But my voice cracked. Lola knew when I was lying. I don't know how she did it. Maybe I just wasn't very good at hiding the truth. It's not exactly a skill that I *wanted* to have.

Lola held up her watch, and the green light spun and spun until it pointed at the passenger seat. Rome drew his daggers just as Lola reached under the seat. There was a loud squeak as she wrenched out a bag of chocolate-covered pretzels with Brixie inside.

"You!" Rome snapped, pointing a dagger at her. "You're the thing that's been eating my snacks!"

I leapt in front of my brother. A tiny part of me didn't trust him not to hurt Brixie. Feeling that way felt like being covered in slime.

"I can explain," I said.

"Please don't hurts me!" Brixie pleaded. "Please, beautiful cheerleader princess! I'm sorry my feathers give you sniffles. I can't helps it."

It was Lola who was stunned. "My allergies. They started when we got to Missing Mountain. You mean to tell me this—"

"Brixie is a colibrix," Ozzy offered.

I wanted to tell him that he wasn't being helpful, even though Lola did look impressed at his knowledge of my little friend's species. *Even* though I'd told him in our Cryptid Kids chat.

"We'll give you some family time," Iggy said, and dragged his brother away.

Brixie, sensing that things weren't settled, flew out of the (empty) chocolate-covered-pretzel bag and into my hands. I cradled her against my chest like a doll. Rome picked up the litter and crushed the bag in his fist.

"Let me get this straight." Lola pinched the bridge of her nose and looked so much like Mom it was scary. "Brixie has been living with us since before we moved to Missing Mountain."

I nodded, feeling extra guilty. I explained about our last job in the strawberry fields and how her whole hive had been killed by hunters. I saw the way Rome frowned when I mentioned them. I pushed the slime feeling away.

"I couldn't leave her. And then everything happening with Dad. And then we moved. Brixie has been my only friend lately."

"She doesn't belong here," Rome said. His hazel eyes zoomed in on Brixie. "She belongs in Finisterra."

"Well, we can't exactly make a portal, can we?" I asked. "Do I need to remind you that the Meridian didn't work because it's missing the core?"

Rome grumbled. He reached for his headphones, but they weren't around his neck. He couldn't hide from us the way he'd been hiding for months. "Fine, we need to find some more then. Because there are two ways to get rid of magical creatures—we either send them to Finisterra or we destroy them."

I felt like I was choking on air.

"Rome," Lola said softly. "You don't mean that."

"I don't?" His voice shook with anger. "The orü

puma killed Dad. The manchani moth would have hurt us. It already hurt a bunch of others."

"I'd never hurts anyone," Brixie squeaked.

Rome pointed a dagger at her. "You ate my snacks."

I held her protectively. Rome wouldn't hurt *me*. Would he?

"Brixie is sorry! Truly. I loves sweetness." And then she started to cry and cry. If you've never seen a colibrix cry, consider yourself lucky. Their tears are like tree sap, all sticky and stuff.

"I hope you're happy!" I snapped at my brother. I returned Brixie to the Scourge, only this time, I nestled her on the cushioned seat and covered her with a scarf. I was so mad, I leapt back out of the van and confronted my siblings. "Brixie isn't hurting anyone. I'll buy you new snacks. I bet you're the one who told the hunters where we were. I bet you wanted us to fail."

Rome looked like I had punched him. He blinked down at the weapons in his fists and he grimaced. He returned them to his ankle holsters. "I didn't."

"You don't even want to be here, Rome. Go home."

"Maybe I will," he muttered.

Lola reached out to both of us, gripping Rome and me by the shoulders. "No one is going home. We have a job to do. Ozzy's getting us a location. We just have a few bumps in the road. Everyone wobbles when they get back on a bike, right? Protect." When neither of us said anything, Lola repeated, "*Protect.*"

"Valor," Rome said.

"Heart," I whispered.

Ozzy cleared his throat. "If you're done fighting, I've got some good news. Follow me."

The three of us turned to Ozzy and Iggy. A few feet away, against the far wall of the garage, was a lean-to, like the kind you see at a park. There were broken computers and multicolored wires spilling out of their guts.

"The building super lets us have our little operation here as long as we fix his appliances for free," Iggy explained.

"What exactly is your operation?" Rome asked.

Ozzy flashed that dimpled smile again. Even though Rome asked the question, he glanced back at Lola and smoothed the buzzed sides of his fade. "Since Dad retired from being a mucker for the hunters, we've picked up where he left off. Only, without the hunters, we run into our own problems."

"What do you mean?" I asked.

"What Rome said was partially true. With magical creatures, you either send them back to Finisterra—which we can't do without the Meridian or a flash portal, and those are too rare and unpredictable to find. The other option, well, we wouldn't even dream of that. Lola's joined me on some local missions. Water bear in the Central Park Reservoir, mammoth snails causing subway damage with their slime, *as if* the MTA needed any more reasons to have terrible service."

"But then, what do you do with them?" I asked. I'd been friends with Iggy for a few months now and he'd never mentioned it. That's how secret he'd kept it. I had to admit I was a little jealous that Lola had found out first.

"We get them homes," Ozzy said.

"But—that's not allowed," Rome said.

"Says who?" Ozzy asked, still smiling. Honestly, how could someone smile so much? "The hunters? They're not in charge of us. The Great Salazar Protectors? Y'all are retired, *if* I remember correctly."

"Well, we're out of retirement," Rome said, crossing his arms over his chest. Next to Ozzy, he didn't look as menacing or tough as he probably thought. "For now, at least. Lola, how could you have been going on missions? You seriously turn these monsters into *pets*? You say we need to set an example for Val and you're being the most irresponsible. What if someone gets hurt?"

Lola shook her head. "I told Ozzy as much. But how is it any different from people who have exotic pets?

Or any pet? Cats will devour a human body once it's dead. A pet python could strangle you in your sleep. A regular dog could bite hard enough to break the skin. All animals have their own nature—normal everyday pets *and* magical beasts."

Rome exhaled like an angry dragon. "You could have used the Meridian."

Lola rolled her eyes. "We don't know how long it's been missing. And no. I wouldn't have used the Meridian. Not—not without you guys."

At that, my anger toward my sister melted a bit.

"Anything truly dangerous," Iggy said, "like the moth, we would have found a safe place in the wild. There's been whispers about a rare-animal collector asking about rare animals. Rare enough that they should be legendary. We get creepy vibes, though, like those über-rich black-market people who like to eat panda burgers or dolphin tartare. That's why we were hoping you'd help with the Meridian, but . . . we all know how that's going."

Standing on that roof with my siblings and friends, I felt like the world was too small and too big all at the same time. Lola was keeping secrets. Rome was sympathizing with hunters. Brixie had been caught. Iggy and his brother were running a magical pet shelter. What else would we find out?

"Look, it's been a long day," Lola said. "Don't you have good news for us?"

"We do." Was Iggy blushing? Holy saints! Was anyone immune to Lola? "Ozzy?"

"Right!" Ozzy plopped down in front of his laptop and typed faster than anyone I'd ever seen. "I had to pull some middle school records for the two Peter Berezas in the same counties as the emporiums. The universe is wild, isn't it?"

Lola smirked at him. It was only for a moment, but I caught it. "I think this is just a coincidence."

"I mean, what are the chances that your sister and my brother would become friends?"

I couldn't be sure, but was Ozzy trying to flirt with my sister? There was a twinkle in his large brown eyes. But Lola only pointed at the screen. "That's our Peter."

Ozzy deflated a little as he turned the laptop around. "He's in Fontana, Florida."

There he was, with his fire-red hair. Peter Bereza, the boy who'd uploaded that video of the orü puma egg.

"There's a new video from a few minutes ago," I said, leaning in closer. I hit play.

The dimly lit room of the Wondrous Emporium came into view. The camera was so shaky it was going to give me a headache.

"Welcome to the shop, everyone! My dad has been collecting marvels from around the world for years. Now it's my turn to add to the collection. I present to you—the Bereza Draconus. Whoever finds it, names it, of course! Starting today, the doors are open for viewing. If you're too far to travel, I've set up this live feed. Dr. Hofheinz from Delaney's Veterinary estimates the egg will hatch within the week, especially with this heat lamp to keep it warm."

Peter flipped the camera onto his face. His eyes were huge with excitement. "Get this—the CDC and animal control both want to get their hands on this bad boy, but we've got security to protect it."

The camera panned in on two tall, beefy girls with red hair, probably his sisters or cousins. They had medieval weapons slung over their backs and something that looked like Tasers at their hips.

"Tune in and get ready to welcome a real live dragon to the world!"

Then Peter Bereza focused the camera back on the egg. The gleaming scales shone under the golden heat lamps.

"Oh, thank the saint," I muttered. "There's only a hundred views. Imagine how people would react if they knew these creatures were real?"

Iggy whistled. "Collectors. Hunters. The government? I don't trust people to form an orderly line when they're trying to score new kicks. Peter Bereza has *no* idea what he's dealing with."

Ozzy made a sound of disagreement. "I don't know, Val. A hundred's pretty good for only an hour."

"Yeah, you've got a ton of videos doing your bachata instructions and only six people have watched it over a month," Iggy said, and doubled over laughing.

"You dance?" Lola asked, smirking again.

Ozzy's face lit up like Christmas. "I'm Dominican."

Iggy rolled his eyes. "I'm Dominican, too, and I have two left feet. You just like attention."

Ozzy reached over and grabbed Iggy's goggles. He pulled them, stretching them as high as they'd go and then letting them smack back on his brother's head. That did it. The two of them started play fighting across the parking lot.

As fun as they were, the whole thing made me feel pretty crummy. I remembered when Rome and I used to play fight. Now things were just weird. I wondered if Lola and Rome were thinking the same thing, because we all just looked at one another real quiet like each one of us was afraid of being the first to break the ice.

"I didn't tell the hunters where we were," Rome said, scuffing his sneaker against the pavement. "I wouldn't do that on our last mission."

I wanted to believe him, but he was so different from the old Rome, the Before Rome. Yet I knew Dad would want us to get along. Even if my brother was being a butthead, I still owed him replacement chocolate-covered pretzels.

"I'll get you new snacks," I mumbled.

Rome chuckled softly. We turned to Lola to see if she had anything to say about lying to us and sneaking off to run around the city with Ozzy and his mucker friends, but she only straightened her shoulders and put on her game-day face.

"It's going to be a long ride," Lola said. "We need to get going."

Ozzy stopped playing around with Izzy and looked from Lola to the Scourge. "You think you're going to make it all the way to Florida without getting pulled over?"

"I'm an excellent driver," she said, jutting out her chin.

Ozzy leaned in to brush away a strand of hair that had fallen over her eye. "I don't doubt it. But the Scourge seriously needs an upgrade. It'll take a couple of hours, but it will save you trouble on the road.

Plus, my dad would kill us if we had you over and didn't make you eat lunch."

Our stomachs rumbled at the barest mention of food. Even Lola's face turned pink at the sound, which I'm sure people across the river could hear.

"What kind of upgrades are you talking?" I asked. No one touched the Scourge without permission.

Iggy rubbed his palms. His brown eyes were wide like a mad scientist's. "Just you wait."

✦✦

While Ozzy and Iggy tinkered with the dashboard, upgrading the system and adding software that would make us undetectable to police scanners and harder to track, Rome and I ordered lunch. We found a Salvadoran restaurant and got fifteen pupusas. The round flour patties were stuffed with all kinds of fillings. I got two cheese and one with meat.

Iggy ate his pupusas in a handful of seconds, then got back to work. He seemed happiest twisting wires and soldering them into place. I have to be honest, even though we desperately needed the update, I felt nervous. No one touched the Scourge except for Dad. But Iggy was my friend, and the way he was so careful really made me think Dad would have liked these two brothers.

Brixie, who'd woken up from her crying-induced nap, didn't care for pupusas because she said they were too savory, and instead she ate an extra chocolate bar Ozzy was saving. It was still weird hanging out with her in front of Lola, but there was something very freeing about it, too.

When we were finished eating, we focused on another problem: the missing kaylorium core that should have been inside the Meridian. We scoured every part of the Scourge. We moved the back seat, which converted into a bed. Under every pillow, the cabinet where we stored our supplies. We sorted through the tools and weapons trunk where it was always kept. We opened up the roof latch where the twin bed was, even though I'd spent most of my time there. It didn't hurt to double-check. Lola even dug her fingers in the plotted succulent plants that somehow had survived months in the garage.

"I wonder..." Lola tapped her chin as she flipped through Dad's old journals. "Could the Meridian have vanished the last time Dad tried to make a portal?"

I shook my head. "I remember Mom looking at it one last time before she put the boot on the Scourge."

Brixie rummaged through the snack box, but I was pretty sure she was looking for sugar instead of the Meridian compact.

I grunted and shut the journal I was flipping through. "Is there a chance that because we haven't used the Meridian, that it just threw *itself* into a portal?"

Lola squinted as she considered this. "We've gone for long stretches without being on the road before. Remember that year when Dad broke his foot and Mom made us rest until he was patched up?"

"That was only four months," Rome pointed out.

"Portals never truly close," Brixie intoned. "They're magical pulses. Perfect tiny heartbeats."

Lola turned to Brixie, whose feathery wings flapped so fast it was like she was floating. "What else do you know of the magic there, Brixie?"

Brixie's eyes lit up. "We had the most beautiful trees with sweet, sweet flowers. Petals melty and tasty like cotton candy. I love cotton candy. Can we get some?"

"Brix," I said. "Focus."

"Oh yeah. I don't know, Lola Lola. I was a hatchling when my hive ran."

"Ran from what?" Lola asked.

Brixie jumped onto Lola's open hand. "Oh yes. There was a terrible volcano that went boom! Our grove was destroyed. And then we came heres and then—but then—" She hiccuped. Her eyes became glossy with her sticky tears. She trembled, so I picked her up and brushed her feathers back.

157

"It's okay, Brixie. You're safe with me."

Lola gave me a look, like I should know better. That we were supposed to send Brixie away. But how could we do that when her forest was gone and she'd lived with me for so long? How could Lola ask me to give Brixie up if she'd been helping others find homes for magical beasts?

"We have to face it. The Meridian is gone," Lola said finally with an air of resignation.

"What are we going to do?" I asked. My heart plummeted right through me and through several floors of concrete. "We need the Meridian to make a portal. We can't exactly raise an orü puma. We definitely can't let the hunters kill it."

"I agree, but we're slim on options, kid," Lola said.

I remembered being in the Scourge. I remembered Uncle Raf rummaging around. He'd been searching for something. I wondered—what if he didn't come to see us because he wanted to have the worst family reunion ever, but because he wanted to steal the Meridian's kaylorium core? But what would a commander of the Order of Finisterra want with a portal? All they did was *kill* magical beasts and monsters. They hunted. They did not protect, let alone return the creatures home safely.

I wanted to tell Lola my suspicion, but would she believe me? Things already felt so delicate because of the lying and arguing. I didn't want to make it worse. So I kept it to myself.

Rome returned to the Scourge from keeping an eye on the egg-video livestream. "We might not be out of options."

"What do you mean?" Lola asked.

For a moment I thought that Rome had the same suspicion as me, but instead he said, "We need a kaylorium core, right? Then we just find some kaylorium."

"But the only kaylorium left is *in* Finisterra," I said. "At least, according to all of Dad's research."

I didn't realize I'd been holding the journal closed against my chest until Rome gently pried it from me. He flipped it to the middle. It made me feel a bit better to know that he'd memorized it just like I had.

"Here Dad wrote about how there are likely still pieces in the world left, even if they're small. Like fossils are remnants of a time gone by. They'd be artifacts or a forgotten vein in a rock somewhere in the Andes. Remember his theory that when the Spaniards invaded South America, they confused kaylorium and the shine of its alloy for regular gold and that's what might have begun the rumors of El Dorado?"

I nodded. It was one of my favorites of Dad's theories.

"Yeah, but where are we going to find artifacts here?" Lola asked.

As I thought about our new problem, Iggy climbed out of the Scourge. His goggles had left imprints around his eyes, and there were grease smudges on his cheeks. "Sorry to break up the family bonding moment, but we're done. Come check out the new and improved upgrades."

Ozzy was in the passenger seat, and the rest of us climbed into the back. Everything looked the same as always, but when he turned the key and Lola said her password, the screen flickered brighter than ever and with new colors.

"Whoa!" I shouted.

"All right, here's the new system," he explained. "Green is the regular navigation. The blinking purple lights are the algorithm that sifts through databases, radio stations, podcasts, any media. If it's public, it pulls it and alerts you to a possible sighting of a critter nearby. It's like your watch, Lola, but this has a thirty-mile radius."

"Sweet," Lola said, then pointed at a new black triangular button. "What's this?"

"You're going to love this. It's a hologram that projects while you're driving. That way anyone who looks into the window can see an adult instead of a sixteen-year-old girl."

"I've also upgraded your maps with my code," Iggy said, like he was competing for which brother had outdone himself. "It alerts you to traffic jams and lets you avoid Five-O, so you don't have to explain monster tracking to clueless mere mortals. But especially hunters. Speaking of . . ."

Ozzy held up a round chip blinking a red light. "We found this in the dash. We can't tell when it was put there, but our dad made trackers like this for the Order of Finisterra."

I snatched the tracker from Iggy and held it in my palm. It was no heavier or bigger than a quarter, its evil red eye winking at me. Anger shot through me at the thought of hunters following us. Could it be that Uncle Raf hadn't tried to take something, but left something behind?

I shoved it in my pocket.

Iggy frowned. "Shouldn't you, like, destroy that?"

"No way, I have a better idea."

We thanked the brothers and said our goodbyes. Ozzy lost the ability to talk when Lola quickly gave him a kiss on his cheek. We buckled in, even Brixie, and peeled out of the parking lot.

We stopped at a gas station, and while Lola filled up

the tank and Rome replenished his snacks (with *my* lunch money), I walked up behind a large truck. There was a sticker on the bumper that read TAKE A HIKE.

I whistled a song that was stuck in my head from Ozzy's playlist and flipped the hunter's tracker into the bed of the truck. "Nice sticker!"

The bearded man filling up his tank looked at me, then at Lola, and seemed confused. "Thanks, kid."

Once we were back in the safety of the Scourge, gassed up and ready to go, Lola glanced at me through the rearview mirror. Rome opened a new bag of sour apple gummies. Brixie perked up her little nose, but flinched back at his brooding scowl.

"Where to?" Lola asked.

I'd been thinking about what Rome said, about how we needed to replace the kaylorium core. I knew someone who might be able to help, but it was a long shot. I shut my eyes and heard Daddy's words, like he was right there with us. *Long shots can sometimes be the most accurate ones.*

So I took my shot and said, "Washington, DC."

12

The Book Garden

Four and a half hours later, we reached Greenbelt Park. Lola parked the Scourge in a campground near the restrooms and showers. Then she built a fire in the metal pit while Rome prepped dinner and I took the first shower. Once I was squeaky clean, even cleaning behind my ears and under my armpits, I ran back across the crunchy road and into our campsite. For a moment, I froze at the sight. Rome was heating up ramen packets and leftover pupusas from that afternoon. (I know it sounds like an unlikely combo, but I was so hungry I'd eat anything.) Lola watched Peter Bereza's live feed on my tablet.

It felt so much like the Before Times, I couldn't stop myself from looking around for my dad, just out of habit. He'd be cleaning the Scourge, and Mom and Andie would have been telling stories around the fire.

But they weren't there, and I swallowed the strange feeling in my throat.

I plopped down on one of the fold-out chairs. "No action?"

Lola shook her head. "No action."

"Good."

"We're sleeping in the Scourge tonight," Lola announced, dusting soot from her palms. She turned her sharp stare at the sky. "It might rain, and I'm too tired to bring out the tents." Soot had gotten on her nose, but on her it looked like dozens of little freckles. "Has your friend replied?"

"Not yet," I said, checking my phone. No replies from Sequoia Thomas.

"How do you know this Sequoia Thomas is legit?" Rome asked skeptically. "You can't just trust anyone you met on the internet."

I rolled my eyes. "I'm perfectly aware of stranger danger. But Iggy and his brother keep the security of the Cryptid Kids club super tight. Plus, Sequoia has been talking about her mentorship program at the museum for months. It's like Ozzy said. The universe is looking out for us."

"I don't know about that, but we've chased after monsters with fewer leads," Lola said, adding another log to the flames.

"If you're talking about the bunny vampire hoax on that Vermont farm from last year," Rome said, laughing, "then yes, fine, I'm on board."

"*Iggy's* an internet friend, and he worked out," I reminded them smugly. Rome was right; there were lots of fake sightings out there. That's why our Cryptid Kids club was small. Not everyone in the group had a close encounter of the awesome kind, but they believed. Better yet, they wanted to know more.

After Lola and Rome took turns using the showers, we ate a hot meal. There was another family a few campsites over, roasting marshmallows and playing guitar. I know Brixie would have loved marshmallows, and I wished we'd thought to pack some. Dad would never have forgotten the marshmallows. Our parents did so much for us on the road, I realized. They built the fire and did the cooking. They put up the tents and inflated sleeping pads. They took turns singing or reading from their favorite books since we rarely had internet to stream any movies or TV. Sometimes Dad would just reenact his favorite scenes from *War of the Galaxies* and do all the alien and android voices.

I found myself wishing that our parents were there more than ever. Nothing about the mission felt right without them. My eyes began to sting and get warm, so I blinked fast. Thankfully, my phone beeped with messages from Sequoia.

M3rmaidLyf3: I've got you covered, @MonsterGrrrl7.

M3rmaidLyf3: Is this what you're looking for?"

I slurped up the last of my noodles and nearly choked. "Look!"

Lola took the phone I offered and zoomed in on the photo. The item was a misshapen lump of gold with a green sheen, sort of like metallic moss. From the look on Lola's face, it was clear we'd hit the jackpot.

She said, "It's labeled under 'Pre-Columbian stone carving from the Chorrera culture, Ecuador.'"

"What's cho-rrreh-rah culture?" I asked, sounding out the syllables.

Rome took my phone and studied the picture. He snapped his fingers like he was trying to remember. "They're the ancient civilization that lived in Ecuador way before even the Kingdom of the Incas, and before the Spanish conquistadors. Mom is better at explaining it. But that looks right. It's a bit misshapen for a carving. They probably don't know what they found."

"Are we really stealing from a national museum tomorrow?" Lola asked, nodding pointedly in my direction.

Why were they so worried about setting a good example for me?

"Dad said that he loved museums," I reminded them.

"But sometimes things are unearthed and taken when they should have been left behind. Besides, that's kaylorium gold. It belongs in Finisterra. We'd be borrowing it until we find who stole ours."

I couldn't help but glance at Rome. I wanted to tell them about my suspicions that Uncle Raf was the thief, but I just waited.

Lola nodded. "Tell Sequoia we're good to go."

I typed faster than I ever had before.

MonsterGrrrl7: Bingo.

M3rmaidLyf3: Come to the Book Garden in Columbia Heights. We're closed on Sundays so use the back entrance.

I was too excited to sleep, so I volunteered to do the dishes. I know! I hated doing dishes at home, but as I scoured leftover noodles in the campground sinks, I felt better than I had in days, months even. Back at camp, Lola had popped the camper roof. Rome and I shared the convertible bed with Brixie. I couldn't tell if the van had shrunk or if maybe I was just getting taller, but I didn't remember the strings of light on the ceiling hanging so low, or my feet dangling from the edge of the mattress.

Just as I was drifting off, the metallic chime of a ringtone woke me up, followed by the hard crash of Lola falling on top of us.

"Mom's calling!" Lola shouted. "She's trying to video chat. What do I do?"

Brixie flew between Lola's phone and Lola. "I can says hello!"

I yanked Brixie by her wings. "And give her a heart attack? You're supposed to stay hidden, remember?"

"Oh yeah." Brixie giggled.

"Uh, if we lie down on the blanket, it'll look like we're in the living room," I said.

I swiped to the right, and my words tumbled out so fast. "Hey, Mom, hey how goes it what's up?"

"Val? Where's Lola? Did I call the wrong child again?" Mom was walking in what looked like a parking lot. The sun was setting and cars honked in the distance.

"I'm right here," Lola said, her voice high-pitched the way she gets when she cheers. I turned the phone to show her face and then Rome's.

"Hey, Ma," he said, in his usual bored voice.

"The three of you are hanging out together?" she asked. I wished she hadn't sounded so surprised.

"Yeah, we're going to watch *War of the Galaxies*."

"Oh, I wish I were there for that." Her eyes got real sad and distant for a moment. Her dark circles were worse than usual, and her eyes were puffy, like she'd been crying not too long before. It made me feel terrible for lying and deceiving her. But I told myself that we were on a mission. When we got back to Missing Mountain, we'd really watch the movie together. We'd get closure, like Lola said. We'd be better than ever. I hoped.

"All right, don't let me hold you up. I'm heading to my hotel and wanted to check in on you. I-I'm sorry things have been the way they are. It will get better. I promise."

"I know," I said. She'd told me that in a whisper when she thought I was sleeping. "They will be."

"I love you all. So much."

"We love you, too." Lola and Rome waved.

She pressed her fingers to her lips and blew us a kiss.

"Well, I feel like garbage on a hot summer day," I said.

Brixie climbed on top of my head and nested in my hair. "That's a terrible way to feels."

The next morning, we packed up our campsite, making sure not to leave anything behind, and went in search of breakfast. We hit the drive-through at Mermaid Cove Coffee. I got a scrambled eggs with sea salt hash browns and the Atlantic Wave Frappe, which was made with spirulina that turned the milk a teal color and lots of confetti sprinkles. Lola got a Super Tsunami Protein shake, and Rome got black coffee and a bacon, egg, and cheese wrap with nori.

Columbia Heights was a suburb in Washington, DC. The Book Garden was a tiny bookstore surrounded by Mexican restaurants and clothing stores. Even though we'd already eaten, there was always room for tacos.

But I knew we had to focus. We parked in the lot behind the store and went around back and knocked twice, then once, then three times real fast.

In turn, someone knocked twice.

I knocked three times.

"What was that?" Rome asked.

"Secret knock we settled on," I said.

Rome grinned. "Nice."

The door swung open. A Black girl around my age poked her head out. She was dressed in a black blazer and a pink-striped skirt, and wore her brown hair in two wide cornrows with striped ties at the ends.

"Monster Girl Seven?" she asked seriously.

"Mermaid life?" I asked back.

Maybe we were both excited or nervous, or maybe we were just happy to be able to meet each other in person after trading stories back and forth in our chat, but we both leapt into a giant bear hug.

Lola cleared her throat, and I realized I was being rude.

I stepped back and motioned in the general direction of my siblings. "Sequoia, these are my associates, Dolores and Romero Salazar."

Lola laughed but shook my friend's hand. "You can call me Lola."

"Rome," my brother said, raising a hand in greeting.

Sequoia's smile got a little bit bigger when she looked at Rome, and she fidgeted with the locket pendant resting between her round shirt collars. "You ready for trouble?"

"Trouble is my middle name," I said.

"Your middle name is Alexander," Rome corrected me.

I scoffed, but Sequoia laughed and waved us inside. We passed a corridor full of towers of boxes, a small office with a desk covered in papers, then made a right into the bookstore. It was small, but there were real potted flowers strung up along the ceiling and all along one of the walls. Dark green ivy twisted along the brick wall behind the cash register. I inhaled the new scent of books, flowers, and green things.

Sequoia led us to the back of the store, where there was a reading nook. A bright purple chaise, a blue-velvet, high-backed chair, and several stools were set around a wooden coffee table with fantastical creatures carved on each corner. On my side I could see the head of a kraken and the horns of a minotaur.

"Is that a griffin?" Rome asked, leaning down.

Sequoia's smile was sad. She'd had tea and cupcakes arranged on a tray and began to pour the steaming liquid into one teacup. "My dad carved it," she explained. "He was a wood-carver. My mom was a florist. But they quit their jobs and opened up this bookstore because they realized there wasn't one in our neighborhood. And then my mom's accident happened."

"I'm so sorry," Lola said softly. "We know the feeling."

Rome accepted the tea and sat back. I wanted to snort because dressed in his black clothes, he looked comical holding a delicate flowery teacup. But he drank and said, "Thank you."

Sequoia stirred extra clumps of brown sugar into her tea and tapped the silver spoon on its side. "That's how Val and I got to know each other."

"Monster Girl Seven?" Rome muttered, and slurped his tea.

I stuck my tongue out at him.

"What happened?" Lola asked.

Sequoia looked into her cup like it had all the answers. "We were in Virginia Beach, and Mom went for a swim. She grew up swimming in the Caribbean side of Colombia and she always complained the water was too cold up here, but she still went in. Every time. Sebastian, my brother, heard the scream first. I dove in and swam after him. He used to call me his shadow because wherever he was, I was there, too. Dad was getting us food or something. I can't quite remember. But anyway, the water was murky and cold, and there was something *in* there. It had tentacles. Big and green with bioluminescent suction cups that lit up. It happened so quickly, but then our mother was gone. Just vanished."

I felt a familiar tightness in my chest and my teaspoon rattled against my cup. We never talked about the day Dad—that day. We talked around it. Uncle Raf bringing it up the other day was the first time in a long time that we said the words out loud.

Then I shut my eyes and tried not to picture my dad's face. *I'll be right back. Andie, Rome, secure the area.* Those were the last words he ever said to us. When I looked down, my tea surface rippled, and I realized a tear had fallen right in. I wiped the side of my face before anyone could notice.

"Is Sebastian still gone?"

Sequoia nodded. "My brother's convinced he can track the beast. He vanishes for weeks at a time.

He became a marine biologist and goes on expeditions. That's where he met hunters from the Order of Finisterra. They promised to help him find the monster that took our mother. But all that's happened is Sebastian's stopped checking in. That's the reason I'm agreeing to help you."

Lola stopped eating her tiny cupcake and sat forward. "Oh?"

Sequoia looked at me directly. "You know about my brother's last trip. He went off the coast of North Carolina with some hunters. He hasn't come back, and I don't know how to get in touch with them. If I help you get into the museum, you have to help me find my brother."

"We don't find people," Rome said. "We find monsters."

"I know, but if you could even ask the hunters—" Sequoia bit down on her trembling lip. "I need answers. *We* need answers. My dad couldn't handle losing him. Not after what happened to Mom."

Rome set his cup down, and he said the words I was dreading. "I'll call Uncle Raf and ask him if he can search for your brother."

"I don't like owing the hunters any favors." Lola admitted the same thing I was thinking. "But we know what it's like to want answers. We'll try as hard as we can to help you get them."

"Do we have a deal?" I asked my friend.

"Deal," she said.

Thanks to Sequoia, we snagged three passes into the History Museum of the Americas and Caribbean. Her mom was from Colombia, and her father was from Texas, and she'd always been interested in the history of her mother's home country, she explained.

"She's the smartest girl in the world," Mr. Thomas said as he came down the stairs. He had the same medium brown skin as Sequoia and wore a soft lavender sweater. He had tight black curls that were sprinkled with silver. His eyes were a little sad, and they reminded me of my mom during our video call, like they were trying but they didn't know how to make everything better. "A little too smart for her own good."

"Good morning, Mr. Thomas," Lola said, turning on the kind of smile that made parents trust her immediately. Like nothing she was part of could go wrong.

"So you three are in this monster business, too?" he said, shaking his head as he poured himself a cup of tea.

"Daddy." Sequoia rolled her eyes. *"Secret* monster business."

He made a zipper motion across his lips. "I'm making an observation, baby girl. Besides, who'd believe me? Not even me."

There was something comforting about Mr. Thomas's presence, even if he didn't agree with what we were doing.

"We have to get going," Sequoia said, and I helped her put away all the tea things. "I don't want to be late for my mentorship."

"Come on, then," Mr. Thomas said.

We followed him to another van, only theirs was a silver family van. I smiled when I noticed bumper stickers from several beaches they'd traveled to. As we drove into downtown Washington, DC, and the monuments came into view, Sequoia went over her plan for us. We had to follow it down to the very last detail, down to the exact minute. Good thing Lola had her Salazar watch.

We pulled up into a crowded street where dozens of taxis and cars dropped off passengers. Sequoia kissed her dad on the cheek, then ran inside.

As agreed, Mr. Thomas drove around the block once more before letting me, Rome, and Lola out of the van. That way, we wouldn't be seen going in together in case we got Sequoia in trouble.

"Thank you, Mr. Thomas," I said.

"Be careful what you chase after," he responded. "Some things might just chase you back."

"Yes, sir," Rome said, his little frown returning with a vengeance.

The three of us stood in front of the building. Out of all the museums that sprawled around the city, this one was relatively tiny. All modern and gray, like what I imagined museums in *War of the Galaxies* might look like.

"Ready or not," Lola said.

And Rome answered, "Let's go steal back some old stuff."

13

Night at the Museum: Salazar Edition

What Rome called old stuff I called heaven. I know museums can seem boring at first, but when our parents took us, they'd tell elaborate stories and reenact famous paintings and statue poses. Lola and Andie would run to the weapons trove and look at all the ancient swords and spears and whatever was on display.

The History Museum of the Americas and Caribbean was brand-new and always packed with school groups, according to Sequoia. As soon as we checked in with the free passes she'd given us, I clocked her across the room with other kids around her age.

"The South American section is all the way in the back," Rome said, using his whispery museum voice. I thought it might look suspicious, but everyone seemed to whisper at a museum. It seemed like an unspoken rule.

The place was laid out like you were traveling through the American continents, starting with the First Nations and Indigenous tribes of North America. A group of kids were gathered around a humongous stone jaguar that came from an Aztec temple.

"You're walking too fast, Tiny," Lola said.

I grumbled at her but slowed to a stop in front of a re-creation of a beautiful Indigenous woman with long black hair and a garland of flowers around her neck. I read it out loud, "Anacaona. Isn't that the name of one of Mom's favorite songs?"

Lola rested her hand on my shoulder. "Yeah. Says here she was a Taíno chief of Ayiti—or modern-day Haiti and the Dominican Republic. She was brave and beloved but had a tragic end."

"She looks younger than Mom," I noticed. They had the same long dark hair, and the same fierce stare that Mom had in the Before Times.

We passed rows of bowls, gold earrings, carved wooden toys. It was so strange to think that centuries ago someone had eaten from that bowl, or worn those earrings, or spent a long evening playing with that toy. I told Lola and Rome as much.

"Dad always said that we honor the places and people that others try to forget. Like us." Lola smiled. "The world has forgotten that there used to be magic on this planet. Very few people know what Finisterra used to be. We guard that memory."

I thought about that. "I guess since we're retired, it'll just be left to the hunters."

Lola frowned slightly at my words and kept walking to a wall-length mural detailing the timeline of the Panama Canal and how it was built.

"Funny story," Rome said. "Panama hats were not from Panama. They're from Ecuador. When the canal was being constructed, Ecuadorian artisans went down there to sell their wares. They became super popular after President Theodore Roosevelt was photographed wearing one."

"Right you are, young man," someone said behind us. "Are you here on a camp trip?"

I whirled around to find a woman with blonde hair pulled into a long ponytail. She wore a blazer and green pencil skirt and official-looking ID tags around her neck.

"Here with the family," Lola said, flashing her bright smile.

"I'm searching for a group to take for a tour test

run! Where are your parents?" The woman looked around, like she was trying to match our faces with our parents.

"Oh, they're resting their old bones at the café gift shop," I said. I'd heard Mom say that all the time when she went to take a bath. She needed to "soak her old bones." This lady didn't seem to like that all that much. "But we can take a tour."

"Wonderful. I'm Ms. Evans and this is— Now, where did she go?"

Sequoia turned around the corner, her pink-striped skirt swishing around her knees. When she noticed us talking to her mentor, her eyes went wide. Rome gave a slight shake of his head, like to tell her to remain cool. "Here I am!"

"Sequoia, I found the perfect candidates to practice your Young Explorers tour on."

"Hello, strange stranger that we've never met before," I said, and held out my hand for Sequoia to take.

I heard Rome hiss beneath his breath and Lola suppress a laugh.

"Fill all your brain noodles with knowledge. I'll have my eye on you!" With that, Ms. Evans clopped away in her blue heels.

We followed Sequoia, who looked super official.

She held her clipboard against her chest and heaved a sigh. "That was close. I was for sure thinking she was going to make us go get your parents resting their *old bones*."

"I panicked!" I said defensively.

Sequoia cleared her throat and gestured to a small, enclosed room that began the South American part of the displays. A banner read ATAHUALPA'S GOLD. An illustration depicted the legendary Inca emperor Atahualpa. Beside him was a Spanish conquistador in silver armor named Francisco Pizarro. Between them lay tons of gold.

I remembered my parents mentioning the names before, but my memory was fuzzy. According to Sequoia, the last emperor of the Incas was invited to a feast to celebrate his kingliness. Atahualpa and his men showed up without any weapons, and surprise, surprise. It was a trap. Pizarro and his men fired on the Inca guests. It just seemed like bad manners to me.

Anyway, the king was captured and a ransom was set. His people would have to fill a room full of gold in order to be freed. The emperor's allies did it. They filled a whole room with gold. But get this. That Pizarro guy still had the emperor killed!

"That's not fair," I said. "He did everything he was supposed to."

Sequoia smiled sadly. "There are legends surrounding the gold itself. Some say it was cursed. Others say the gold was lost. All gold, whether in the king's ransom or from the mines, was sent back to Spain."

"Dad would have loved this," Rome said, standing in front of a mask made of hammered gold in the shape of the sun.

A few tourists wandered into the room and Sequoia turned on her über-professional voice, the way Lola does when she's cheerleading, and then relaxed when they wandered away.

"Some archeologists are disputing that because the gold is tinged green," she said, "that it isn't pure and it's some kind of fool's gold. That's what we're researching at the moment."

Lola, Rome, and I exchanged a look. They weren't going to be able to keep researching after we got our hands on the kaylorium.

"Thanks again," I whispered to my friend.

"Good luck," Sequoia said, then left us to find another tour group to practice on. "Don't forget our deal."

I gave one last glance at the item on display, then followed Rome and Lola back the way we'd come from. We headed past the café and gift shop, just like Sequoia had instructed us. There were two doors marked EMPLOYEES ONLY. One was a janitor's closet and one was their mess hall. I almost froze, unable to remember which one was which. Up on the corner of the wall was a security camera. But it was pointing away, slowly making the trajectory in our direction.

"It's the left one," Rome hissed.

Lola shook her head. "No, it's the *right one*."

Rome looked over his shoulder. "Come on."

The camera was moving again. I had to make a decision. There was no room to doubt myself. I grabbed the handle to the door on the left and held my breath as I turned.

It opened and I came face-to-face with cleaning supplies.

We hurried inside just in time for the camera to make a full rotation. Inside the janitor's closet, it smelled like wet mop and lemon cleaner.

"This smells familiar," Rome said.

"It smells like your *room*," I muttered, and Lola clapped her hand over her mouth to stop from laughing.

"Very funny," he said.

Lola tapped the screen of her watch. "According to Sequoia, we have exactly seven minutes from the moment they shut the doors at one p.m. and everyone on staff leaves, and when the security guards change shifts."

"That's a pretty big window," Rome said. "They might want to call Ozzy to up their security."

Lola and I traded a curious glance. "Was that a *joke?*"

Rome shrugged. "I'm a funny guy."

"Funny like Brixie eating all your chocolate-covered pretzels." I snorted.

As soon as I said it, I wished I hadn't. When we replaced the kaylorium core in the Meridian, I knew they'd bring up the subject of sending Brixie back to Finisterra.

Instead, Lola asked, "Any updates on the egg livestream?"

"Can we call it the Egg Stream?" I asked.

"No," Rome and Lola said at the same time.

Older siblings ruined everything.

Rome checked his phone, where he already had the video pulled up. "No action."

We still had one hour to kill, and so we changed into black shirts and watched the video. There were ten more viewers than last time, and the number dropped up and down a tad, just like my nerves. Sometimes Peter Bereza would pop on and remind "viewers" to visit the shop. Then he'd zoom in on his bodyguards and make them take bets on what the dragon would look like. Pink, or furry like how dinosaurs were supposed to have feathers or something. I wanted to scream, *It's not a dragon! It's an orü puma!*

The egg remained perfectly still. I kept thinking, *Don't hatch don't hatch don't hatch don't hatch.* I must have thought it for nearly the whole hour because then we heard the shuffle of people outside the door. Ms. Evans's excited voice and high heels clicked away until they were nothing but a distant echo.

"Five minutes," Rome announced, rubbing his palms together the way he did when he was all nerves.

I nodded and repeated the plan and reached into my backpack for our baseball caps. "We can't do anything about the cameras, so make sure your caps are pulled over your eyes. See, Panama hats would really be helpful."

"And conspicuous," Lola said.

"Your *face* is conspicuous." I tugged her visor lower. "Then, Rome picks the locks, and we grab the kaylorium and hightail it to the door in the back that leads to the loading bay. From there we make a run for the subway and back to the Scourge."

Rome cracked his knuckles. "Done and done."

"Two minutes," Lola announced.

You know when you're waiting for something to happen and it's like the clock is dragging, like the whole world is moving at a snail's pace? That's what those two minutes were like. My stomach felt like chocolate melting on a sidewalk, but somehow I was sure I could run a mile in a second. That's how nervous and charged up I was.

There was a knock on the door. Just a single rap from Sequoia.

"That's the signal," Lola said. "She's the last one out the door."

She tapped the side of her Salazar watch and a green countdown began. I stepped out of the janitor's closet first, because I was the smallest, and if I got caught, I could just say I got lost.

Saint Pakari was on our side because the museum was empty. All the lights were out except the ones inside display cases. You could hear a mouse hiccup if you listened closely enough. With the coast clear, I held up two fingers to signal for Lola and Rome to follow.

We crept back to the South American section. The entire time, my heart was lodged in my throat. Lola's watch beat a steady pulse of green light. We had five minutes before the security guards returned.

"There you are," Rome said.

He was the best lockpick in the family, which Mom argued wasn't something to be proud of, but Dad always said, "That's my boy!" He said you should never steal from those who need it, but some things called for exceptions, like how once, we freed an entire cage full of ofilibonagas (fuzzy salamanders with elongated snouts) from a cosmetic test lab who'd gotten them from a black-market website. We couldn't have done it without Rome's skill.

My brother rubbed his palms together, then withdrew his lockpick from his back pocket and went to work. He crouched down and behind the display case, where a metal lock reflected Lola's green light. Rome held two thin metal pieces with slender tips and inserted them into the lock mechanism. A tiny bead of sweat rolled down his temple.

I thought I heard something, so I crept carefully back and around the corner. The place was quiet. Light reflected from all the glass surfaces. I would have thought being alone in a museum would be cool, like in the movies, but it was more like a horror movie with the eyes from paintings and replica statues following you around. I whirled back around but froze.

There it was again.

Keys. Jingling keys! A door opened.

I pulled my cap low and ran, so fast my shoes squeaked, despite the suede we taped on the bottoms. Lola and Rome glanced up at me with desperate alarm.

I made a cutting motion across my throat and whisper-hissed, "Ms. Evans!"

Her clicking heels echoed through the halls. Her bright voice seemed louder in the empty museum, and there was a tall security guard with her. "Thanks, Robbie. I'd lose my head if I didn't have a reminder on my phone. I just have to pop back in my office real quick."

Rome didn't stop working. Lola stared at her watch. Two minutes were left on the clock, but now the security guard was in the building early.

"Abort mission," Lola whispered, and waved her hands frantically. Was she trying to cheer the words out?

No way. We *needed* that piece to make the Meridian work.

Then we all heard it. The clear, beautiful click of locks falling into place. Rome pushed the glass container door to the side and reached in to grab the kaylorium gold.

Lola looked up as her watch stopped pulsing. "Time's up."

"I swore it was in my office," Ms. Evans said. "Let me retrace my steps."

That's when I noticed a glossy rectangular ID card on the floor. One of the dozen cards that'd been hanging from the museum curator's neck. The footsteps hurried in our direction. Even though we had what we'd come for, we would be caught trying to get away.

What would Dad do? I wondered.

The thought came to me as fast as lightning. I grabbed the kaylorium from Rome.

I didn't have time to explain. I opened the Meridian and placed our stolen gold in the center with a sharp snap.

"What—" Lola began.

"This is our only way out," I cut her off.

The glow of the portal split the air open with a circle of light. I always thought it was like being surrounded by the rings of Saturn or Jupiter.

All the light and sound drew attention. Voices shouted in the distance, coming for us. I grabbed my brother and sister by their hands, and we escaped into the place we were never supposed to enter.

We stepped into Finisterra.

The Patron Saint of Finisterra

If you've ever fallen through an interdimensional portal, then you know the first thing that happens is, your ears pop. Since it was my first time, I wasn't prepared to fall. I wasn't prepared for the way my head spun. One minute I was there, and then the next I was somewhere else. I was surrounded by streaks of colorful light. The sound of a howling storm. And then, for a few seconds, when the wind was at my back and I was alone, there was nothing but black and pinpricks of stars in the distance. Everything that made my world *my world* was sucked out into a vacuum and replaced by Finisterra.

The landing wasn't smooth. I wish I could say that I landed in a crouch, like a superhero, or even a cat. No, I, Valentina Salazar, landed on my tailbone.

Ouch.

I waited for a second before opening my eyes. I had to make sure I wasn't going to throw up. I could hear how fast my heart was beating in my eardrums. Grass tickled the palms of my hands. At least, I hoped it was grass. I was afraid to look.

All my life, Finisterra had seemed like a place that was so far away. It was on the *other* side of the portal. I remembered asking my dad why we couldn't go through the portal, and he always said, *We don't belong there, little bug. Promise me that a long time from now, when I'm old and gray and the Meridian falls to you, that you won't try.*

I promised. So did Rome and Lola and Andie.

That day came sooner than we thought, and now, I'd broken that promise.

I opened my eyes. The first thing I noticed was the sky. It wasn't the blue I was used to. It was lilac fading into pink. Mammoth clouds floated across a white sun, and just below that was a crescent moon. Both winked in the sky at the same time.

When I breathed deeply, my lungs ached, like they were stretching to fill with the sweetest air I'd ever smelled. I wanted to look at everything all at the same time. Giant hills rolled in one direction. Behind me was a rocky path that led to a forest made of black pine trees, and behind that a mountain sparkled and shined like it was made out of crystal. The grass was just a little bit greener, the yellow flowers just a little sunnier.

I spun around in circles, each time seeing something new. There was a path through the grass, like someone, or something, walked it enough to permanently leave their mark. To my right was a skinny river with shimmering fish that jumped out super high.

"Whoa." I sighed.

After making sure none of my bones were broken, I looked around for Rome and Lola. I walked in a small diameter from where I'd fallen, but they were nowhere to be found.

Then it hit me. The Meridian. It must have fallen out of my hand when we fell. I sucked in a gulp of air. We needed that to go home. To complete our mission. I dropped to my knees and searched in the tall grass.

Moments later, I found it nestled in a patch of dirt. The grass around it was burned off, which was weird. When I touched the compact, it was cool. Our stolen piece of kaylorium was still in the core. I was careful not to press it down and activate another portal without Rome and Lola.

"Thank you, Saint Pakari," I said to myself.

"Oh, I don't think I had anything to do with it," someone responded.

I froze and nearly dropped the Meridian again. I inched around to come face-to-face with a boy about seventeen years old who looked incredibly familiar. His tunic was ink black, with gold stitching along the collar and sleeves. He had burnished bronze skin, and jet-black hair half tied up in a knot. His eyes were black and kind. They crinkled at the corners with a word my mom used to describe me. *Mischief.*

Who was this guy? There were not supposed to be any humans in Finisterra. It was a place for magical beasts and monsters. A place from long ago, when there was still magic in the world.

"Who are you?" I asked.

"Don't you know?" he asked with a smile. "You were just thanking me."

No way. There was *no way* that teen boy was Saint Pakari. I opened my mouth to speak, but all my hundred questions tangled into one "Hrrrhhhhwhaaa?"

The boy who claimed to be Saint Pakari glanced around. His movements were so slow, it was like he was used to taking his sweet time. "You're a long way from home, little one."

I made a T with my hands like Lola. "Time out. *You're* Saint Pakari?"

He crossed his arms over his chest and flashed

straight white teeth. "Last time I checked. Though I never dared to call myself any sort of saint."

"You're the guy who guards the gates to Finisterra?" I asked, my brain still struggling to process all this.

He shrugged one shoulder. "That's me."

"And walked the great Andes Mountains?"

"Guilty."

"And sealed the last door of magic to protect humans from magical beasts!"

At that, Saint Pakari tapped his chin. "I wouldn't put it that way exactly, but . . ."

I couldn't decide if I believed him or not, but no one had seen Saint Pakari in centuries. Maybe no one wanted to give all the credit to a boy, so he just kept getting older and older as the story was retold over the years. "I thought you'd be old."

He scratched the side of his head. "Well, I *am* six hundred and eighteen, I suppose. But I've been seventeen for about six hundred and one years."

"*Wait* until Lola and Rome meet you." Then I had that sensation of falling again, like when you're about to go to sleep and you feel like you've dropped off a cliff and jump awake. Where were Lola and Rome? They should have found me by now. "Have you seen a boy and girl? They kind of look like me. I don't know how many kids you get coming through here."

"No, actually," he said. "You're the first I've seen in, well, time passes differently here, but let's just say years. As for your companions, I noticed the break in the sky. It scared my flock, but you're the only visitor I've encountered."

"I have to find them," I said. "They'd be lost without me! What if they got stuck in the portal? What if they got sucked out into space? What am I going to tell my mom? Oh no. This is all my fault—"

That's when something landed on my shoulder. I felt its claws dig into my skin, but not so much they'd hurt. More like it had found a perch. The creature had the face of an owl but the plumage of a rainbow parrot. A skinny reptilian tail with a feathery tuft at the end plonked me on the head.

"What the—"

"Rayo, be nice," Saint Pakari said. He clicked his tongue and the bird flew from my shoulder to his. "Our new friend needs to find her family."

He drew a shiny green beetle from his pocket and Rayo, the rainbow owl, snatched it up between its beak. I gulped. I wanted to ask if Saint Pakari just carried around beetles in his pockets, but that seemed a little rude, so I let it drop. Besides, I had bigger worries.

"You'll help me?" I asked hopefully.

"Of course. Did you come through together?"

I nodded quickly and showed him the Meridian. "We used a portal."

Saint Pakari's eyebrows rose with surprise. His gaze unfocused, like when I zone out in class because I'm remembering all the adventures we had in the Before Times. Then he looked at me with interest. "I haven't seen that device in years."

"You've seen it before?" I said, surprised.

"Years ago, quite long ago. I was out for my morning stroll when, much like today, the sky broke open. Out fell two boys. One of them told me he'd discovered a way between the worlds. If you're in possession of his invention, then, oh dear."

"What was his name?" My mouth went dry.

"His name was Arturo Salazar. Where is he?"

My mind was racing, but I found the words to say, "I—I'm his daughter. He's gone."

Saint Pakari bowed his head. "My deepest condolences, Young Salazar. Come, we have to find the rest of your brood. And we have much to discuss."

We trudged up a steep green hill. Saint Pakari used a long staff to help him walk. It was carved with geometrical patterns and magical animals. I found a big stick, which also did the trick.

"My dad never told us that he'd been here before." I thought back to all his journals. I knew I'd read them all. Every single one. We kept a family library for a reason. I was starting to realize that we were keeping secrets. Me with Brixie. Lola with the muckers. Dad and Finisterra. Mom, Andie, and Rome might have been the only ones who weren't.

Saint Pakari nodded. "I see. What did he tell you?"

"Only that he'd created the Meridian to help hunters from the Order of Finisterra stop killing magical beings. But when he presented the invention, they wouldn't listen to him. They didn't want to change their ways. My dad ran away and became a protector instead." I told him about my parents meeting, and my siblings. About how we drove across the country and sent creatures back here.

"Hunters," Saint Pakari said sadly. "I've seen their kind before. They are the reason I sealed the gateway between the worlds."

I felt a little out of breath the more we trekked up the hill. "But I thought—"

"That I was protecting humanity?" He chuckled. Rayo flew off his shoulder and circled above. That made me wonder—where were the other big animals? If this was Finisterra, why was it so quiet?

"What really happened?"

Saint Pakari stopped, planted his staff in the grass, and looked back the way we'd come. It was like no matter how often he saw the trees and sky, it was all new again. That's how I felt about the Scourge.

"There were those following the legends of cities filled with what they called green gold even before the conquistador invaders arrived to my part of the world in search of riches. They called themselves the Order of Finisterra." Saint Pakari tapped his staff and the etching in the wood came alive with a pulsing green glow. There was kaylorium inside. "For a time, I believed the Order wanted to help me keep Finisterra safe, help me guard the gateway. Then they began taking animals out."

"Why?" I asked as we kept walking.

"They claimed it was for knowledge. For preservation. But it was all a lie. They slaughtered countless creatures and experimented on hundreds of others. My sister had the same gift as I did. We were imbued with the magic of Finisterra. We had to do something. She helped me close the gateway, but she would not leave with me."

"But why?" I asked.

"Because our people would not leave either, and they were rooted to the place. I was always a wanderer. And so, the way was shut. Not entirely, of course. There are small pockets, like rips in a seam, all over the globe."

"Swiss cheese," I told him, and explained my theory.

He laughed at that. "Right you are. And then, of course, an age later, there was your father."

"I can't believe he never told me."

"He kept his promise after all." Saint Pakari smiled up at the sky, like Dad could see him. "I taught him everything I could about my time here. The animals I watch over. The time before."

Even Saint Pakari had a Before Time. The thought made me happy that I could have something in common with a saint, but sad for him, too. Sometimes you miss the Before too much, and there is nothing and no way to get it back.

We were almost up the hill then, sweat trickling down my temples. The clouds were thinning, and the sun and moon were making a diagonal journey across the powder-pink-and-purple sky.

"You said animals you watch over, but I haven't seen anything. Except your rainbow owl and some fish."

"That's because you didn't know where to look," he said.

Saint Pakari walked a little bit faster, and I hurried along. We came up on the crest of the steep hill. A breeze spun around me, and I stuck my arms out to catch my balance.

"Whoa!" I shouted.

Down below were hundreds and hundreds of creatures gathered around the wide bend of the river. In the water was a water bear, like a tardigrade, but it had six fins instead of six claws. It floated on its back past a huge sea monster with a long neck and horns made out of coral. Shimmering fish jumped out of the water and the sea monster gobbled them up like when Rome used to throw a handful of popcorn in the air and try to catch as many as he could before they hit the floor.

Off on the shore, land creatures grazed. I recognized a cluster of chupavacas drinking from the river, then running and howling at the moon. Fuzzy pink abelitas floated lazily in patches of wildflowers. I'd never seen an abelita before, only confused one with a fuzzy scrunchie in Maritza Vega's hair. I could barely contain myself when a neon-purple snake jumped out of the grass and swallowed an abelita whole. The rest scattered.

"I've never even heard of some of these creatures," I said. "I wish Lola and Rome could see this."

My stomach tightened with fear. Where were they?

Then I heard the screams carried by the strong wind. Lola and Rome. It had to be them. I scanned the area in the direction of the noise, but there was too much movement for my eyes to focus.

"There!" Saint Pakari said, then gasped. "Oh, Blessed Mother."

Down at the bottom of the hill, inside a deep crater, were Lola and Rome, and they were about to be skewered by a giant two-headed scorpion.

15

Legend of the Orü Puma

Stop, think, see the best way out. That's what Dad used to say when we trained in the woods or the desert. Panicking led to messy mistakes. Panicking led to danger. Death. Had my dad panicked when he came face-to-face with the orü puma? Was that why we had to figure out how to be without him?

All those thoughts crowded my mind. But there was something more important. Lola and Rome were in danger, and they needed my help. So, I did what I wasn't supposed to do. I panicked.

"Valentina, wait!" Saint Pakari shouted behind me.

I pushed my legs as hard as they'd carry me down the hill. I kept my eyes trained on my siblings. The double-headed scorpion had a deep blue carapace with oozing lemon-yellow spit dribbling from its two mouths. It scuttled side to side, the pincer wagging in the air like it was getting ready to strike.

Rome held up his twin daggers in the air, but as he threw them at the creature, it was clear he didn't know how to use them. They were not supposed to miss their target, but they bounced off the scorpion's claws. Lola pushed Rome behind her. She was the older sister and she had to protect him, even if it was just as a shield.

I screamed and pumped all my strength into reaching them. I couldn't lose them. I just couldn't.

The ground was so steep I practically slid the whole way down on the muddy trail. They must have heard me scream because they turned my way.

"Val! No!" Lola shouted.

But I was moving too fast to stop. I opened up my ring shield as I slipped right onto the crater. This time, I didn't land on my tailbone. I landed in a crouch just as the scorpion pincer attacked. It slammed into my shield so hard the force field made a warping sound.

The creature scuttered back to its shadowy corner, readying for a second strike.

"It won't hold a second impact," Lola said, taking my hand in hers. The shield flickered and then faded.

"Not with that attitude," I said, wrapping my arms around her waist. She was alive. Rome was alive. Now they just had to stay that way. "I have never been happier to see you."

Rome bent down on one knee and put his palms right side up. "Celebrate when we get out of this hole. Salazar ladder, come on!"

I got on my knee, too, and stacked my hands on top of his. Lola stepped on our palms. It didn't hurt exactly, but no one likes getting stepped on with muddy sneakers. When Rome counted to three, we pushed up with all our might. Lola got the jump she needed to reach the ledge.

That's when Saint Pakari appeared and offered his hand.

"Who in the saints is that?" Lola shrieked.

"A friend," I shouted. "Just take his hand!"

Thankfully, Lola did as I asked.

"You next," Rome said. "You're bleeding."

His frown was so serious, I knew better than to argue. I realized for the first time that I had a cut on the top of my hand. There was too much blood to see the damage even if I had too much adrenaline in my body to feel the pain yet. I climbed up on Rome's palms and looked up. Bits of dirt fell into my eyes.

"Hold on to the staff," Saint Pakari ordered.

I could barely see. The chittering sound of the scorpion threatened behind us. I climbed up on Rome's shoulders and he gripped my ankles with his hands, then grunted as he stood and raised me closer to the ledge. I reached up blindly until I grabbed hold of the staff. Seconds later, I felt Lola and Saint Pakari pulling me up.

There was no time to catch our breath. Rome was still trapped down there. But instead of trying to reach for Saint Pakari's staff, Rome spun around to face the two-headed scorpion.

"What are you doing?" I shouted.

Normally, I would have prayed to Saint Pakari, except Saint Pakari was right here with me. As if on cue, he pulled back his staff. He moved a little slowly for my liking, but maybe I was just so used to wanting things to be fast. I reminded myself to *stop. Look. Don't panic* (anymore).

Saint Pakari leapt into the pit and positioned himself between Rome and the scorpion.

"Get out of my way, stranger," Rome said, his words shaking with anger. He ran for his daggers and picked them back up, ready to attack. "That monster hurt my sister."

The double-headed scorpion bit at the air, but as Saint Pakari twirled his staff, the creature seemed transfixed by the spinning green light.

"And you're in her nest," he said. "She's protecting her young."

That's when I noticed the bright yellow eggs, barely visible in the corner shadows. Rome and Lola had fallen right into a nest!

"Here," Lola said, and took off her sweater. I slid out of my jacket and we tied the sleeves together. We threw it over the side of the pit. "Rome! Grab it."

Rome looked up at us and then back at the creature. The frown between his eyes pressed down, like he was torn. I'd seen my brother cranky and sad and brooding. But I'd never seen him so angry.

"Rome!" Lola shouted. "Val is fine! But you won't be if you don't get out of there."

Rome shouted his frustration, but he made up his mind. He lowered his weapons, but it wasn't fast enough. The scorpion was pretty ticked off. Saint Pakari tried his spinning staff trick, but the creature knocked him off to the side, then it charged at my brother.

Lola and I screamed. I couldn't look. I just couldn't. I shut my eyes so hard and held my breath, but the next thing I knew there was a loud *thump*, and the ground in front of us shook.

Behind me, the scorpion had crept back up into the

shadows. Saint Pakari propelled himself from a huge jump back onto solid ground. And in front of me was Rome, dangling by his jacket collar from the mouth of an orü puma.

My body froze and my mind shot back to the last day I ever saw my dad. We never saw the creature then. All that was left behind was blood and feathers. Mom hadn't even let me look.

After the accident, I'd imagined what I would feel if I ever saw an orü puma in person. I figured it would be sadness, because something so rare and beautiful was tied to my dad's death. I wondered if I'd be angry *because* of my dad's death. Rome was angry. Lola was—well—she was always too busy being perfectly organized to show her emotions. But me? I didn't want to be sad or angry or fearful or anything like that. Dad would have said to remember our favorite scene in *War of the Galaxies* where the Galactic Knight defeats the fear in his heart and uses hope to wield his flaming sword.

Anyway, the best I can describe what I felt as I faced the massive orü puma was relief. That's right. I was relieved that it had *saved* Rome from the two-headed scorpion below. It released my brother, who fell on his back and tried to crawl backward. Its golden fur shimmered and its blue-and-green wings expanded on either side. And then the orü puma did something none of us expected.

It licked Rome's face.

"Disgusting," Rome muttered.

The enormous winged cat purred as Saint Pakari came around and rubbed at a white spot shaped like a sunburst between its ears. "Good boy, Sami."

"Sami?" I asked. More like shouted. I had so much adrenaline pumping through me that I was shaking.

Lola helped Rome stand. All around us, the animals of Finisterra were going about their dinner hour like we hadn't almost just been shish-kebabbed by a mommy scorpion protecting her young.

The orü puma walked around Saint Pakari and plopped down at his feet, like it was a regular cat instead of a ginormous mountain lion with wings and a serpent tail.

Lola tried to straighten her shirt and tuck back the stray hairs from her French braids, but we'd been through a lot. I liked her better looking less perfect. She glanced from the saint to the monsters and back to us. "Okay, I need some answers. Who in the realms are you?"

Saint Pakari nodded in that slow, thoughtful way of his. "I will try to explain as best as I can. But I will start with the easiest part. I am Saint Pakari."

Lola and Rome reacted the same way I did.

"Yeah," I said. "He's been seventeen for six hundred years!"

"A teenager forever?" Rome made a face. "Bummer."

Saint Pakari chuckled. "I rarely notice anymore. Come, it's been an exciting day. Let's patch you up before you return home."

We hurried down the trail. Thankfully, we didn't have to go very far. Along the river where jackalopes grazed and herds of wapi-kapi (reptilian warthogs) raced was a small stone house with a clay tile ceiling. Behind it was a firepit. Charred logs still had a few embers in there.

"I'll be right back," Saint Pakari said, and left us in the yard with the orü puma, Sami.

The big cat made itself right at home scratching on a log that was almost torn to shreds by its giant claws.

We were in Finisterra! I gulped the sweet air and was hoping to share my excitement with my siblings, but Lola pressed her hands against her eyes.

"Lola?" I asked. "What's wrong?"

She made a strangled sound that could have been a laugh. I'd never seen her look so disheveled, so uncertain. She flexed her fingers like she was look-ing for something to do—dishes to wash, breakfast to make, homework to finish. She saw a wood pile in the corner and retrieved three logs, like she had to keep moving.

When she dropped the logs in the pit, she asked, "What were you thinking back there?"

She didn't yell, which was the scary part. Just arranged the wood neatly and dusted her palms.

Rome sat on a crudely carved bench and rotated his arm. He winced but bit down on his lip. "I was thinking that I needed to protect my family. Even if I'd gotten out of the ditch, that thing could have followed us."

"You could've gotten hurt."

"I did get hurt." He winced. "*Val* got hurt."

"Protecting *us*," Lola added. "It shouldn't be that way. We're the ones that should be taking care of her."

"I'm fine," I said, but my finger was red and angry, the cut beginning to throb. "Besides, we take care of each other."

Rome didn't seem to be listening to us. You know when you're so angry you want to cry? That's how Rome looked at that moment. He tossed one of his daggers in his good hand and stared at the lazy orü puma. A cold sensation crept along my spine, like when I caught Uncle Raf skulking around the van.

"Rome," I said softly. "Sami helped us. Sami *saved* you."

Rome stood and faced the tall forest behind Saint Pakari's cottage. The black pines were strange, but Finisterra was supposed to be strange, wasn't it? Now that we weren't in immediate danger—at least I hoped not—I perked my ear to the cries of birds zooming across the sky. The low rumble of a sea monster nearby. I started to notice more and more flowers with impossible colors—like the in-between shades of a rainbow we couldn't see in our world. Even the orü puma, a legendary monster, was incredibly beautiful.

"That *thing* killed our dad," Rome said. His voice was so full of hurt, I wanted to hug him. "How can we just sit here watching it sleep? How could it just—"

"Save you?" I offered.

Rome's lip trembled and he repeated, "It killed our dad."

"It didn't," Lola said. "If Dad had been attacked by a shark, would you blame all sharks?"

Rome turned to Lola like she'd slapped him. "Are you defending it?"

Lola fanned the flames in the pit until they roared. I shivered and stood closer to the fire.

"I'm being logical," Lola explained. "I know you're angry—"

"Why aren't you? Only Andie understands. You— you don't know *anything*." Rome started to walk away. He weighed another dagger in his fist and then glanced back at the orü puma, who sneezed at the grass. Rome's eyes were filled with tears. For months I'd thought that my brother hid in his bat cave room and under his headphones because he didn't want anything to do with us. But when I looked at him then, really looked at him, I saw something different. I saw someone who was keeping a secret, and the only way he could do that was by hiding, by being distant.

"Tell us," I said encouragingly. "Tell us what's bothering you, Rome."

He shook his head. "I can't."

Saint Pakari's valley felt awfully quiet, like the whole world was holding its breath just for us. "You're our brother. You can tell us anything."

Rome stepped closer to the fire. He looked from me to Lola and then away. "Dad's dead because of me."

Lola's mouth fell open and I froze. Even Sami raised his head to stare at Rome.

Rome, who held those daggers he didn't know how to use. Rome, who taught me how to ride a bike without the training wheels. Rome, who could clean our cuts and scrapes, and they never hurt. Rome, who used to laugh and tell jokes and never frowned. Rome, who had a connection with animals the rest of us didn't, like he spoke their quiet, strange language.

"What do you mean?" Lola asked softly, finally breaking the silence.

"Andie and I were supposed to have his back. But I left my post. I heard a noise down along the ridge, and I went to check it out. I left my post, and Andie couldn't find me when Dad screamed. There was no one to help him. No one." Rome shut his eyes, and tears streamed down his face.

Lola dusted her hands and walked around the firepit. She hugged him. Rome tried to push her away, but then I jumped on him.

"It's my fault," he cried.

I shook my head. My own eyes burned. "No, it's not," I said fiercely.

"It was an accident," Lola said. "Neither you or Andie could have reached him in time. And if you had, we might have lost half the Salazars."

We squeezed Rome into a Salazar hug until he stopped crying. His eyes were red and puffy, but he took a deep breath and looked at Sami. The orü puma tilted his head at my brother, like he was waiting for his own hug.

Yeah, baby steps.

"I'm sorry to intrude," Saint Pakari said. He held a tray with two ceramic bowls, strips of clean linen, and needle and thread.

"It's all right," Lola said, wiping her eyes. "We never thanked you enough for saving us."

Saint Pakari set the tray down on one of the wooden benches. He smiled and pointed to Lola's arm. There was a thick cut already scabbing. "May I?"

She sat down on the bench, and he knelt in front of her. I don't think I'd ever seen Lola blush. *Ever.* She was so cool and collected around the mouth-breathing boys at school, and even someone as nice as Ozzy. Being a teenager sounded terrible and I wanted no part of it if it meant I couldn't control my own blushing face.

"I haven't had a day this exciting since your father fell through that portal."

"What?" Lola and Rome asked at the same time.

Saint Pakari chuckled as he used one of the linen strips to clean Lola's wound. "Valentina, will you do the honors?"

So I told them everything the saint had told me. I started at the beginning, of course. How I fell and he found me. How he told me Dad had been here and the promise that he'd made. "I guess we broke that promise."

"You couldn't have known his reason," Saint Pakari said. "And it sounded like you were in dire need of help."

Lola winced as he spread some green smelly-looking stuff on her cut, which he said would help with healing. "What was he like? Our dad, I mean."

"Spirited," Saint Pakari said. "Truth be told, I had no idea the world had changed so much, but that's the way of things, I suppose. He told me the Salazars were from my region of the world—now you call it Ecuador. They were here for six days before they returned."

"Six days?" I repeated. I tried to imagine our dad right here in this place, around this firepit with this same boy. Even now we were having adventures together, even if it wasn't at the exact same time.

Saint Pakari took a clean linen and wrapped it around Lola's arm, tucking in the extra fabric. He smiled at her and said, "There we are."

"What did he do in those days?" Rome asked.

"What *didn't* he do." Saint Pakari rinsed his hands with one of the bowls of clean water. "Mostly he wrote everything down. He wanted to walk the length of Finisterra, something I said I'd never done. Finisterra was named so by the Order because they believed it was where your world ended and the magical one began. But this land existed long before the time of humans, simply in another realm. Even so, there are parts I have yet to explore."

"I'm sorry," Lola said, frowning slightly. "You said *they*. Was Dad not alone?"

"Yes, what was his name . . ." Saint Pakari motioned for me to sit next in Lola's place. My hand was throbbing with pain, but so much had happened, I was a little too distracted to feel it. He started cleaning the drying blood and gently took off my ring. I squeezed my eyes tight and breathed through the stinging pain. "Ah, I remember. Rafael. His brother, I believe."

I yelped, partly because the green paste he slathered on the top of my hand and between my knuckles stung, and partly because I couldn't believe it. Uncle Raf had been to Finisterra, too?

"He's never told anyone," Lola said. "Not that we know. I feel like if the Order knew that Dad and Uncle Raf had actually been here, there would have been consequences."

I made a raspberry with my tongue. "More Salazar secrets."

Rome gave me a pointed look. "We have to ask him. We promised Sequoia we'd call anyway. He'll tell me the truth."

I rolled my eyes. "Why would he tell you the truth? He's visited us *once* in eight months."

Rome rubbed his palms together over the fire. "Actually . . . we've been talking for a while now."

My heart gave a squeeze. "Why?"

"*Because,*" Rome said harshly. "He wants me to be a hunter."

"And you said no, right?"

Rome went real quiet. Saint Pakari raised his brows but kept dressing my wound.

"You said *no*, right?" I repeated.

"I said I'd think about it," Rome admitted. "That's why he came to see us. To see if I'd made up my mind."

I said a bunch of words I *definitely* needed to put money in the swear jar for. How could Rome have kept that from us? How could he even consider being a hunter? They were the exact opposite of what protectors did!

"Enough of that!" Lola said, giving us a stare that rivaled our mother's. "We'll talk about this later. First we have to get back home and continue the search for the egg."

Saint Pakari's attention snapped up at that. "What egg?"

I told him about Peter Bereza and the live feed set up to watch the hatching. I winced as he finished wrapping up my bandage.

"This is highly unusual," he said, casting a glance at where Sami slept. "What do you know of the orü pumas?"

I shook my head and tested my middle finger. The bandage felt weird, and I'd have to switch my shield ring to the other hand, which seemed unatural.

"Only what was in our father's journals," Rome said. "Although now it makes sense how he knew so much about them if he'd been here before. Why, what are we missing?"

Saint Pakari's brow furrowed thoughtfully. "Even in my old world, the orü puma was a creature of legend. It has the body of a puma, great wings like a condor, and the tail of a serpent. It was a creature that embodied the heavens, the earth, and the afterlife. When the Order first came, they wanted to train orü pumas as weapons, but my sister and I closed the gateway before they could trap any. Most have dispersed deeper into the unknown parts of Finisterra, but Sami and his mate, Sunku, remained by my side."

"Sun-koo," I said, feeling out the word. Sami raised an ear at the sound of her name. His cat eyes scanned the skies, but he made a yowling sound when he didn't find her.

"She vanished one day. Orü pumas mate for life. Only death could have separated them." Saint Pakari pressed a hand against his chest, over his heart.

"Swiss cheese," I said, and Saint Pakari nodded. "If Sunku accidentally slipped into a flash portal—"

"I fear Sunku and Arturo met a terrible fate," Saint Pakari said.

We were silent for a long time. Rome took my place and had Saint Pakari bandage a cut on his palm and a couple on his cheek.

I lay back on the grass and watched the lilac-and-pink sky get a little darker as the silence stretched. It was like someone had let out a bomb and the dust was settling. I imagined Dad and Uncle Raf writing things down in a journal around this fire, looking up at this same sky. For the first time I wondered—could Uncle Raf have been on Dad's side after all?

I didn't know what to think anymore. All I knew was that we needed to get back home. We still had a mission. A quest. A long way to go.

"I apologize I'm not a faster healer," Saint Pakari said. "It's not often I get visitors. As much as I've enjoyed your company, I hope you understand why it's important that you keep your father's promise."

"We'll make sure the egg gets back here," Lola said.

The three of us stood and gathered around. We shook Saint Pakari's hand. Sami came around and nudged the side of my leg with his cold nose. I stood still for a moment, then I petted him between the ears. It was strange, but sort of nice.

I fished out the Meridian from my pocket with my good hand. I opened the latch and thought of the Scourge as I pressed down on the core. Light exploded in circles around us. This time, I was ready for the fall.

16

The North Carolina Detour

We stepped out of the portal and onto the parking lot behind the Book Garden. My ears popped again, and my legs felt like the green Jell-O they served at school. Lola and Rome weren't in a ditch, which was a relief. The Scourge was parked where we'd left it. I ran around it and hugged the front of the van.

"Come on, Val," Lola said, glancing at her watch. "We were only gone for half an hour in Earth time, but we need to get a move on."

I glanced back at the Book Garden one last time, and for a moment, just a little moment, I wished we could see Sequoia and tell her what happened. We could drink more tea and cakes and talk about our favorite monsters. I'd never hesitated before getting back on the road, and it only lasted for the blink of an eye. Besides, Lola was right. We had somewhere to be. I pulled up the video stream, but not much had changed in the half hour we were gone. The viewership was steady, but I noticed a bunch of new comments.

Are you selling tickets online?

Got any merch?

Convinced my mom to drive us down all the way from St. Paul!

It seemed like we weren't the only ones who were making the drive. I told Lola as much, and we hopped into the Scourge.

"We need to load up on gas. No more detours," she said.

The gas station was near the highway. We charged the van and added a gas reserve for backup. When we parked and Lola got out at the charging station, Brixie pointed at a brown paper bag.

"Your nice friend left you this," she said.

I raised my eyebrows. The bag looked a little ripped. "Brix—are you sure you didn't already see what's inside?"

Brixie hiccuped and burped. It smelled like chocolate, but not in a good way. She squealed an "Oopsie!" and then darted to the back to hide under her favorite pillow.

"What's left that your scavenger didn't pick off?"

Rome asked, turning the passenger seat completely around.

I crossed my arms over my chest. "Nothing for *you*." I still couldn't believe that Rome was thinking of becoming a hunter. How *could* he?

Rome frowned. "Don't be like that, Val."

"Like what? Annoyed? Angry that my flesh-and-blood brother is a *traitor* just like the traitorous Andromeda?"

"I didn't say yes to Uncle Raf," he snapped.

"You also didn't say no!" I felt the sting of angry tears well up in my eyes. Why did being angry also make me want to cry? "You'd have to leave us. Is that what you want? You want to leave us just like Andie did?"

"No. I don't want to leave you. But maybe I should." Rome combed his fingers through his hair. "Maybe you'd be better off without me."

I thought back to moments before, in Finisterra. Rome's confession couldn't have been easy. I knew telling the truth was hard because, sometimes, it wasn't what we wanted to hear or have happen.

"The accident wasn't your fault," I told him. Sometimes, when people were sad, they needed to be reminded of the good things. I had to remind Rome that he couldn't blame himself for what happened to Dad.

224

Rome nodded. "I'm sorry I didn't tell you all. I wasn't going to say yes."

I wanted to believe him.

I rummaged through the mostly empty snack bags. "Sequoia left us chips, cheese puffs, string cheese, beef jerky, and—cool—café con leche in a can! Catch."

I threw one at my brother and he caught it. Even coffee in a can wasn't cheering him up. I'd never seen him look so miserable. His eyes were still puffy from crying. Mine felt the same. We were covered in dry mud and bandages. All in all, we'd been better.

"I'll go get us some ice cups," he said, then hopped out of the van.

While they were gone, I pulled up my chat with Sequoia. I sent her a message thanking her for all her help and for the snacks. I did not tell her that Brixie pillaged it. I also needed to make sure she wasn't in trouble after we left.

MonsterGrrrl7: Thanks again. We couldn't have done it without you.

MonsterGrrrl7: Any trouble? I'm afraid we gave your boss a heart attack.

M3rmaidLyf3: ❤ It worked! Tell me everything!

M3rmaidLyf3: The official report is that three high-tech treasure hunters robbed the gallery. No suspects.

MonsterGrrrl7: *dies of relief* I'll give the group a full report in the morning. Charging now.

M3rmaidLyf3: Hey . . . don't forget about my brother.

MonsterGrrrl7: We won't. Promise.

I thought about the promise we'd made to Saint Pakari and the one Dad and Uncle Raf made to him as well. How could people keep promises when they were just words and words can be changed all the time? Dad had promised to love us forever. But we didn't get forever. I plugged in my phone to charge and left the van to find Rome. He was standing near the pay phone, his hands stuffed in his pockets and his head bopping along to his terrible heavy metal. When he saw me approach, he pulled his headphones off.

"Hey," he said. "I was about to call Uncle Raf. Ask him about Sebastian Thomas."

My heart pounded like a kickdrum. I wanted to ask if he was going to give Uncle Raf an answer, but it bothered me that I wasn't sure what my brother would say. Yes to being a hunter. Or no.

Instead, I reminded him, "You know Ozzy and Izzy installed anti-tracing chips in our phones. Plus mine's a million years old, I don't think you *can* trace it."

Rome nodded, then mussed up his hair. "I know, I'm just feeling a little paranoid."

"Why?"

"Why didn't Dad or Uncle Raf tell us that they went into Finisterra?"

"The Order of Finisterra is a secret society," I said, and shrugged. "They have a million secrets."

"I know but something is feeling off. I can't put it together."

"Usually," I said, "when I have that feeling, it's because I know I'm missing a clue."

He laughed. "I taught you that."

I grinned. "I know, just reminding you. Sometimes, when you're not a butt face and hiding under your music, you can be smart."

Rome grabbed his earphones defensively. "I *like* my music."

"You *do?*" I shook my head. Then I pointed at the pay phone. "We should call Uncle Raf now before we get on the road."

Rome fished out a quarter and dialed. The receiver was so old and loud that I didn't even need to crowd my brother to hear. After so many rings, Uncle Raf finally picked up.

"Whoever this is, you have the wrong number," Uncle Rafael growled.

"Uh—it's me." Rome's voice practically squeaked. "Rome."

"Rome! My favorite nephew," Uncle Raf answered in his scratchy voice. "Why're you on a pay phone?" He sounded suspicious.

Rome blanched for a moment, but then he said, "Val's playing a game on my phone, and I didn't want her to hear me. You know how nosy she can be."

I raised a fist and waved it at my brother, and Rome gave me a warning glare, pointing to the phone.

Our uncle laughed. "Don't I know it."

I rolled my eyes, but Rome shot me a warning glance. He mustered a chuckle. "Hey. Uh—thanks for those daggers again."

"What did I tell you? I bet they'll come in handy. They always hit their target."

I wondered if Rome was remembering how he didn't even scratch the scorpion with them, but he just kept going. "I was actually calling for a different reason."

Uncle Raf's chuckle was like the rumble of thunder. "Good news, I hope. You accepting my offer to train with the hunters? It's your birthright, you know that, son?"

"I know . . . I'm still thinking about it. My mom's on a work convention, so I want to talk to her about it."

A warbling fancy lady's voice interrupted and said, "Please deposit twenty-five cents for another three minutes."

I pushed in the quarter.

"Now, what can I do you for?" Uncle Raf asked.

Rome cleared his throat nervously. "I have this friend. He's an apprentice with the Order. His sister hasn't heard from him in a while. She doesn't know details about the society, but she found an email between us and emailed me."

"What's the name?"

"Sebastian Thomas," Rome said.

Uncle Raf was quiet for a few beats. I didn't know if we had any more quarters, so I dug through my pockets. "Thomas. Yeah, rings a bell. Still out on assignment. He's a bit older than you, how do you know him?"

Rome hit his forehead with the ball of his palm. "Uh—don't tell Mom. I've been searching for cases. Small world, you know."

"I know, kid." He chuckled. "Believe me, I know. Anything else I can help with? You say the word and I'm right in Missing Mountain to pick you up."

Rome glanced at me. This time he didn't look like he had to lie. "I'm all right for now. If you hear anything, can you let me know?"

"Sure thing, son. I'll do some digging and get back to you. Now remember. Honor, strength . . ."

"Blood," Rome finished.

Then the call flatlined with a long beep.

We got some ice cups and hurried back to the Scourge, where Lola was eating chips and a gas station burrito for dinner. We told her about our call with Uncle Raf.

"I hope he bought it," Lola said between bites. "Uncle Raf can sense lies like a bloodhound."

"I hate lying," Rome said quietly.

"Well, the hunters aren't going to offer up the truth now, are they?" I asked.

Lola and Rome didn't disagree with me. I picked up my phone and pulled up the egg's live feed on the dashboard projector. The egg was still in its display case. Now that we'd seen the orü puma in person, I knew that its wings matched the color of the egg's scales.

Lola sighed with relief as we watched the video and ate a quick dinner. Brixie came back out of hiding to sniff at my canned café con leche, which we poured into ice cups. She tipped herself so far that she almost dunked her own head in. She grimaced, then sat on my shoulder, eating a honey stick.

"All right," Lola said, pointing at a map. "We can make up some time if we keep driving straight through North Carolina. We'd reach a campground around midnight, have a cat nap, then get back on the road by sunrise. That would leave us with ten hours to get to Fontana, Florida, and right to Pete's Emporium. Then Val makes a portal, and then the three of us take the egg to Finisterra. I'm not taking chances getting separated."

"Then we just drive home before Mom comes home from the airport," I said.

"We got this." Lola held out her palm, and we each gave her a congratulatory slap even though it was covered in cheese dust.

"I can't wait to get this mud out of my hair," Rome grumbled, and flicked a piece of crud at Lola.

She squealed and flicked one right back. Brixie leapt off my shoulder and saw the opportunity to dive into Rome's last bag of chocolates.

"No!" he shouted, and protected the bag against his chest. Brixie's lips trembled like she was going to let loose with the sappy waterworks, and so Rome relented. "Fine."

I dug through one of the cabinets and brought out one of Dad's ancient Polaroid cameras. I hit the button, and it made a mechanical whine as it spat out a rectangular picture. I watched the black spread and reveal Lola laughing harder than I'd ever seen her and Brixie flying away with a piece of chocolate right out of Rome's hands. Poor Rome's face was twisted with shock. I felt a warm glow right under my rib cage that ached a little. We were filthy and beat-up, but we were together.

I didn't have too much time to relish the moment. A movement caught my eye. While Brixie rode out her sugar high and Rome made Lola listen to one of his horrible songs while cleaning up the van, I turned to the live feed on the projector.

At first I thought Peter was back giving his tour of the emporium. But the egg was still. So still. The shiny scales reflected the lens of the camera.

And then it moved. Wobbled from left to right.

"Guys!" I shouted.

They stopped, and I pointed. We stared for a few minutes, but it didn't repeat itself.

"I swear it moved."

"Look at the comments." Rome pointed. Others had seen what I had and were taking bets on what kind of dragon it would be. I blinked *once*, and the viewers jumped by ten, twenty, fifty, two hundred. It hovered at about one thousand and stayed there.

This wasn't good.

This *really* wasn't good.

Lola brushed the cheese dust from her fingers and

chugged her coffee. "Forget stopping at the campsite. Get your bathroom break in now because we're not getting out of this van until we reach Pete's Emporium."

◆✦

We blazed out of the gas station. Normally, Lola wouldn't have sped, but we didn't have a choice. We *had* to find the egg before it hatched. The Scourge shot down the highway like a great big surf-green bullet. Thanks to Ozzy and Iggy's tech, we were undetectable to speeding cameras.

In the back seat, Brixie and I watched the map on the dashboard as we crossed into Virginia and toward the North Carolina border. After the first hour staring at the dark road, I updated my Cryptid Kids chat. Almost everyone was asleep except for Iggy, who I'm pretty sure never slept.

MocoLoco88: You'll get there in time. Thanks to my upgrades.

MonsterGrrrl7: Obvi. What's up by you? Any new sightings?

MocoLoco88: Quiet as a cemetery. Kind of creepy actually. Ozzy's heading to Louisiana with a group of ex-muckers. There's a mammoth snugslug absolutely shredding the landlines outside New Orleans.

MonsterGrrrl7: Snugslugs smell like cat pee and Rome's gym locker.

I must have snorted too loudly because Rome glanced back. "What's so funny?"

I smiled innocently. "Chatting with Iggy. How's the egg?"

Rome clicked over to the feed on his phone. "No action. Maybe it was like Braxton-Hicks for eggs."

Lola, who was so focused on the road she was nearly hunched over, took her eyes off the highway to snicker at Rome. "That's only for pregnant women, Rome."

I thought about asking what that meant, but it seemed like baby stuff I didn't want anything to do with. Animals I could handle. People were strange.

"I pray to Saint Pakari that we make it there in time," I said.

"Isn't it weird to say that now?" Rome asked. "I mean, now that we know the guy. And Lola practically had cartoon hearts bulging out of her head every time he looked at her."

Rome and I burst out cackling.

"You take that back!" Lola shouted. "I was concussed and disoriented. Wait until I tell—"

Then she caught herself. Would she have said Andromeda? Dad? Mom? The missing Salazars. She cleared her throat and straightened her hands on the wheel.

"I will admit, it *is* weird knowing he's still alive and that Dad and Uncle Raf met him." She eyed Rome. "Did you ask Uncle Raf about it? Now that you're his best friend and all."

"Not you, too." Rome shook his head, but I smiled smugly that Lola was on my side.

"What do you expect?" she asked. "I'm trying to see the reason behind you becoming a hunter and nothing adds up. I'll support you no matter what, but I won't like it."

"I've been thinking—maybe—I should join the hunters."

"What?" I shouted, so loud Lola got jumpy and swerved a little bit. Brixie rolled across the table and landed in my lap, still drooling.

"Relax! I mean, I could go undercover. Like a double agent." Rome picked at the mud under his nails.

I frowned. "Well, you could have *said* that."

"I was never going to say yes to them, you know. I was just so angry. At everything. At Dad for letting the orü puma get him. At the orü puma. Then I realized— remember when we were in that ditch?"

"It was more of a crater," I said,

"Whatever. Crater. And the two-headed scorpion protected its eggs out of fear. What if—the orü puma that got Dad was just doing the same?"

235

We listened to the sound of the road for a while. We were the only car for miles and it had begun to drizzle.

"I can't stop wondering if maybe this egg that Pete kid found belongs to the same orü puma that got Dad. And deep down I know that it was what Saint Pakari said. A horrible accident."

How would things have been different if we'd only gotten there a few minutes earlier? A few minutes later? If Dad hadn't raced off alone. He *knew* he shouldn't go alone. That was his rule, not ours.

"What does that have to do with being a double agent for the hunters?" I asked.

"There's so much we don't know about the Order of Finisterra because Dad always warned us that their mission was the opposite of ours."

"Rome, think about it. You'd have to hurt things. Train to kill. I know you're angry. I am, too. But it's just not you."

Rome shrugged. "I know that. But I also hate being in the dark. I hate that Dad lied. I hate that Uncle Raf lied. I hate that the Order is the reason Saint Pakari closed the gates between the worlds in the first place. It's just a thought."

"Keep it a thought," I told him. "We can deal with

them our own way. Protect. Valiant. Heart. You're the heart, Rome."

I caught his smile in the rearview mirror. With that, he went back to watching the live feed. I joined Brixie in taking a nap even though the music was loud enough to keep Lola alert.

Suddenly, there was something louder than the music. The Scourge's new systems started wailing. A yellow hazard light blinked on the map. I rubbed my eyes and realized we were deep in North Carolina, on the way to the state's border with South Carolina.

"Warning," the Scourge said. "Unidentified equine species detected. Warning."

"What? Where?" I climbed to the front between Lola and Rome, but there was nothing in sight. We were surrounded by dark trees on both sides of the road.

"It keeps blinking out." Rome tapped the screen, where a light appeared and disappeared like a ball in a pinball machine.

I tried to remember the types of monsters that liked to inhabit this part of the country because of the balmy heat and sprawling green terrain. But the Scourge said equine. That meant horses. I let out a squee of excitement.

"What?" Lola asked.

Before I could give her my theory, the alarm stopped. The lights on the dash blinked out.

"Close call," Rome muttered, just as a bright silver flash darted out of the trees and right across our path.

We screamed. Lola swerved hard to avoid hitting it. She righted us back onto the middle of the road, but then there was another creature leaping out of the trees. Lola hit the brakes, and we lurched, running right over something hard. The Scourge trembled to a screeching stop.

Brixie woke up, disoriented. She pulled her small pile of foil-covered chocolates and gathered them around her. "They're coming for my sweets! Protect the candy!"

"*Quiet*," I whispered. "Something's out there."

"This is not good," Rome grumbled.

Lola turned the key and hit the gas, but the Scourge sagged slightly to one side. "This is very much not good."

"I think the front bumper fell off," Rome said.

Lola grabbed the flashlight under the driver's seat. She was breathing hard but her eyes were sharp. "I'll go check it out. The Scourge isn't detecting anything."

"This is the part of the horror movie where we get eaten," I said.

"They can't eats my candy!" Brixie added.

Lola huffed, "No, Brix. They won't."

Rome and I followed Lola with our own flashlights to assess the damage. The road stretched on both sides for miles. There was not a soul in sight. Our flashlights and the van's headlights were the only things illuminating the highway. When I looked into the surrounding trees, it was impossibly dark. Even if we couldn't see, I could hear the chitter of night creatures.

I'm not going to lie. If Lola hadn't made us make that bathroom stop, I might have peed my pants. I know, I know. We went to another dimension! We faced a two-headed scorpion and saw hundreds of magical animals. This was different. This was the middle of an empty road in the dead, dead dark after getting run off the road by two super-fast "unidentified equine species."

The cool night air made me shiver, and I wished my jacket wasn't covered in Finisterra mud.

"What's the damage?" I asked, teeth chattering.

We pointed our flashlights to illuminate the van. "Right wheels down. We have one spare, but we'll need another. Front fender hanging on by a hair."

Rome swore.

I shushed him.

"I'll add a dollar to the swear jar when we get home," he grumbled.

"No, just—*listen*."

The sound was distant at first. We spread the light on either side of the road, but there was nothing there. My heart matched the rhythm of the hooves on the asphalt as a blazing-red creature appeared from the direction we'd just come.

"Is that a—" Lola started.

I could hardly contain myself and screamed, "That's a unicorn!"

But this unicorn was different than the fluffy rainbow-farting kind I'd imagined. This one had eyes that reflected our flashlights, and red-and-orange hair. As it barreled toward us with its head lowered, I realized it didn't have one horn, but three.

"Oh, sugar," I said. Well, I didn't really say *sugar*, but I'm not allowed to tell you what I actually said. I'll just have to borrow a dollar from Rome for the swear jar.

"It's not slowing down," Rome said with alarm.

"Aren't unicorns supposed to be friendly and help lost kids get back home?" I asked.

"Get back in the van!" Lola ordered.

Rome shone his flashlight at the flat tires. "We'd be sitting ducks!"

"I'll make a portal," I said. "Send it through to Saint Pakari."

I dug into my pocket for the Meridian. My fingers

shook something fierce, and I already knew I wouldn't be fast enough. Lola yanked me and Rome out of the way, and we dove into a muddy ditch off the side of the road.

"More mud," I spat.

The unicorn skidded to a stop, then clapped its hoof on the road, like it was announcing it was coming back around.

I wanted to try for the Meridian again, but how was I supposed to make a portal without getting impaled?

The answer arrived with a blaring sound of thunder. Rome scrambled out of the ditch and onto his forearms. "I know that song. That's 'Hammer of the Gods' by Golden Jet."

It was too dark to see, but I rolled my eyes. Thankfully, the unicorn wasn't preoccupied with staking us. Instead, it faced down the huge black van that had crested the hill at the end of the road and was blaring Rome's favorite song. The red three-horned unicorn charged.

"We have to do something," Lola said, unable to take her eyes off the road.

As the truck closed the distance, a girl climbed out of the passenger side window. In her hands was a rifle.

"No!" I shouted, but they kept driving toward us.

The three of us scrambled out of the ditch, but it

was too late. The unicorn went down. Its legs still twitched, and I realized it wasn't hurt. Not exactly. A bright yellow dart hit the red-eyed unicorn right between the eyes.

"Oh, thank the saint," I said. "It's a tranquilizer dart."

The van braked to a stop and the rifle-girl, who was about my age, climbed out. Her hair was loose, and her, pale, round cheeks were bright red. She looked from the unicorn to the van to us.

"Oof. Erik really did a number on y'all, didn't he?"

Lola brushed a branch that had tangled in her hair. "Erik?"

The girl laughed. She had a big laugh that boomed in the empty road. I decided I liked her instantly. "Like the Viking on account of its coloring. What do you think, Mum?"

A tall woman with black hair streaked with silver approached. Her scuffed boots crunched on the loose pebbles on the road. She had a serious set to her eyes as she took in the state of us.

"I think they're very far from home." She rested her elbow on her daughter's shoulder.

My stomach twinged as I thought about our mom, somewhere in Los Angeles, probably tired from her convention. I wondered if she missed us.

Lola started to explain, saying how the creature

had run us off the road, but the serious lady shook her head.

"Say, you don't seem surprised at this unicorn here," the girl said.

Her mother pursed her lips. "They sure don't."

That's when the girl's eyes darted to the Scourge, like she was only just seeing it correctly. She took out a high-beam flashlight from her pocket and shone the light at the bumper stickers.

"Wait a minute—" She turned to me. "Are you Valentina Salazar?"

I crossed my arms over my chest. "Who wants to know?"

"It's me! Rainbow Poops!" She tapped her chest. "From"—she lowered her voice to me—"Cryptid Kids!"

Then we screamed. From joy, of course. We hugged each other fiercely, and she rattled off a dozen questions about our journey so far, then realized we were in trouble because of the flat tire.

"Mum," she said. "This is my friend—"

"Valentina."

"And you are?" Rome asked, scratching the back of his head.

"I'm Sarah Ellie Elwood, and this is my mum."

We did a round of handshakes and introductions.

"Like I said," Mrs. Elwood muttered. "You're very

243

far from home. Come, we'll tow you back to the farm and get you fixed up. But first, have you ever loaded an unconscious unicorn into a horse van?"

The three of us shook our heads, even Sarah Ellie, who caught herself and then nodded.

"Well, I'm sure as monster protectors, you know there's a first time for everything."

Unicorns Are Kind of Jerks

The Elwoods had a farm about six miles south in an area called Whispering Valley. We couldn't see much in the dark, but the headlights illuminated a metal arch that read ELWOOD HORSE FARM. The air smelled of freshly mowed grass and dirt, and something earthier that I figured was just the stench of horses.

I wanted to explore every part of the property and see what other kinds of horses there were, but it had to wait until morning. Mrs. Elwood stopped the truck in front of a giant barn.

"Get our guests settled and we'll figure things out in the morning," Mrs. Elwood said.

"Yes, Mum," Sarah Ellie chirped.

The Scourge, which we'd tied to the back of their horse van, would remain at the barn until someone could assess the damage in the morning. We grabbed our to-go duffel, and I smuggled a sleeping Brixie into the farmhouse.

We were trying to be polite, but everyone was falling asleep standing up. We followed Sarah Ellie, who explained that the house was usually packed with summer students, but we were lucky because the season didn't start until after Independence Day.

"You can have a whole dorm to yourselves," she said.

We shared one last quick hug. "Thank you. Seriously. I don't know what we would have done if you hadn't been there to tranq that unicorn."

"Don't worry about it. You'll meet the others tomorrow."

With that, she left us in a room with four twin beds. As tired as we were, we took turns showering, if only because I was pretty sure there were bugs in the mud drying on our skin. While Rome was in the shower, Lola plugged in her phone and turned on the livestream. She bit her bottom lip nervously.

"There's three thousand people watching now," she said grimly.

My guts twisted into a knot. I placed Brixie on the fourth bed. She muttered in her sleep and reached out for ghost candy that wasn't there. "We'll leave first thing in the morning."

"We can't. The repairs will take time. I'm so sorry,"

Lola said, resting her head against the wall. "I thought if I could just push hard enough, I'd get us there. Then this would all be over. It was dangerous driving in the dark."

"We're all right," I reminded her. Then I winced a little. "Do you really want this all to be over? Is being on the road again so bad?"

Lola sighed like a deflated party balloon. "It's not that. Part of me wants to be out here. I think I just got so used to sneaking off with Ozzy and the others, and making cheer practice, and keeping my grades up. I was doing the work of three people and it sucked, but I told myself that the busier I was, the less I would think about all the bad stuff. I would stop thinking about how we couldn't bury our father and how Mom was acting different and Rome was so sad and we were letting you down." Lola brushed a tear from her cheek before it could fall.

"And now?" I scratched under my bandage.

"Now I have the mission to focus on, plus all that other stuff." She laughed and cried a little at the same time.

I went to sit next to her and wrapped my arms around my big sister. "You've never let me down. Ever. Plus you make the best breakfast."

When Rome came out of the bathroom, squeaky

clean and in his *War of the Galaxies* pajamas, he froze. "Everything okay?"

"We're going to be okay. Go shower, stinky," she told me.

So I did.

A little later that night, we got a text from our mother saying how much she loved us. I started to type *I wish you were here.* But I fell asleep as soon as my head hit the pillow and never got to send it.

◆✦

"It's MONNNN-DAY!" Sarah Ellie's voice rang through the whole house.

I startled awake. "What's happening?"

"Are we being attacked?" Rome said, falling out of his bunk while tangled in his sheets.

Lola laughed. She was already dressed and in clean jeans and a pink tie-dyed T-shirt. "It's just wake-up call."

I rubbed my eyes and realized Brixie was perched on my sister's bed frame, scooping out a fingerful of Lola's cotton-candy-flavored lip gloss.

"Yeah," Brix said. "Youse sleepyheads."

I let out a horrible groan. My whole body felt like I'd, you know, traveled to another dimension, gotten in a car accident, and then fallen into a crater. I stretched my arms and peered out the window. It was barely even sunrise and Sarah Ellie was ringing a— was that a *cowbell*?

"*Less* cowbell," Rome said, drool and eye crud still caked to his face.

We got dressed, packed up our dirty clothes, and found our way back downstairs. In the daylight, I got my first real look at the house. It was exactly what I imagined a farmhouse might look like, even though I'd only ever seen them in the movies. It was decorated in soft pink flower wallpaper and tan wood. We passed a living room full of riding trophies and pictures of the family's generations of horses. There wasn't anything out of the ordinary that said, *Hey, we caught a unicorn in the middle of the night*, though. I was beginning to feel like I had dreamed the whole thing.

When we entered a large kitchen, Sarah Ellie was there making breakfast. A tall man with reddish hair and a bright red mustache grinned from behind his coffee mug. On the front of the mug was a picture of a brown horse in a regal pose and above in cartoon letters it read STUD. I didn't get it, but I greeted him good morning.

"Morning!" he bellowed. "How are our mystic travelers today? My wife tells me you got into a bit of a pickle."

We sat around the coffee table, where Sarah Ellie had laid out breakfast. A tower of waffles, bacon and sausages, cheesy scrambled eggs, and a slab of butter that already looked melted.

"That's one way of putting it," Rome said, then Lola flicked his arm.

"Thank you for the rescue last night," Lola said with her bright smile. "Sarah Ellie said she'd explain about the—" I knew she hesitated because we'd grown up not talking to other families about what we did. When we stayed a little too long in a town, people always shot curious glances at our van, or my parents, who worked odd jobs when we weren't on a mission. No one really got to know us well, except the neighbors in Missing Mountain, even if we still got curious glances.

"The unicorn?" Mr. Elwood finished for Lola. He grinned; his sun-freckled cheeks were pink and round like his daughter's. "Oh, I'll let Sarah Ellie explain. You look hungrier than a toothless pirate lost at sea."

He was right. We dove in. It was pretty hard to have table manners when you hadn't eaten dinner the night before. Being on missions really burned a lot of calories. While I slathered syrup on my waffles, Sarah Ellie told us about the Elwood Farm and how it truly was a place where people could take riding lessons. They kept dozens of real horses in the main stables.

"But out back"—Sarah Ellie wiggled her eyebrows—"is where we keep the infirmary."

Rome was eating so fast he began to choke. I clapped him on the back and Lola shot him a warning glare as if to say *Chew your food.* "Infirmary? Like a hospital?"

"Sort of. We call it the Enchanted Equus Infirmary. That's where we take in all kinds of equine beasts. Unicorns, pegasi, and even some other four-legged friends. Word gets to us, we drive out, find them, and bring them back for a bit of an extended recovery spa."

"That's amazing," I said. "I knew from our group that you knew all about unicorns, but I wasn't expecting this."

"Is this a family business?" Lola asked, taking in the dozens of family portraits that decorated the walls. Macaroni art and something that looked like a unicorn made out of glitter and glued toothpicks was taped to the fridge. I realized that none of us had ever made school arts and crafts. Rome and I would have *rocked* at it.

"Oh yes." Sarah Ellie beamed with pride. She waved her hands in the air like the scene was unfolding right in front of us. "Thousands of years ago, all the way across the Atlantic Sea, there was a young girl who dedicated her life to protecting unicorns. No one knows where she was born, but for a period of time she lived on the Isle of Skye, in Scotland. No one even knew her name, because she was a hermit, but they began to call her Saint Skye. She would only talk to and be around the unicorns. That's how her legend started. Saint Skye gathered the unicorns of the island for their protection."

"Who would want to hurt unicorns?" Lola asked.

"Hunters," Sarah Ellie and I growled at the same time.

Mr. Elwood nodded emphatically. "There were folks who helped Saint Skye. Those lucky souls were inducted into the Guardians of Skye. My ancestor Magnus Elwood was among them. He was the youngest son of a family of twelve, and he set off on his own. Learned how to care for magical creatures and found he had an honest-to-God gift of healing. When folks began to realize what he could do, powerful and rich men wanted to buy his services. So he ran to Ireland, then to Iceland, and eventually, right here to Whispering Valley, North Carolina, where we still honor Saint Skye."

"Our family isn't so different," I said. I explained to

him our family's story about splitting from the Order of Finisterra. "Now this kid Pete's got his greedy hands on the egg for the world to see, and we have to rescue it before it hatches."

I pulled up the livestream on Lola's phone because it was newer. The egg was in the same position as it was when I'd gone to sleep, which was a relief. But the viewership had climbed another few thousand. There were a total of five thousand people watching and discussing monster lore in the comments.

"So you see, we have to get on the road as soon as possible," I said.

Mr. Elwood tugged at his red mustache. "Hmm. I see. I see indeed. If ordinary humans knew of the existence of these beasts—well, that would be a sorry day indeed. Poachers, governments, heck, *circuses*!"

"Daddy hates the circus," Sarah Ellie explained.

"Don't get me started! Point is, everyone'd be clamoring to get their hands on these things. We'll get you there, don't you worry."

"Don't forget the hunters from the Order of Finisterra," I said.

Mr. Elwood frowned for the first time since we'd met. "They tried to buy the infirmary from me once, but I told them to stick it where the sun don't shine."

I looked at Rome, who pressed his lips together to stop from laughing.

"Mum already drove into town for an extra tire. You'll be patched up in no time," Sarah Ellie said brightly. Her mood was contagious, even if it *was* six in the morning. Then she tapped her fingers together and leaned forward. "Do you think—can we meet Brixie?"

At the mention of her name, Brixie flew into the room and arced a flight path to Sarah Ellie. "Good morning, pretty unicorn fellow! Can I has tasty treats?"

And that's how Brixie spent her morning, practically diving into a bowl of maple syrup with clumps of waffles and maraschino cherries. While Brixie regaled Sarah Ellie with her favorite facts about living with us, Lola and I helped clean up.

"What are these?" Rome stood in front of a shelf stacked with clear bottles in individual compartments.

Mr. Elwood got up, nearly towering to the ceiling. "Medicine."

"Is that glitter?" Rome asked, unconvinced.

"Sort of. Did you know that there are eighteen breeds of unicorns alone, and seven of those have healing properties in their horns?"

Rome looked impressed. "I did *not* know that. We've never come upon any unicorns."

"They're also regal but kind of jerks." Sarah Ellie giggled.

Mr. Elwood inspected the bruise and cut on Rome's cheek, the bandages that all three of us sported from our trip into Finisterra. He clicked his teeth and shook his head. "Oh dear, I should have treated you sooner. Can't have you out there looking like you fought a giant chicken and lost."

Before we could stop him, he unstoppered a bottle of red liquid that shimmered like glitter. He let a single drop fall on Rome's face. My brother squeezed his eyes. It must have stung. Then he ran to a mirror on the wall. The cut and bruise were stitching and fading right before our eyes. All that was left was a thin pink scar.

"Whoa," Rome gasped. "Thank you."

"It's no trouble." Mr. Elwood treated my cut next where the scab had opened during the scuffle the night before.

"This right here is why the hunters were after the farm. What they don't realize is these serums, they heal. But they can't cure everything. They can't reverse old injuries with a snap of a finger. They'd take our free medicine and jack up the prices. The unicorns they come from are already endangered. I fear what would happen if they were in the wrong hands."

"Your secret is safe with us," Lola assured him.

Mr. Elwood clapped his hands. "Now that that's settled, it's time to get to work. Marie should be on her way back by now and it'll take you time to clean out the stalls."

Rome made a horrified face. "Stalls?"

Mr. Elwood chuckled and dragged his fingers along his mustache. "That's right. Everyone who stays on the farm has to lend a hand. We fix your tires, you clean out the stalls. Deal?"

I suppressed a groan and shot a quick glance at Rome and Lola, who nodded. We all understood how much we owed the Elwoods. "Deal."

Sarah Ellie led us deep into the grounds. We passed a wooden signpost half covered by ivy that read ENCHANTED EQUUS INFIRMARY. The sun shone on the grass fields surrounded by bushy trees. At the farthest end was what looked like the stable, and then I saw the most magnificent sight.

I tried to say "Unicorns!" But it came out as "AHHHHHHH!!!!"

Unicorns grazed. Pegasi stretched their shimmering wings under the shade of trees. Tiny deer no taller than me jumped around dandelion patches. They had horns made of flowered branches. There was even a

256

small hippocapus—half horse with a tail fin for hind legs—splashing in a pond. There was an albino caribou with a metal leg, which Sarah Ellie said her father made after they freed it from a bear trap.

That's when I noticed that each creature had some sort of scar. Unicorns with cracked or broken horns. A zebra with gold stripes missing an ear. Pegasi with broken wings. I hated seeing them that way, but at least they had a quiet place to rest on the farm. It reminded me of the way Saint Pakari looked after the creatures of his realm, and the way my dad had changed his whole life to protect magical monsters. Now, my siblings and I were going to Florida to do the same. I wasn't looking forward to scooping tons of equine *manure*, but if it got us closer to our mission, I was ready.

Sarah Ellie walked us through our morning task. She handed us each a pitchfork (which reminded me of a giant kitty-litter scooper) and opened the doors to the stalls. There were mountains of rainbow-colored poop.

"Huh." Rome said, amused, "Unicorns really do poop rainbows."

Lola pinched her nose. "Doesn't smell like rainbows."

With that we got to work, cleaning out stall by stall. We filled wheelbarrows with the stuff and took turns rolling it out to where Ellie said they used it for compost. Nothing went to waste at the Elwood Farm. I started to sweat, but Sarah Ellie came prepared with bottles of cold water.

"Iggy and the others are insanely jealous that you're here, by the way," Sarah Ellie told me as we shoveled. She didn't even seem tired.

"I know. Sequoia would die if she saw the hippoca-pus, and Iggy would love Erik the Red."

Sarah dug her shovel into the hay-littered ground and leaned on it. "Sure would. Erik the Red is an interesting case."

Rome brought the empty wheelbarrow back and asked, "How come?"

"Well, when we rescued him, we thought we'd found a never-before-seen species of unicorn. Three horns is just—excessive and not a *uni*corn, right? But when you see the X-rays, it's like Frankenstein's monster."

"What do you mean?" I asked, my gut queasy. I wasn't sure if it was because of the heat, eating too fast, or because I had a bad feeling about what she was going to say.

Sarah Ellie's eyes got real wide. "You can see where the horns were grafted into the skull."

"You mean someone *made* the tricorn?" Rome asked.

Sarah Ellie picked up her pitchfork and kept scooping the rainbow poop. "Yup. Can't tell you who or why. There have been two other cases in the last year. A wolf with two heads and torn wings, like they'd been ripped off at the nubs. And a strange chipmunk with a raptor tail."

I gasped. Firemunk! Could it have been the same as my fiery little friend from the last day of school?

"Neither of them made it." Sarah Ellie untucked a gold horseshoe pendant she wore and gave it a kiss. "The wolf died before we could get her to the farm. The chipmunk died the day after. Couldn't eat. It just—got radioactive hot and exploded. It was awful. I cried all day. Daddy said he's never seen or heard about anything like it in his whole life."

Rome puffed a sigh. "We have."

I nodded. I told her all about my encounter a few days before with the firemunk. "Hunters! It has to be the hunters! Who else would do something so monstrous?"

Rome shook his head. "No way. Why would they do something like this?"

"Uh, because they're *bad guys*?" I suggested.

"I agree with Rome. Hunters think they're saving people," Lola said. "They kill magical beasts. Creating whole new ones would go against their creed."

I couldn't believe it. After all we'd been through the last couple of days and they still didn't give me the benefit of the doubt. My gut was telling me that the hunters had something to do with these Frankenstein's creatures, but I wasn't sure how.

Sarah Ellie whistled. "Well, like my mum always said, I don't believe in two things—a sink full of dishes and coincidences."

We kept working in silence for another hour. The day grew warmer as the sun perked up in the sky.

When we were done, I sat on the ground and caught my breath. "Is it over?"

Sarah Ellie crouched in front of me and bopped my nose. "It's over. Come, Mum should be finished with the repairs by now."

We were heading back to the main house when I heard a rumble in the distance. I told myself that it must be tractors or traffic from the nearby road. But as we walked across the green, the unicorns stopped grazing. Ears twitched in the direction of the noise. A pegasus tried to flap its good wing.

Then there was the whistle of an arrow, so fast it was a blur.

It slammed into the thigh of a unicorn.

"No!" Sarah Ellie screamed and ran to it. She threw her body across the beast as it fell.

I spun around in the direction the arrow had launched from and shielded my eyes from the sun. Someone was standing at the top of the hill with a bow and arrow.

A hunter.

"How did they find us?" Lola asked.

The hunter drew another arrow, then aimed from side to side to confuse us as we positioned our bodies in front of the creatures. But there was only the four of us and we couldn't protect them all. We still had to try. I tapped my ring shield and held it out in front of me.

The hunter loosed another arrow. This one landed true, into the side of a Pegasus too far out of reach. Purple blood oozed from the wound and then it went down hard and struggled to get up.

"No!" I screamed. My insides roiled with anger. I knew that it was the same hunter from Fort Washington Park. It had to be.

Then she took off her helmet. Her short hair tossed in the wind.

The hunter was my sister Andromeda.

And she wasn't alone.

18

Battle at the Enchanted Equus Infirmary

Six sleek motorcycles roared over the hill and flanked Andromeda.

"Oh sugar," I hissed.

I'm not going to lie, they were intimidating, all dressed in black and red leather jackets with shiny black helmets that blocked out their eyes. We were outnumbered and separated from Sarah Ellie's parents. But we stood together and formed a line between us and the animals behind us. Rome crouched down to retrieve his daggers, and I raised my shield.

"We're not here to fight," Andie said. "Not unless you want to make things difficult."

"You shot my friends!" Sarah Ellie yelled, and even though it was our first time meeting in person, I knew Sarah Ellie never yelled.

"They'll live. And monsters aren't your friends." Andie's voice was flat, like she was reciting words from a script.

"What do you want, Andie?" I said, shaking with anger. "Other than to be *the worst*."

"Uncle Raf sent me. Rome called asking for help last night." Andie sat on her bike like we were all having a perfectly normal conversation. Like she hadn't just killed a pegasus and injured a unicorn. "He was so disappointed that you lied right to his face. But he's not angry. He knows you're conflicted, Rome. Just do as he asks. Come back with us."

How had they found us? Iggy's tech was good. Plus we'd called him on a pay phone. *Plus* I'd already ditched the tracker Uncle Raf had left in the van. Unless . . there was another.

"You came all this way to ask me to *join* you?" Rome asked, his words full of frustration and hurt. He looked back at the dead animal. Rome squeezed the daggers in his fists. He breathed fast as he took one last look at me and Lola.

I shook my head. I wanted to tell him that he couldn't join the hunters. Not even to be our spy and learn all their secrets.

Then Rome dropped the daggers. "Forget it. You drove all this way for nothing."

Motorcycle engines revved and Andie held out her fist. The noise stopped instantly. If I wasn't so angry, I would have been impressed at her leadership skills.

"Don't be like that," Andie told Rome. She examined her nails like she was bored with us. "I came all this way to tell you that Uncle Raf did as *promised*. He searched for your little *friend*, Sebastian Thomas. He's MIA. Ship went down around the Bermuda Triangle. Shame. Would have been a great new recruit."

"You're lying," Lola said. "You might have chosen to leave us, but I *know* you, Andie. I know when you're lying."

"You don't know anything," our eldest sister snapped. "The only liar in our family was Dad. He filled our heads with useless monster trivia instead of preparing us for what was really out there."

"That's not true," Rome said.

"Well, thanks for stopping by and being the biggest jerk in all the realms, Andromeda!" I shouted. "Now run off on your ugly bikes. Rome isn't going with you."

"You guys don't understand," Andie said. "You're still kids."

"You're a kid, too," Lola reminded her. "You're still part of our family. Come *home*, Andie. You said it's not too late for Rome—well, it's not too late for you either. This isn't you."

"What home?" Andie spat. "Not that stupid van. It's ugly and old and it smells. Mom and Dad could have done better for us and given us a normal life, but they didn't."

"The Scourge is ours. It's our home."

Andie shook her head. "That's not a home. Home is what you have in Missing Mountain. Home is what Dad couldn't give us."

Lola and Rome gasped and staggered back, like she'd decked them. But me? I screamed. I picked up the daggers Rome had dropped in the grass. Under my touch, they roared to life, vibrating a metallic sound. These daggers couldn't miss their targets. I threw them at the motorcycle wheels, and they sank into the front wheel of Andie's bike. Then another.

We were never, ever supposed to fight with each other. That was a Salazar rule. But Uncle Raf and Andromeda broke that first.

The hunter whose wheel I'd popped hopped onto the back of another bike. Another one gave up their motorcycle for Andie and doubled up with someone else. In seconds, their bikes came alive, kicking up dirt and grass. I could feel their agitation. Behind us the animals neighed and darted into the trees for safety. If the hunters were let loose, it would be a bloodbath.

Sarah Ellie stepped forward. I did a double take

because I had no idea where she got the tranquilizer rifle from, but she trained it toward the hunters. "Now that you've said your piece, I'll kindly have to ask you to vacate the premises as you are trespassing on private property. Didn't you read the sign out front?"

"Oh, I forgot to mention," Andie said, "you have something that belongs to us, Horse Girl."

"Horse Girl is a *compliment* to me," Sara Ellie harrumphed.

I didn't realize what Andie was talking about until I heard the familiar, heavy stomping of Erik the Red. He galloped into the clearing then, pounded the ground with his hooves. Steam billowed out of his nostrils with a wild shake of his mane.

Sarah Ellie turned to us. "They can't take him back. We found him hurt and nearly dead. Whatever they want with him *can't* be good."

I knew there was only one thing we could do. "The only way to save these animals is to send them to Finisterra."

We were out of time. The hunters raced down the hill. Sarah Ellie shot a tranquilizer dart and hit one of the hunters. He dozed off and crashed into another. That left two doubles and Andromeda. They drove in a circle, shepherding all the scared creatures to the center of the pasture.

266

"Finisterra?" Sarah Ellie repeated.

"It's the only way," Rome said. "Right now, we're sitting ducks."

"Do it!" Then she fired another shot. The hunter on the back of a bike fell right off, but their partner just kept on going.

"All right. Keep them away from the portal," I told everyone. "Rome, help me corral the animals my way."

"What am I supposed to do?!"

"You know!"

I ran farther into the clearing and opened the Meridian. I pressed down on the core, and this time, instead of holding it firmly and letting the spinning circles take me to Finisterra, I dropped it onto the grass and jumped out of the way. Light flared as cylindrical spheres spun in place. They started off slow, then opened like the rings of a faraway planet or an atom. The gateway to Finisterra was open, and we could see right through to the other side.

"What?" I heard Andie say, followed by the crash of motorcycles and rearing cries of magical horses.

I scrambled off the grass just in time to see Rome herding unicorns and pegasi in one long line. The creatures galloped through the portal with Rome speaking gently to them. Rome understood the language of wild magical creatures in a way the rest of us didn't. I think he tried to forget that while we were in Missing Mountain, but it's part of who he is. In that moment, I had never been prouder of my big brother.

"Stop!" Andie shouted. She parked her motorcycle and realized that she was losing. Three of her hunters were snoozing in the grass from Sarah Ellie's tranquilizer darts. Lola picked up one of the bikes and kicked it into high gear. I had no idea she could ride, but she rode in circles, cutting off the two hunters who followed after Erik the Red. "Stop them!"

The remaining hunter made a direct path toward Sarah Ellie. She tried to reload her dart rifle, but the bike was moving too fast.

"Not on my watch!" came the booming voice of Mr. Elwood. He jumped the hill on a four-wheeler with Mrs. Elwood at the helm. He tranquilized the hunter threatening his daughter. Sarah Ellie and I threw our fists in the air and hollered a victory cry.

Across the meadow, Lola managed to corner the two hunters. I didn't realize what she was doing until the hunters, too busy trying to get the tricorn, crashed into a giant mountain of rainbow poop.

It was too early to celebrate. Rome was shouting for our attention. The portal was getting smaller and smaller. Most of the equine beasties had gone, but one great red blur still stomped around the green.

"Erik isn't budging," Rome said. "There's something—different—about him."

I wanted to say that whatever was different was the fault of the hunters, but I knew when to choose my battles.

Erik lowered his three horns in Andie's direction and charged. As mad as I was with her, she was still my sister. Only I got to fight with her.

I ran as hard as I could, double tapping my ring shield. I leapt in between them. Erik reared his head, blazing eyes transfixed on me. "That's right. Follow the pretty green light."

I held up my shield and ran backward, toward the open portal. Erik was like a bull, hurtling right for me, the bull's-eye. He followed the green light, his steaming breath so close on my face I wanted to scream. But I just ran faster and focused on getting him to safety. I could feel the pull of the portal. It was like a magnet sucking me into Finisterra. I glanced back and saw the pink-and-purple sky.

"You'll be safe," I told Erik, then at the last minute, I dove to the side.

Erik jumped into the portal. I grabbed the Meridian and closed it, placing it against my racing heart.

"Did we win?" I croaked, sitting up on my elbows.

A hunter I didn't know crawled to a shaky stand

and took off her helmet. The girl had golden hair and a face full of freckles. A smile split her face like a jack-o'-lantern. "Missed one."

I glanced around but didn't see any magical horses. Then I caught bright blue and purple feathers above me. Brixie.

"Fly, Brixie, fly!" Rome shouted.

But she was trying to help me stand.

The hunter girl had her arrow and bow ready to fire. I felt everything freeze: The Elwoods tying up the hunters with rope. Sarah Ellie helping Lola pull the arrows from the unicorn and pegasus. And Rome running, leaping, throwing his body in front of Brixie, before he went crashing to the ground.

I don't let myself think about the day we lost Dad. Remember how I said sometimes memories turn out fuzzy? That terrible, horrible day is like that in my mind. I remember being at the head of the trail with my mom. I remember thinking we were so lucky that Dad figured out the strange activity in the Joshua Tree National Park was an orü puma. I remember hearing screams but convinced myself they were eagles. Mom said that when something hurts too much to remember, things get fuzzy so that we can protect ourselves.

As I watched Rome fall to the ground, my vision got

blurry and strange. I heard screams, but this time I knew they weren't birds. It was Lola and me and even Andie. I ran to my brother and stopped. I didn't see any blood or anything, but my brother wasn't moving.

"Rome?" I asked, my voice breaking.

"Rome?" Lola repeated.

I swear those were the longest seconds of my life. Lola crying and me holding my breath. Behind us Andie was in a fistfight with the blonde girl who'd shot the arrow. Sarah Ellie was trying to stop them, but I would have just let them fight. I was that angry.

Finally, Rome turned over. Brixie was clutched against his chest in a trembling ball of feathers, crying her little sap tears. Rome touched his arm, where the fabric was ripped. One millimeter to the left and it would have done some serious damage.

"Thank the saint," Rome exhaled, and flashed a real, honest smile.

I laugh-cried with relief and we helped them up. Brixie clung to my shoulder like a sugar glider. Lola found the arrow sticking out of the ground and snapped it in half with her bare hands.

"It's over, Andie," Lola said.

Andie dusted herself to a stand. She saw that she was outnumbered. Her hunters were tied up and gagged, or passed out from the tranquilizer darts. Sarah Ellie seemed to take great pleasure in making sure the hunter girl who'd almost shot Rome and Brixie didn't get away. Their weapons and phones were in a pile on the ground. I picked one up. I knew it was Andie's because it had a *War of the Galaxies* sticker on it.

"What are you doing?" she screamed as I guessed her code—typical, Captain Alonso's birthdate—and typed in a text to Uncle Raf.

"We'll have none of that, girlie," Mrs. Elwood said, wagging her finger in front of Andie's face. *"Sit."*

Andie scowled but did as she was told.

I kept typing.

Me: Got the goods. Meet you at base.

Uncle Raf: I knew you wouldn't fail me. Bring test subject 0133 back as soon as possible.

Me: Roger that.

Uncle Raf: And the rest?

The rest? Did he mean Rome? I needed to be careful of what I said so he didn't get suspicious. I looked up at Andromeda and read the texts out loud. "What is the rest? What is he talking about?"

Lola pulled down Andie's gag. "Talk, Andie. No lies."

Andie's eyes were smudged with her eyeliner. She spat a piece of grass that had gotten in her mouth. "Why would I tell you anything?"

"Because we're family," Rome said.

Andie looked at Rome and her anger softened. She shook her head.

"Fine," I said. "I'll just ask him."

"You do that," she scoffed. "He'll realize that I'm compromised and burn the phone line."

"Then tell us," Lola said. "Why have you been tracking us?"

Andie glanced at her defeated hunters. She must have realized she'd lost this battle because she finally said, "Uncle Raf wants us to keep tabs on Rome. He's obsessed with Rome joining the fold. Something about how the family line has to pass through male heirs. It's so—"

"Sexist," Lola and Andie said at the same time. Lola gave a shy smile but Andie rolled her eyes.

"But then you vanished," Andie continued, "and I didn't pick up your trail again until last night. When I saw you come here, I knew I had to get back up. You even did me a favor and found test subject 0133."

"His name is Erik the Red!" Sarah Ellie yelled, and her dad held her back by the shoulders.

"He's a monster," Andie said robotically.

"No, Andie," Lola said sadly. "Whoever cut him up and stitched him back together? Whoever gave him all that pain? They're the monsters."

"Look," Mrs. Elwood said, doing the Supermom

pose. You know the one—when she puts her hands on her hips because she means *business*. "I'm sure you've got a lot of family drama to work out, but I've got damages here. Your bikes broke my fence and shredded my grass. Do you know the cost of grass, little girl?"

Andie's anger deflated under Mrs. Elwood's Supermom stare. "You can't keep us. That's kidnapping."

"We're not trying to keep you. We'll let you go soon enough. You've already traumatized my animals and sent them saints know where!"

"Finisterra," Sarah Ellie offered in a whisper.

"I don't care about your Order," Mrs. Elwood continued. "I care about the creatures I'm responsible for. Now you'll get your toys back once you and your little friends are done fixing the fence you destroyed, do I make myself clear?"

The hunters looked at one another. "She can't do that," one of them hissed.

"I *could* always turn you over to the sheriff, though he doesn't like to come to the farm on account of his allergies, which would make him put out. I'm sure your *Order* will get you off scot-free, but that'll be lots of paperwork and records. Who knows what they'll find on you, especially since some of you have the look of runaways."

"Fine," Andie spat.

"Fine what?"

"We'll fix your stupid fence. Ma'am."

Mrs. Elwood was terrifying when she smiled. "The rest of you get going. Get that egg. We can buy you a head start but not much."

I found myself wavering between staying to try to get more answers from Andie and the hunters, and leaving. They were all young. One kid as young as Rome. Runaways, Mrs. Elwood had called them. What if they were only hunters because they didn't know they could be something else? But then I thought of the egg, the video racking up views. I knew that we needed to get down to Florida, and fast.

"One last thing," I said. "Sebastian Thomas—is he really MIA?"

Andie narrowed her eyes at me and shrugged. "That's what Uncle Raf told me."

Unlike the other times, she didn't sound sure. I thought about sending a message through Andie's phone, but it beeped. The signal cut out. My traitor sister had been right. Uncle Raf knew something was wrong.

I had a sinking feeling as I walked away from Andie. What would I tell Sequoia? What would we tell Mom about Andie? I wondered if my sister was so far gone that there was nothing we could do to bring her back to us.

"You'll learn the hard way," Andie shouted after me. "Dad broke your heart, Valentina. Only the Order can put it back together."

I ran faster and faster, until I couldn't hear her.

Pete's Wondrous Emporium

With the time Mrs. Elwood bought us, we cleaned up quickly and packed up the Scourge with containers full of leftover waffles and bacon for the road, plus a jar of sweet tea just for Brixie.

"I'll let you know when we cut them loose," Sarah Ellie said. "Stay on comms, all right?"

"I feel terrible leaving you with them," Lola said, biting the corner of her lip.

"We've handled worse," Mr. Elwood assured us.

Sarah Ellie handed me a sticker. It read ENCHANTED EQUUS FARMS inside a family crest with a unicorn, a staff with a snake wrapped around it (the staff of the ancient healer Aesculapius), and an elder tree.

"Wait!" I said, just as Lola turned on the engine.

The Elwoods turned around. Something inside me

gave a little squeeze at the sight of them together—complete and whole—a family.

"What did you mean when you said you knew their kind? The runaway hunters?" I asked.

Mrs. Elwood's face softened and a distant look came into her eyes. "I don't come from fancy secret societies. My great-grandmother immigrated from Sicily to New York City, running away from a bad situation. My mom ran away, too. So did I. Suppose I come from a family of people who run away, which isn't a bad thing. You just know that the place you're supposed to be isn't safe and you're looking for a place to land. I found my place, but not everyone does. Those kids, they're just following orders. They're lost and scared, and they're looking for something to believe in. The Order of Finisterra, much as I don't agree with what they do, is giving them that. I hope we can offer another way."

I felt my eyes sting despite my smile. I shut the door and wondered—did Andie not feel safe with us? Then a worse realization hit me—*I'd* been about to run away, too, before Lola and Rome caught me. So maybe Andie and I weren't so different after all.

"Let's ride," Lola said as the engine rumbled to life.

Rome hit play on "Hammer of the Gods," and we listened to that song on repeat for the first *hour*. It was almost as much torture as fighting with the hunters. Brixie, who was now practically in love with Rome after he saved her life, kept offering to share her sweet tea and the caramels Sarah Ellie gifted us. They became so insufferable, Lola made me sit up front to help her navigate.

I changed the music to one of Dad's playlists, and this time, we all sang along. So did Brixie, even though she didn't know the words. When we hit the song "Werewolf Moon Rising" (Dad and Andie's favorite), we all got real quiet.

"Do you think Andie's a lost cause?" I asked as the song ended.

Lola squeezed the wheel. We were in the carpool lane, going as fast as the speed limit would let us since the alarm system spotted so many patrol cars along the way.

"We can bring her back," Rome said. He'd brought out a magnetic chessboard and was playing against Brixie, only she didn't know the rules and was making them up as she went along.

I turned around and glared at him. "Still want to join them as a spy?"

Rome rested his fist under his chin. "It would be good for us to know what they're doing. You were right, Val."

"Hey, Lola, what's that word Mom uses when she

proves to her boss that she's been right and they didn't listen to her?"

"Vindication?" Lola asked.

I cleared my throat, and as loud as I could, I shouted, "VINDICATION! Boom!" I danced in my seat and ignored their eye-rolling. "Valentina VINDICATION Salazar. I'm only answering to that from now on."

Rome shut his eyes. "No one likes a gloater, Tiny."

I scoffed. "What did I *just* say my new name was?"

"*Anyway*," Rome grumbled. "Something's still off. Why are they making monster hybrids if the sole purpose of the Order of Finisterra is to get *rid* of monsters? And why does he want me to join them so bad?"

"He gave you those daggers. It's the Order's backward tradition of male heirs. Since Dad exiled himself, they're trying to win *you* in his stead." Lola winked at me. "Nice throwing, by the way. Which proves that *anyone* could wield them as long as they found a reason to aim."

"How do you know that?" I asked.

She shrugged. "Magical Weapons 101?"

It had felt pretty cool, but I didn't like how angry I got. I hated feeling that way. It gave me a stomachache.

"At least the Elwoods bought us time. The gas reserve will keep us fueled the whole way to Fontana. Update on the stream?"

I clicked on the video and then zoomed in. "No way . . ."

As I watched, the egg gave a little jump. It was how I imagined a heartbeat twitched the muscles of an exposed heart. The crowd inside the emporium went wild. Peter Bereza's security kept the tourists at bay and ushered them out, saying their timed ticket was up.

"No cameras!" Peter Bereza yelled. "Petra, I said no reporters unless they're real believers. I don't want another reporter calling me a liar."

The redheaded boy turned to the camera and said, "As you can see, we're getting closer to the moment of truth! The Bereza Draconus egg hatching!"

Have you ever seen a slot machine before, when you pull the lever and all the numbers move? That's what the viewer number was like. The video skyrocketed to ten thousand, then twenty thousand.

"This isn't good," I said.

"It's up to fifty thousand viewers," Rome said grimly. "And now there are several offshoot reaction videos."

Lola kept her cool and drove, but her eyes flicked to the livestream. I held my breath for almost a whole mile.

"What's the plan when we're there, Capitán?" Rome asked.

Capitán was what Dad called himself on missions.

It meant that he was the captain and we were his crew. I closed my eyes and pictured his face. No blur, no forgetting. I imagined that if he were with us, he'd say, *Don't panic, we got this. Together.*

Together. I had an idea, but I'd need help. I typed up a long message to Iggy detailing exactly what I needed. Then I told my crew the plan.

Rome crackled his knuckles. "I'm going to make that lock my b—"

Lola cleared her throat.

"Best friend. I'm going to make that lock my best friend," Rome corrected himself.

We'd break into Pete's Wondrous Emporium, take the egg, and safely take it to Finisterra.

"Easy peasy," I said.

Then I had to do the hard work. I messaged Sequoia about her brother. I told her what Uncle Raf said about him being MIA and that I would find out more. The Order was like a giant tower of secrets—their experiments on monsters, their obsession with Rome. Something was going on and I had a feeling that it was all connected. I just didn't know how. Sequoia went quiet, but I let her know I was there. I wouldn't leave her alone. That's what friends and family were supposed to do when things were bad.

About halfway through the ride, Lola put the van

on training wheels to help her drive since her hands were cramping and she didn't want to chance getting into another accident. Though hopefully there would be no stray unicorns on the I-95.

I couldn't take my eyes off the live feed. The egg hadn't moved again, but I could no longer keep track of the comments.

Fifty miles out! We can pay to hold it, right?

I've got an all-cash offer.

Would you trade three purebred pixies for them?

Ever wonder what dragon meat tastes like?

Chicken, I'm guessing.

Quit it! This is a miracle from nature! The monster needs to be caged in a zoo for its own protection.

Lola told me to stop reading the comments, but I couldn't help it. People were saying all kinds of things. All of it made one thing clear—the orü puma egg did not belong here.

A message came up on the Scourge's dashboard.

"It's Sarah Ellie," I said, sitting up. "They set the hunters free."

"Should we be worried?" Lola glanced at Rome through the rearview mirror.

Rome shook his head. "I'm not joining them. I'm a Salazar protector. Not a hunter."

He had no idea how much I'd wanted to hear those

words. Even if we had agreed that it was our last mission.

✦✦

When we arrived at Pete's Wondrous Emporium in Fontana, Florida, we were greeted with the most unexpected sight. The cottage lights were still on, and a neon light that read MERMAIDS MERMAIDS MERMAIDS blinked against the balmy night. A coin-operated ride shaped like a dragon was chained outside. All that was fairly normal to me.

The strange part was the dozens and dozens of tents on the sandy strip behind the emporium. Cars, which clearly had people sleeping inside, were parked and double-parked, spilling out from the garage on the dead-end street.

"There's nowhere to park," Lola whisper-hissed, like her voice would wake up the sleepy campers. It didn't matter. There were some tents with silhouettes of people still awake, and when we circled around back, groups of excited kids dressed in dragon pajamas were gathered around tablets and phones broadcasting the livestream inside.

"What are we going to do?" Rome asked, rubbing his palms together. "We can't break inside with so many witnesses!"

I hit my head on the dashboard. We were so close.

We had the Meridian. We had one another. The egg was just inside. I thought about Mom sitting in this exact seat. Of Dad driving and leading our charge as capitán. Did they always know what to do when things got hard?

Somewhere out there, I heard music coming from one of the cars parked nearby. "Hammer of the Gods." It was a sign.

"Plan B," I said. "Follow me."

"We have a plan B?" Rome asked.

"We do now! Dad always said that if we want to be in the field, we have to think on our feet. Like that time he was removing ratbats from the light fixtures at Rock Valley Rocks '05 but the only way he could get backstage was by pretending to be an act and then—"

"He had to perform in front of a crowd of hundreds?" Rome finished, raising a fist in the air. "Legend."

"So are we," I said. "Follow me."

We parked the Scourge and left Brixie as lookout. Lola reminded me that it was a big responsibility to put on a creature that had the attention span of a kitten in a box full of strings, but I trusted her.

I grabbed my table, an ancient camera that my dad had from a hundred years ago, our portable karaoke microphone, and one of Mom's Panama (Ecuador) hats. I was real glad we'd changed out of our unicorn-poop-covered clothes before we left the farm.

"I don't know where this falls in the plan," Rome said, "but I've had to pee since Georgia."

"Maybe Peter will let us use his bathroom," I said hopefully.

"Before or after we steal his egg?" Lola quipped under her breath.

I shushed her as we gathered around the back door. Some of the kids gaped at us as we walked by. I kept my head up and took a deep breath. I knocked on the door.

No one answered.

I knocked again.

"Hey, they're closed until seven. Get in line," someone told us.

"We're from the *famous* Cryptid Secret Society," I said loudly. "We don't wait in line."

There was movement at the window. Eyes peered out, but there were too many shadows to see. Then someone opened the door.

It was Peter Bereza himself, dressed in glow-in-the-dark alien pajamas. In another circumstance, I would have definitely asked him where he got them. But I had to focus.

"Who're you?"

I cleared my throat. "Good night, young man. I'm—Tiny Salamander—and these are my associates."

"Tiny Salamander?" he asked skeptically.

"We at the Cryptid Secret Society change our names after initiation," I said, raising my eyebrows.

"*Secret* society?" he asked, now curious. "How come I've never heard of you?"

I smiled. "Well, we're very good at the secret part."

"How do I know you're legit?" He crossed his arms over his chest.

"Check out our website."

I felt Rome anxiously fidgeting beside me. But I wasn't worried. On the ride down, I'd asked Iggy to make us a fake website and online profiles to match. If everything went according to plan, he'd be seeing our page documenting rare and exotic magical animals.

"Awesome," Peter whispered. "But if you're here for an exclusive, I can't help you. I already promised Channel Ten a first look at when the creature hatches. I'm going to be the first dragon owner in the world!"

I waved my hands in the air. "We're not here for that. We're here for something else."

"What, then?" he said, quirking his eyebrow. "I've had a zillion offers. The egg *isn't* for sale."

"Our secret society is recruiting."

"We are?" Lola asked, through her smile.

"You are?" Peter asked with wide eyes. "Because I know *loads* about mythical beings."

Rome snorted and I shot him a warning glance.

"That's why we're here." I let the words dangle in the air like a sugary treat for Brixie. "To induct you into the Cryptid Secret Society."

"Why not in the morning?" he yawned.

"Uhh—because—"

Lola stepped a little closer and flashed her winning smile. "Because secret societies only meet at night, of course."

"Duh," Peter said to himself. He stepped aside. "Come on in."

I fought the urge to fist-pump the air. I had to keep my cool.

"Yeah, come on, *Tiny*," Lola said, enjoying herself way too much.

I regretted using my most hated nickname in a moment of panic. But maybe, just maybe, it was growing on me just a little.

We followed Peter inside. The Wondrous Emporium wasn't very big. It was full of overcrowded display cases of taxidermy, tiny bones, eggshells, and even something that claimed to have been a mermaid but definitely looked like a rubber tail with glitter.

The stuff gave me the creeps, especially the skulls that claimed to have been from a yeti. All of it was covered in a fine layer of dust, like whoever did the cleaning only wiped in one direction but not back and forth.

I stepped farther in, and there it was, smack in the middle of the room—the orü puma egg in a special case, getting toasty under the heated lamp. The camera propped up for the livestream didn't show the red velvet ropes, like the kind they have at the movies or special award shows.

Behind us, someone cleared their throat. "A little *late* for guests, Pete."

I turned around, and it was Petra, his sister. She came down the stairs in unicorn pajamas. I tried not to grin at her. I was really starting to like these kids.

"Sorry," Peter said, scratching his head sheepishly. "I know Mom needs her rest."

The girl sent me a distrustful stare. "That's right. She's sick. Which is why we shouldn't be entertaining a bunch of school reporters. I swear, Pete, you'd just let anyone in the house if we weren't paying attention. What if they're secretly serial killers?"

"Oh, we're not, Miss—" Rome offered.

"Petra," she said, pursing her lips. "And you're

entirely too pretty. I read online that serial killers tend to be handsome."

Lola and I burst out laughing as Rome frowned and turned pink at the cheeks.

"They're not reporters," Peter said in our defense. "They're part of a secret society and I'm about to be a new member. Don't ruin this for me, Petra."

The tall redheaded girl shook her head. "You can't be serious."

"It is! Look!" Pete held up his phone for inspection of our credentials. "Between this and all the money from the ticket sales, we're going to be able to pay for Ma's hospital bills."

I lowered my camera. My siblings and I exchanged conflicted stares. I knew they were feeling just like I was. All of a sudden, it all felt too real. Lying felt different when Peter was just an annoying kid on a video. But now he was kind of nice and we liked the same things (minus taxidermy and fake oddities). He was a kid just like me trying to have a big sibling pay attention to him or just be nice. He had a mother who was sick and he was going to take care of her.

I took off my hat. I couldn't go through with it. No matter how close we were. There were other options. So, I moved to plan C. I pulled the plug on the livestream.

"Hey!" Peter shouted.

"Please listen." I help up my hands. "Look, we're not serial killers or wannabe journalists, though I do keep a journal of our adventures. We're protectors. We protect monsters, magical creatures, cryptids, critters that shouldn't exist but they do. Like this egg. And if it hatches for the world to see—you'll be unleashing something ancient into this world. The monster that laid this egg? It got our dad. You won't know how to control it. If people watch this and believe it, if they have proof, then you'll never be able to rest. Read your comments. Everyone wants a piece of this creature and it hasn't even hatched yet. But we have a way of getting it back home."

Peter and Petra stared at us. They didn't even blink. They just gaped at me. Peter stammered and pointed. Petra began to reach for the handle of a baseball bat. I went to tap my shield ring, but then I heard the heavy stomp of a boot. A sound I was unfortunately familiar with.

I whirled around and came face-to-face with Uncle Raf and his hunters. Two of them had a hold of Rome and Lola, covering their mouths with black gloves.

I balled my hands into fists and screamed "Let them go!" as I lunged for them.

My uncle shoved me aside. Two more hunters flooded the emporium and grabbed the Bereza siblings.

"You can't have my brother!" I spat.

"Rome will see what's best for him, in time," Uncle Raf told me. "But I'm not here for him this time."

I glanced at my brother, who looked just as confused as I felt. "What do you want?"

"You know, it didn't have to be this way, Valentina," my uncle said. He crossed the small room and picked up the egg in his gloved hands. He tossed it in the air and caught it before I had a chance to beg him to put it down.

Pete struggled against the hunter, kicking and screaming, but these hunters were bigger, older. They weren't Andie's crew of runaways. This was Uncle Raf's own squadron. He threw the egg in the air again and pretended like he wasn't going to catch it at the last minute.

"Stop it!" I hissed.

"Andromeda told me what happened at the farm. We'll have to deal with those pesky veterinarians one day. But I'm more interested in what she saw."

I tracked Uncle Raf as he slowly stomped through the room. I considered charging him and snatching up the egg. After all, I was eleven and a half and he was old. But I couldn't take a chance of the egg getting crushed.

"She saw a bunch of your junior hunters get their butts kicked."

The hunters snickered, and Uncle Raf curled his lip. "She said you made a portal."

My heart skipped a beat. "And?"

"Which is impossible because when I searched the Scourge and opened up the Meridian, it was missing. So, tell me." He tossed the egg in the air. "Where'd you hide the kaylorium core?"

The core? I was right. I, Valentina *Vindicated* Salazar, was right. Again.

"Why do you want it?" I shouted. "So you can go back to Finisterra and say hello to Saint Pakari?"

That's when he looked up, shocked. I wished I could have captured it because I'd never surprised my uncle.

"We met," I told him. "He told us all about how you'd been there with Dad."

Some of the hunters looked at one another, like it was news to them, too. Uncle Raf held the egg between his fists and pressed. The Bereza siblings screamed through the hands holding them back.

"You don't know anything, little brat," he spat. "I suspected you were the one who'd hidden the kaylorium core, but when you didn't use it, I knew something was wrong."

I snorted, just because I knew taking that tone

would make him mad. "You're the one who doesn't know anything. I didn't hide the core from you. This whole time I thought *you* stole it."

"Then how—"

"We found a new piece," I confessed, terrified that he'd hurt the egg. "There was a piece misidentified at a museum and we stole it."

Uncle Raf smiled. He ran his fingers through his graying hair, and he looked like a meaner, angrier version of my father. I had to look away. "You *are* your father's daughter, Valentina Salazar. You even have his cowardly heart."

Lola slammed the back of her head into the hunter holding her. She got loose for a moment and picked up the nearest item on display—a scepter, the kind queens get during coronations. "Don't talk to her like that. You *wish* you were like our father. He was kind and thoughtful. He was—"

"Your father is shortsighted, my dear Dolores." Uncle Raf flinched slightly, then his eyes grew sad for a moment. "*Was* shortsighted. He was unable to see the bigger picture. But I can. Now, give me the kaylorium core."

"Why?" I asked. "Why do you want this so badly?"

"If you were in the Order of Finisterra, you'd know.

But your father denied you your birthright. He denied you the glory of being a monster hunter."

"I am *not* a monster hunter." I was getting *real* tired of having to repeat myself.

"That's right. You protect." He took pressure off the egg, then tossed it in the air one more time. "Give me the kaylorium."

What would Dad do? I didn't even have to ask. I already knew. He would have chosen the egg. But I wasn't Dad. I wasn't Lola or Rome or Mom or even Saint Pakari. I was me. The only question that I needed to answer was *What would I do?*

I took out the Meridian from my pocket and removed the kaylorium core. "I give you this and you let everyone go?"

"On my honor, Valentina."

I shut my eyes and took a deep breath. There was only one choice I could make that would be right. I removed the core from the Meridian and squeezed the kaylorium. The green-tinted gold was cold in my fist. I could sense its powerful properties, the ancient metal that came from another realm. Then I dropped it in my uncle's waiting, calloused palm.

I reached for the egg, but Uncle Raf held it above my head.

My limbs felt weak as I jumped, and a hunter grabbed me by the back of my shirt and shoved me to the floor.

"My dear Valentina." He licked his canine tooth, then glanced around the room. He looked pale and gray in the shadows and bad lighting of the shop. "This egg was and has always been mine."

I didn't understand. I looked to Lola and Rome, but they shook their heads. "What are you talking about?"

"Who do you think sent you on your journey from the beginning?" he asked. "I'd been searching for the Meridian for months. I figured your mother had hidden it from me, or it had been entrusted to one of you. But your retirement from being feeble protectors kept you in Missing Mountain. Like I said, you are your father's daughter. All you needed was the right—what's the word?—*motivation* to get the band back together."

My eyes burned with angry tears. I glanced at Peter. "You're a hunter?"

He shook his head and loosed a muffled scream.

Uncle Raf rubbed the boy's head. "Don't be cross with Pete here. According to our data, he was the best candidate to profit off something so rare. Something like a *dragon* egg."

"You're lying," I cried.

Uncle Raf beat his fist over his heart. "Every decision you've made is because *I* led you there, Valentina. I knew one of you had hidden the core. I assumed getting you back on the road meant that you'd use it again. We didn't think we'd have to wait until Washington, DC, but now I know how clever you were. Not to mention resourceful."

Hot, angry tears coursed down my face. I didn't want to believe him. But he'd been at our house *coincidentally* checking in on us after months. At the same time I found that new species. A species that looked stitched together, like an experiment. Like the unicorn. I was certain he'd unleashed the firemunk to get me excited about going on another mission. Was anything real? I was tricked.

"You said you'd let everyone go," I said, but my voice was barely a whisper.

"This?" He held up the egg. "This is not someone. This is a thing. Well, maybe it's my future omelet."

"I hate you!" I shouted after him.

He chuckled, then motioned to the hunters. "Move out."

We remained on the floor of the emporium for a bit longer. Peter Bereza cried into his sister's shoulder. Her ruddy face was pinched, and she stared daggers in our direction.

"You need to leave. You've done enough," she said.

"I'm sorry," I said. But I felt like I was numb from head to toe. Like I was running the Scourge's auto-pilot on my whole body.

We closed the door behind the Bereza family and hurried past excited hordes waiting for a hatching that would never happen.

"Let's go after them," Rome said. His anger was back. Only this time, it was aimed at the hunters, at Uncle Raf. "We can't let them get away with this."

"They already have." I shook my head, silent tears spilling down my face as we opened the doors to the Scourge. "You got your wish, both of you. Mission's over."

"Val—" Lola reached for me, but I stepped back.

"Just go." My eyes were blurry and my heart hurt.

But the night wasn't over yet. As soon as I opened the door to the Scourge, there was an awful, high-pitched wail.

"Brix?"

Brixie had been tied up with shoelaces on the steering wheel. She was in a pile of sap. I set her free and gathered her in my arms. I couldn't even promise her that she'd be okay, because I didn't feel okay. How could any of us be okay after that?

"Where do we go?" Rome asked.

"Missing Mountain," I said, biting my lip to stop it from trembling.

After a long silence, Lola drove us out of the sandy street and down a dark road that ran along the beach. I recognized it, but I couldn't remember why. I wanted to point out that it wasn't the way home, but the next moment Lola hit the brakes so hard everything rattled.

"We've got company," Rome said.

Up at the end of the road was a motorcycle. At first we thought it was another hunter. But when she took off her helmet and the headlights illuminated her face, I couldn't believe it.

"Mom?" Lola asked.

I didn't care if we were going to get in trouble, we all spilled out of the Scourge. Mom opened her arms and embraced us. She didn't even yell. At the time, I was so happy to just cry on her shoulder that I didn't even question how she had found us and why she was dressed in jeans and her blue leather jacket.

"Mom, I can explain—" Lola said, but our mom put her hand up.

"Please, I have to show you something." She cupped my face in her hands. Then Rome's. She was crying and, by the looks of it, had been for a while. Mom *never* cried. She cut onions like a boss and when she sprained her ankle chasing after a raptor-pig she called it a boo-boo. Whatever she wanted to say was so serious she was in tears.

"You're scaring me. Tell us what's going on," Lola said, then held her breath for our mother's response.

"I can't—" she said. "I have to show you."

She pulled up her phone and pressed play on a video in her camera roll. It was three seconds long. Scratchy and black and white like a security video. In it, a bearded man was sitting inside a cage. He grabbed the bar and leaned forward, but the video stopped.

It was—

No, I was imagining things.

"Play that again," Rome said. His voice sounded far away.

I couldn't believe it. I wouldn't let myself be fooled. But I knew what I was seeing. I couldn't move. I couldn't do anything but replay those three seconds over and over and over again until my heart felt like it'd been punched out of my body.

Lola gasped. Rome fell on one knee and clutched his chest.

"This was taken two weeks ago," Mom said. "Your father is alive."

300

20

Suzie Q Rides Again

"Dad is alive."

I said it over and over because I couldn't believe it. We hugged and cried and hugged some more, until a car came up on the road and honked at us.

Lola wiped her face and steadied her breath. "How did you find this?"

Rome was still sitting in the middle of the road with the headlights so bright I couldn't see the features of his frame. Me? I'd like to say that I was the brave monster protector I'd always been. But I felt like I was in a dream. You know when you want something to be real so badly, you're almost afraid of it being true?

"It's a trick," I said. "Uncle Raf is tricking us like he tricked us to get the kaylorium core."

Mom touched my cheek gently. She gave a tiny

shake of her head. "It's real. I'll explain everything. But first let's get settled at the campground."

"How did you know that's where we were going?" Lola asked, looking out at the dark water on the other side of the highway.

"When I pinged your phone and saw you were here, I had a feeling. We always stayed at this campground when we had a case down here."

That's why the area had seemed so familiar. Dad always said that his favorite place to camp was near the beach because he loved the sound of the sea, and that one day, he'd take us on a sea voyage. I let myself hope. It was a tiny firefly right in the middle of my chest. Maybe we could finally do it. Maybe we could get to do all the things we hadn't yet.

We got to the campground and parked in the same spot as we always did. Mom and Lola built a fire. Rome and I made sure we had something to eat, even though I wasn't hungry. You ever get so nervous it's like there's a giant rock in your gut? Well, it's not fun. Especially because I love food.

Mom rubbed her hands together over the fire. "I don't know where to start."

"You always say you have to start somewhere," Lola told her.

"A few months ago," Mom said, "I got a location

ping on my emergency phone. It's one only your dad and I had for each other. I don't know why I still kept it charged. I suppose I was having a hard time letting go. For a moment I truly believed there was a ghost in the house. That's how nutty I was."

"I mean, Great-Aunt Hercilia Salazar's house *is* a hundred years old," I said, and she reached out to brush my hair back.

"But it wasn't a ghost," she continued. "It was him. He was sending me a message. I couldn't backtrace it, and neither could some of my best contacts."

"Wait a minute." Rome looked so much older under the flames of the fire. His frown mark appeared as he looked at our mother's clothes. "You've been out there, too. You never stopped."

She bit her bottom lip. "Guilty."

Another Salazar with a secret.

"Are you even a lawyer at the magazine?" Lola asked.

"Yes," she said. "Lauren is really my coworker, but the conventions became an excuse to do some research and follow any lead that could take me to where your father is being held. I helped other protectors and muckers around the country in exchange for their help."

"Why didn't you tell us?" Lola asked, stoking the fire.

"Yeah," I said, getting angrier by the second. "Lola's

303

been sneaking off to the city to help muckers, too. Rome was thinking about joining the hunters."

Lola and Rome looked like they were going to throttle me. I know, I know. Snitches get stitches and end up in ditches. But I'd already been in a ditch on the side of the road and in a crater in Finisterra, so why did I care? They'd all lied to me.

"You all told me not to lie. To tell the truth. To stay home and learn to love Missing Mountain. But none of you could do the same!" I blinked back the angry tears that flooded my vision. "We could have been out there, together. We could have—"

"Querida," Mom said as I finally cried ugly, ugly tears. You know the kind—with snot and hiccups and that feeling like you'll never be able to catch your breath. "I'm so very sorry. I realized that I was failing you. All of you. I didn't know how to be a mother without him. Rome, I didn't know how to pull you out of that darkness. Lola, I thought you were fine without me. That you didn't need me anymore."

"I did need you," Lola said. "I made myself so busy to make sure things worked out, but I'm so tired. Being perfect is *exhausting*."

"Val—my sweet Valentina. I hoped you'd forget about this life. But you're your father's daughter.

You've got his strong heart. You're a fierce protector of the magical and your family."

"I wish you'd told us about Dad," I said.

"I hated lying to you all, but I would have been devastated if it turned out I was wrong. Having that kind of hope is terrifying."

I felt that tiny burst of hope. The firefly in my chest. Being with my family, *for really real*, it doubled so there were two lightning bugs.

"If you're telling us now," Rome said warily, "does that mean you know where he is?"

Mom nodded once, her lips set in a serious line. "Home base . . . for the Order of Finisterra."

I thought about how Uncle Raf never visited us after the accident, or what we thought was an accident. He was so cold, even knowing his brother had died. I remembered how he'd corrected himself at the emporium. *Was.* Uncle Raf had known all along. I had a few words I wanted to call him, but I couldn't say them out loud in front of my mother.

"He knew and he didn't tell us," Rome said, resting a hand on his stomach like he was going to be sick.

"Don't," Lola said. "Don't let him get in our heads. He already tried with Valentina."

"What did he say?" Mom asked.

We told her about our showdown with Uncle Raf and the hunters at Pete's Wondrous Emporium. What he said about me and Dad having cowardly hearts. We told her what Andie did at the farm.

"I'm going to—" Mom made a strangling motion with her fists. Then she took a deep breath. "This is good."

Lola, Rome, and I traded confused stares.

"How is losing good?" I asked.

"Let Rafael and the Order think we've been defeated. Let them think they've won."

"But they *have* won," I emphasized. "They have Dad. They have the orü puma egg. They have our only way to make a portal."

"No," Mom said, reaching into her inner jacket pocket. She withdrew a round, perfectly molded kaylorium coin with an *S* at the center. "They don't."

"You're the one who stole the core!" I shouted, and jumped on her with a huge hug. "You're brilliant. It made us do extra work and steal from a museum, but now it's your fault instead of ours."

Mom frowned, but the corners of her mouth fought to smile. "We'll deal with that later. Right now we have a new mission. Operation Great Rescue of Arturo Salazar."

"Oh my saint." I clapped my hand over my mouth.

"It's just like when Captain Alonso and the Galactic Knight went to rescue the Solorian princess at the Shadow Moon Empire's lair."

Mom kissed the top of my head. "Exactly. Only, unlike them, we have to be very careful. It'll be dangerous."

"Mom, that's like our middle names," Rome said.

"Please, do you know how hard I had to push back so your father wouldn't actually middle name you Danger?"

Rome looked like he might have liked that. For a moment we shared a long laugh. It felt like exhaling after holding my breath underwater. Now, we were only missing two Salazars, and perhaps there was a way we would get them both back.

"Why would they do this to us?" Lola asked, stirring her noodles and taking a bite for the first time. My hunger was beginning to return, too.

"Because they're ugly butt faces," I grumbled.

Mom suppressed a smile. She didn't like it when I called anyone names, even the hunters, but she made an exception. "This might be one of the worst things they've ever done. They've kept Arturo for eight months. They let us believe he was dead. They've kept him alive all this time for a reason."

A thought scratched at my head. I thought of what Mrs. Elwood had said at the farm. There were no such things as coincidences. "It has something to do with Frankenstein's animals."

Mom almost choked on her cup of noodles. "The what?"

I explained about Erik the three-horned unicorn, and the other animals the Elwoods had found. "Not to mention the firemunk. A fire-breathing chipmunk shows up at *our* school on the same day the hunters did? Now that we know Uncle Raf was matriculating us, I'm positive the hunters set that thing loose so one of us would find it."

"I think you mean *manipulate*," Lola said. "But I agree."

"By the way, Mom, my new middle name is Vindication; I just thought you should know."

Rome rolled his eyes. "So, they kidnapped Dad. They took the kaylorium core. They've been creating new monsters. Why? The hunters value tradition. They were created to protect humanity *from* monsters. Not make new ones. What do they gain from this?"

"Power," Mom said. "The Order of Finisterra has more secrets than we'll ever know. But one thing they've always prized is power. If they can control monsters, then they have even more power."

"But monsters are rare," Lola said. "Sure, there are

some invasive species like snugslugs and abelitas, but they're still rare. Otherwise we'd be on a case every single day and we're need an army."

I gasped. I remembered everything Saint Pakari had told us, about the reason he and his sister had closed off the gates to Finisterra. The Order had arrived to their mountain and they wanted to take animals *out*. What if—"They want the kaylorium core to get into Finisterra. It all makes sense. They'd have an infinity amount of magical animals from there! Which means infinity power! Dad probably won't reveal how to make it! That's why they've kept him alive this whole time!"

"We have to get to him," Rome said. "Like, yesterday."

Eight months. Dad had been in that cell for eight months. What was he thinking? Would he even recognize us? Did he hate us for leaving him behind? Then I had a terrible thought. Did my sister know about it?

"What do we do about Andie?" I asked.

"Does she know about Dad?" Rome asked.

"There is *no* way Andie would be with the hunters if she knew they were lying to her about Dad being dead." Lola squeezed her soda can so hard it exploded. "We have to tell her. Only . . . would she believe us?"

"She seems to be drinking the Order of Finisterra brainwashing juice," I muttered.

Rome nodded quietly. "I could go to her. Uncle Raf wants me to join. Double agent, like I said."

"No," I said, crossing my arms over my chest. "I don't trust them."

"But do you trust me?" Rome's hazel eyes were serious. Rome had put his life on the line for Brixie. He'd come on this quest with me, even though he wasn't sure about it from the start. Yes, he'd considered joining the hunters, but he'd done it because he was blaming himself for something that didn't happen.

"Of course I do," I said. "You're my favorite brother."

"I'm your only brother."

We laughed, then got back to planning. The fireflies of hope in my chest multiplied.

"All right, so we need to break into the hunter's home base, rescue Dad, take back the kaylorium core, and send the orü puma egg home." As Lola ticked off our to-do list on her fingers, worry poked and prodded at my nerves.

"I have an idea." Mom took us all in, like she was seeing us for the first time. "But we're going to need a lot more help."

"Leave that to me." I pulled up my chat and sent an SOS to my Cryptid Kids group, and a few others.

Operation Great Rescue of Arturo Salazar was on.

Despite our complaints, Mom insisted we needed rest, showers, and food. We couldn't launch an offensive attack on the Order of Finisterra on empty stomachs. We set up our tents and air mattresses. I fell into a deep sleep and dreamed I plunged through the portal to Finisterra again. This time, it was burning, and my dad was on the other side. It was a horrible video game scenario because every time the portal burned, I was just an arm's length away from him, but I'd fail. In the dream he looked just how I'd last seen him, tall, with dark wavy hair and eyes that crinkled with smile lines at each corner. When I began falling again, I'd scream, then start all over. It's safe to say I did not get the beauty sleep intended before the mission.

When I woke up, my family was already awake and making a racket. "What *is* that?" I groaned.

Was that—

"Cowbell?" I said, brushing my hair out of my eyes.

I hurriedly opened my tent flap and crawled out. Sarah Ellie was there with Brixie flying at her side.

"You're really here!"

Sarah Ellie thumbed in the direction of where her parents were having coffee with my mom and two other people I didn't recognize. "After the hunters

311

threatened the farm, we decided to follow after you. We were already on our way when we got your SOS. We're happy to hear about your dad."

Fireflies pulsed in my heart. "I still can't believe it."

Sarah Ellie lightly punched my shoulder. "Believe it, Monster Girl. We're ready to fight back."

21

Cryptid Kids Alliance

As the sun rose over our campsite, more and more cars pulled up. We assembled picnic tables together into one long table for tech and blueprints of the Order's headquarters, courtesy of Ozzy. He showed up with his group of muckers covered in slime from the oozing ollifantes they were tracking.

"So who is everyone?" Rome asked. He was in charge of cooking up hot dogs while everyone prepped.

I was applying moleskin strips on the soles of my boots. "You know Sequoia. She got a ride from Iggy and his cousins, who help Iggy with tech. Ozzy and the muckers were on a job in New Orleans and came right over when I sent out the call for help. The Elwoods, of course, brought some of their neighbors who know about their farm and want to teach the

313

hunters a lesson. Then there's some of Mom and Dad's old protector friends."

I couldn't believe it. All those people had rushed right over to help us get him back. Then I corrected myself. I could believe it. The impossible was real. I'd started off my quest alone, and then Rome and Lola had joined. But we'd had help along the way. We couldn't have gotten as far as we did without Sequoia or Sarah Ellie. Now we were an entire alliance, and my dad was coming home.

"You really brought us together, Tiny."

I smiled and didn't even mind that Rome called me that. Yeah, I was small, but I had something Uncle Raf didn't. Friends. Probably a conscience, too.

"All right, listen up everyone," Mom said, whistling between her fingers. "Gather 'round for one last run-through."

Everyone did as she asked. I huddled between Sequoia, Sarah Ellie, and Iggy. Brixie sat securely on my shoulder, munching on a chocolate-covered pretzel and leaving the pretzel part behind.

"Val, care to do the honors?" Mom asked. "Capitán?"

My nerves felt like the insides of a pinball machine. I took a deep breath. My hands trembled. I couldn't stop tapping my foot. Yes, I was nervous, but more than that, I was ready. Ready to see my dad again.

Ready to prove to Uncle Raf that he was wrong. I was brave. I was a Salazar. And I was the capitán.

I clapped my hands and used a stick I'd whittled into a pointer. I used it to move around pieces on the map that represented us. We mostly had old *War of the Galaxies* toys and whatever action figures that were in the car.

"We know that the hunters are in their evil lair," I said. "We have three objectives. Number one is rescuing my father. He's here in the western corridor."

"That's where they keep the monsters they capture instead of kill," Joey Rivera, one of the muckers, said. He was about my age and had fingerless leather gloves and cracked his knuckles whenever he talked about the hunters. The hunters had destroyed his building after a hunt gone wrong and never helped them rebuild as promised.

"I didn't know they did that," someone said.

"Neither did we until recently," I said, trading a look with Sarah Ellie. "The second objective is retrieving the kaylorium core."

"I mean, we went through all that trouble in stealing it," Rome muttered under his breath. But he piped down with a stern look from Mom.

"The kaylorium core will be with Uncle Raf." My nerves twisted just thinking about him and the terrible things he'd said to me. But Dad was counting on us. He was alone and didn't even know we were rescuing him. I wished more than ever that we could get a sign to him. To let him know that we were on our way. I needed to stay strong. "There are two extraction teams. Team one is Suzie Q—" Mom cleared her throat and I nervously chuckled. "*Mom* and me. We'll lead stage one: the rescue." I pushed two action figures onto the board. "Stage two will be the core retrieval headed up by team two. Lola and Rome."

Lola slapped Rome's open palm.

"Iggy, you and Sequoia will be the comms team." I moved a toy car slightly off the map, where they'd be stationed close enough for us to catch their signal.

"Ozzy, you and your crew will be in charge of human containment," I said.

Ozzy raised his hand. "Uh—what's that again?"

I pressed my lips together. But Joey Rivera answered for me, slapping a fist against his palm. "We crush hunter heads, bro."

Ozzy nodded, a big grin on his face. "Right on, right on."

"The rest of you will be animal containment, aka stage three." I moved the final action figures on the board. "Once we have the kaylorium core, I'll be able to use the Meridian and send animals through the portal. It's highly important that no humans go through."

"What about the egg?" Sara Ellie asked.

I winced. I still felt the sting of the moment I'd handed the egg over to Uncle Raf and he'd betrayed me. Again. "Hopefully, it's still safe. That'll be among your animal containment task force, Sarah Ellie."

She gave me a salute.

"The Order of Finisterra kidnapped my dad," I said. "They let us believe he was dead. They manipulated us into handing over the kaylorium core. They're experimenting on magical animals and who knows what else. They claim they're the ones that keep people safe, but what they really do is lie and hurt families like mine and yours. I know that's why you're here. So we Salazars thank you. Now." I looked at all their faces. I wanted to combust from excitement. I was really leading my own mission, and my father was waiting. "Let's ride."

Operation Great Rescue of
Arturo Salazar

Mom drove the Scourge like a speed demon all the way to Beaumont, Texas. She let Rome pick the music, which was terrible for my eardrums but good for my adrenaline. We cut across the tail ends of Alabama and Mississippi along the coast of Louisiana until we crossed into Texas late that night.

The area was surrounded by oil refineries and metal warehouses. The headquarters for the Order of Finisterra was a huge gray building that looked much like any of the others in the dark.

Iggy climbed over the seats and nearly plastered his face against the small window of the van. "If I had a secret lair, I'd definitely paint it neon green and have a slide entrance."

Sequoia unbuckled her seat belt and smoothed

down the jean jacket she'd borrowed from Lola. "Then it wouldn't be secret, would it?"

"All right, Cryptid Kids," I said, gathering everyone's attention. "Everyone's in position. Brixie, you know what to do?"

My little colibrix flew back and forth in place. She saluted me. "Stay close by for when youse needs me."

"Right," Iggy said. He unfolded a tool cloth and held up the hunter Salazar daggers. Sarah Ellie had returned them, and Iggy had removed the tracking microchip that had led the hunters to us.

Rome hesitated, but he needed them. It was part of the plan. He pulled on one of Dad's old blade holsters and sheathed the daggers. "Ready."

I gulped a big breath and stuck out my hand. "Protect."

Lola and Rome stacked their hands on top of mine. "Valor."

Iggy and Sequoia placed their palms on top of ours. Then my mom went last. Together, they said, "Heart."

My friends hid. It was a good thing Iggy was so skinny because he fit in the gear trunk. Sequoia tucked herself under the back seat, and I threw the wool blanket over her. The rest of us filed out of the Scourge. The air was hot and sticky from the second I hit the parking lot asphalt, even though it was sunset.

I rested my hand on the back doors of the Scourge, right where Dad's OLD GUYS RULE sticker and my *War of the Galaxies* sticker were. "Thanks for getting us here, old friend."

Then I heard a familiar voice say, "I *really* hope you grow out of your obsession with this stupid van."

I snapped around to find Andromeda. At her side was the blonde hunter who almost shot Rome, and another boy with a crew cut and jagged scar along his jaw. They aimed stun guns at Lola and Mom.

Scar Boy opened the back door and looked inside the back of the van. I held my breath as he scanned the area, then said, "All clear."

"Thanks for the tip, Rome." Blonde Girl flashed a smirk. "Sorry I almost killed you last time. No hard feelings?"

Rome frowned but left our side to stand next to Andie.

"Rome!"

He didn't look at me, only kept his head down. "Andie was right. This plan of yours is going to fail."

"I know you said you didn't want to see me again, Val," Andie told me. "But we just keep meeting like this."

I scoffed and gathered all the anger I'd felt for months. Rome's silent treatment. Lola choosing to do a million things instead of spend time with me, with us. Mom lying and keeping a huge secret. Every bad feeling I'd had rose to the surface as I shouted, "You *told* her? How could you?"

"I'm tired of us fighting," Rome said, looking down at his feet. "I'm tired of being a protector. Andie's right. We need a fresh start. We need a normal life."

I couldn't even look at our mother as Rome spoke those words. But they had to be said.

"Aww," Blonde Girl said. "Your brother's such a soft teddy bear."

"The Order will cut that right out," Scar Boy promised.

Rome straightened his shoulders and stared the boy down. He pointed at Mom. "Mom had Dad's kaylorium core the whole time. She's the reason Uncle Raf couldn't find it."

I kicked him hard in the shin. Mom and Lola shouted for me to stop, but the hunters covered my mouth with a cloth and tied my hands behind my back.

"Andie." Mom said her name. "Andromeda."

"Hello, *Suzie Q*," Andie said, using Mom's nickname from when she was younger. "That's what you are, isn't it? You're more of a *protector* of monsters than you are a mother."

"Don't talk to her like that!" Lola shouted.

"You know, I was glad that Rome called me on

321

your way here. He's finally chosen the winning side. This was inevitable. We were always supposed to be hunters."

"Maybe," Lola said, raising her head high. "But do you know what?"

"What?" Andie snapped.

"When this is all over, no matter what we are, we will still love you."

Andie's face fell. She looked like she'd been ready for cruel words, not ones of love. She ground her teeth and motioned toward the big gray warehouse.

"Miguel, Cali, take them inside," Andie commanded. "I'll have maintenance tow this hunk of *junk*."

I lashed out and kicked and fought as we were blindfolded and dragged inside the warehouse. It was thirty degrees colder inside. The lights were the same ugly yellow ones they used at school, only up high on ginormous ceilings. We were pulled down a long hallway, left and right. I tried to remember the way we came but there were too many turns.

"Did Andie say which cell to toss them in?" Cali asked.

"Throw them in with the pets they love so much." Miguel laughed.

The next thing I knew, we were shoved into a dark room. Before the doors clicked closed, I heard the hum of wings. Then a scratching sound. Tiny little claws on the other side of the door, followed by a beep.

The door crept open, but no footsteps followed.

Brixie flew in a sweeping arc, holding a key card in her tiny hands.

"You should have seen me, Val! I hid in Rome's hoodie like you said and no one saws me. Andie was like, 'I'm a bad mean hunter,' and she didn't sees me take her magic key! I was awesomes!"

I made a noise through the cloth covering my mouth.

"Whoopsies!" Brixie dropped the key and untied me first, then we helped Mom and Lola.

"Excellent job, Brixie," Mom said. "I so wish my daughter had introduced us sooner. But I'm glad that now I know why we went through a hundred jars of honey in eight months."

Brixie beamed and flew around even faster.

"What *is* this place?" Lola asked, rubbing her wrists.

The room was entirely gray and full of cages. Most of them were empty, but a few had tarps covering them. I pulled one back and covered my nose at the stench. A horned llama was nearly starved and sitting in its own filth. Its wool had been shaved completely off so we could see the bones of its ribs. The shimmering horn weighed its head down. It only blinked at me. I started to reach for it when a sound crackled.

"*Capitán, do you copy?*" The voice came alive in my earpiece.

I pressed down on it like Iggy had instructed me. "*Roger, roger, Rat King.*"

Lola snorted and pressed down on her own. "*Did you really choose Rat King as your code name?*"

"*I've got to represent my city,*" Iggy said. "*Now, Rome got us in. The Scourge got towed into some sort of garage lot inside the warehouse. No one seems to be around, but we're still keeping a low profile. This was a good call, Val. There was no way we'd have access to the warehouse grid if they didn't* capture *us first. You really sold it, like blam pow!*"

Rome's alto voice crackled over the comms system. "*A little too well, I might add.*"

"*Suck it up.*" I started to grin but shrank with a stare from my mother.

"*Where are you, honey?*" Mom asked.

"*Mom. It's Alpha Two,*" Rome grumbled. "*Someone's coming.*"

His line cut off, and I felt like my stomach was a bunch of open sparking wires.

"*Speaking of where you are,*" Iggy said. "*The chips in your earpieces allow me to track you and guide you through this maze, all right?*"

"*This compound is huge,*" Sarah Ellie chimed in

from where she was waiting with her animal control team.

Sequoia made a sound of agreement. *"You're in the west sector already, but you have to get all the way from the south bay to the north bay. The hunters on patrol are spread out, which makes it tricky to maneuver, but we'll get you there."*

Mom shook her head. *"The things you kids have learned these days. When your dad and I did this alone, we had two walkie-talkies and sheer luck."*

"And each other," Sarah Ellie added. She was the hopeless romantic one in the group.

"Ready?" Iggy said.

I picked up the access key Brixie had stolen for us. She flew close to me. As we opened the door, I glanced back and made a silent promise to the creatures in these cages that we'd get them home.

"Ready," I said.

Iggy's voice came in loud and clear. *"Make a right. You're going to be clear for three corridors and then there's going to be a group of hunters. They look to be gathered in front of a storage closet. But there's a hall to the left that's all clear."*

We did exactly as he said. As we crept past, my mind raced with the realization that I was going to see my dad. What would I say to him? Would he even recognize me? I mean, I hoped he would. It had only been eight months. What if I was too different? I'd tried so hard to stay the same. The Before Valentina. But maybe I'd changed, just like the rest of my family. Would that be okay?

"Stop," Sequoia alerted us. *"This is where you diverge. Lola, you go straight ahead for the kaylorium extraction. I'll separate our comms lines. There's some interference, so there may be moments when you're in blind."*

"I'll go with pretty Lola," Brixie said. "I have good eyes at night from all the sugar I eat."

"We're going to have to talk about this sugar intake later," Mom said softly.

"Capitán, good luck," Sequoia said. *"Over and out."*

Lola left, with the promise that we'd see each other soon. It made me think that "see you soon" was something everyone said. Dad said it before he vanished—before he was taken by the hunters. What if "see you soon" became "see you never because I got kidnapped." Or was it "dad-napped"?

I shook the thoughts away. Mom and I had to focus to rescue Dad.

Iggy, I mean, *Rat King*, walked us through a maze of passageways. How much space did these hunters really need? The warehouse seemed endless.

"You're at the nest," Iggy said. *"I repeat, you're at the nest."*

My hands trembled so hard Mom had to take Andie's key card from me. She tapped it against the scanner, but the light flashed orange and wouldn't unlock.

"Andie doesn't have clearance," I said.

"Val, get out of the way, you have a booger."

"I do not!" I hissed.

"I think he means *bogie*," Mom corrected him.

But then I heard it. Boots.

We skirted around the corner and pressed ourselves against the wall. I peeked around the bend. Two big hunters keyed themselves in. I knew it might be our only shot, and I had to take it. The door was inching closed.

I leapt and slid on the floor, thanking Saint Pakari that I'd taped moleskin to the bottom of my boots. I stuck my arm out. I'm not going to lie, having a door shut on your hand hurts. Like, real bad. But Mom appeared over me and released the barest pressure so I could get free.

"You've got two bogies! Watch out!"

Mom held up her fingers and counted down. Three, two, one. She slammed the door open, confusing the two hunters. They stared at us with mouths wide open. With their black uniforms and buzzed hair, they could have been twins. Their Salazar crest tattoos peeked out from their collars.

I grabbed the first thing within reach—a metal bedpan (thankfully empty)—and flung it at one hunter's head. Mom fought the second hunter. She kicked, blocked, and brought up her knee to his stomach. He fell on his knees, turning red from trying to catch his breath.

"Mom, I didn't know you could do that!"

"Well," she said, breathing fast. "Now you know."

"Anyone copy?" the hunter I'd hit sputtered. Blood trickled into his mouth from a cut.

I had to think fast. But I froze. There was nothing I could do.

Then I heard the unmistakable chatter of a creature I hadn't seen in days. I yanked off the tarp. Inside a small cage to my right was a firemunk. It looked at me, gripping the bars with its tiny paws, and I knew it was *my* firemunk. The cage didn't have an ordinary lock. I tried Andie's key card and it worked.

The creature scuttled into my hands and sniffed me. Then it turned in the direction of the hunter and bared its terrible little pointed teeth.

"I might not have a stun gun or killer weapons," I said. "But this little guy could incinerate you in seconds."

The hunter raised his hands in the air while Mom tied up the second hunter.

"Drop your comms," I ordered.

He did as I asked and dropped the slim walkie. On the other line, someone was chattering. *"Raúl, do you copy? What's your status?"*

"Lie your pants off," Iggy stressed.

I cleared my throat and picked up the communication device. *"Uh, status normal. False alarm. Over and out."*

I set the firemunk down, and it began to scratch the walls. The sound seemed to wake up the other creatures in cages.

"They'll never buy that," the hunter said. He looked like he was going to reach for his stun gun, but Mom removed it first. "Who are you?"

"I'm—" I was going to say awesome, but then my whole world tilted upside down. I know a lot of people say that when something incredible happens, but it really felt that way. Like I was falling through the portal to Finisterra, the moment when there's a tunnel of stars and light and sound. Because my dad was calling my name.

"Val?" he asked. "Valentina?"

Mom and I yanked off tarp after tarp covering the

cages. There were unicorns, chupavacas, raptor-pigs, and all sorts of other creatures. Behind a set of bars, all alone, was a man. In my wildest dreams I'd imagined seeing him again. That the accident had never happened. That I'd wake up and be in the Scourge instead of Missing Mountain. That we'd found the orü puma and returned it to Finisterra and then driven to our next mission. But never, not once, did I imagine I'd see him like this.

He'd lost so much weight. His clothes were ripped. His facial hair had patches of white. There were bruises under his eyes and cuts on his arms. He gripped the bars and shook them.

"Daddy?"

"Oh, my girl." He shut his eyes and reached for me through the bars of the cage. Then he saw my mom and he made a fist over his heart, like it hurt him too much to see us. To have us see him that way.

"Arturo!" she cried, and fell right in front of him. She touched his face and he flinched. What had they done to my father?

I hurried and slapped the key card. Andie's didn't work, so I tried the ones that belonged to the other hunters. Orange lights blinked.

"That won't work, Val," Dad said. His voice was scratchy, like one of his favorite CDs he played too often. "Only my b—only Rafael can open my cage. There's an override switch on the wall. But it'll open all the cages in this room and the others in this sector."

"How many more rooms are there?" I asked.

Dad winced as he tried to sit up. "The entire western sector is lined with cages, but this is Rafael's room. His office is back there. That's where he comes up with his creations."

"Creations," I repeated. "The firemunk."

When I said its name, the little monster looked up. I dug into my pocket and found a cookie left over from lunch. I threw it at him, and he caught it, devouring the whole thing in one bite.

"Firemunk. Good one." Dad laughed at first. I had forgotten what that sounded like. He'd laughed at everything. He'd loved everything. Then it became a sob. I'd never seen my father cry, so I did, too. "I'm sorry. I'm so sorry. My girls."

"What do they want with you?" Mom asked. "Why did they do this?"

Dad ran his hands through his tangled waves. "My brother wanted my design for the Meridian. The kaylorium core."

"I did as you asked," Mom told him. "I kept it hidden in case anything happened to you. But your brilliant children hunted down another piece."

"I'm sorry, Daddy," I said.

"I should have known." He wrapped his hand on top of mine. "We'll figure it out. We always do."

I reached into my pocket, the inner pocket that Cali missed when she searched us. "But I have the Meridian right here. They can't—"

"They built another one," Dad confessed. He wouldn't look at us. "I had to. Rafael had Andromeda. He threatened her life when I wouldn't cooperate. He throws me in here when we disagree. There are more of us. Doctors. Experts. They work on the animals. I work on the portal."

"We were right," I said. Though this time, I didn't want to feel *vindication*. I just wanted him out of that cell.

"Rafael wants to create a permanent door to Finisterra. The Order has been manufacturing hybrids. But they're unwieldy. We have to—" Dad shivered and had a coughing fit.

"We have to stop them," I said.

My comms crackled with Iggy's voice. *"Hate to break up the family love, but you're about to have company. I don't think they bought your guard voice, Capitán."*

"Rat King says we have incoming," I told them.

"Rat King?" Dad asked.

"I'll explain later." I ran across the room to the control panel. The hunters on the floor shook their heads and tried to scream. I couldn't help but smile as I gave the order. "Extraction one complete. Time for phase two."

"Copy, Capitán," everyone responded.

I flipped every switch across the board. Cages dinged and hissed open. An alert wailed throughout the warehouse as chaos erupted.

23

Finisterra Strikes Back

The first thing my father did when he crawled out of that cage was hug us. Was he shorter or was I taller? He was shaking, and he looked like it hurt to take his first step. He'd always had a beard, but now it was extra long and scratchy. His clothes were shredded like he'd been left to die on a deserted island.

"What did they do to you?" Mom asked, cupping his cheek. Alarms blared all around.

Dad smiled, deepening the lines at the corners of his eyes. He moved her hand over his heart. "Nothing that could ever change the way I feel about you."

And then, Suzie Q, Dad's partner in crime and my leather-jacket-wearing mom, who could beat up a guy twice her size, ugly cried. Never in my whole life had I seen that. Like at all.

"We're all right, querida," Dad whispered. He kissed her forehead, and then mine.

I rummaged through my pockets and handed him a chocolate bar. "It's not much."

Dad unwrapped it and ate it in two bites. "Oh, sweet merciful saint. I'm starving."

That sounded like my old man.

A crying sound came through the comms. *"Are you crying, Rat King?"*

"Me? I'm cool. It's just so beautiful. I love reunions."

"We're all crying," Sequoia said. *"Now hurry!"*

Slowly, the animals emerged from their cages. Wolves with wings. Another horned llama. There was a howler monkey with five tails who barreled out and jumped on the hunter, pummeling him with his tails.

"I didn't realize how much it stinks in here," I said, scrunching up my nose.

"Well, this isn't exactly the five-star Scourge of Land and Sea." Dad winked, but it turned into a wince when he stretched his leg. Mom was right at his side, helping him shoulder his weight.

I opened the door. Animals poured out of the room, merging into the hordes of other animals in the way. Their cries were beautiful and terrible, full of pain and fear. Over the comms I heard Ozzy and the Elwoods make their way into the warehouse for phase three: containment.

"Stay close," Mom said. "We have a plan."

We moved down the warehouse maze with Iggy directing the way. My heart raced faster with every turn. I held my dad's hand, afraid to let go. With every room we passed, more monsters joined the fray. I caught a glimpse of Sarah Ellie corralling a golden zebra and soothing it. We nodded at each other and gathered toward the center of the warehouse.

"Wait," Dad said, stopping in the middle of a hall. Three mammoth snugslugs slunk past us, leaving a sticky trail. "I have to find her."

"Find who?" I asked.

"The orü puma," Dad explained. His eyes focused. His frown returned. He winced when he stepped on his left foot, but the Before Times version of my dad was there. Determined. Brave. "Rafael took her egg."

It struck me that the orü puma was still alive. "Sunku?"

"How do you know about Sunku?"

I shook my head. "Explanations later. Uncle Raf has her egg. It hasn't hatched yet."

"We need to find her." Dad looked at us, then at the traffic of monsters we'd unleashed. I recognized that look. He was scheming, planning. My stomach twisted into knots as he said, "I'll meet you at the rendezvous point."

"No. Absolutely not. You don't even know where it is!" Mom said frantically.

"It's where Rafael is. He's at the center of the warehouse. That's where they're building the door." He tapped Mom's chin, brushing away one of her tears. "I need to do this. I need to finish this."

"He's right," Rome said. His voice cracked. I could tell he was barely keeping it together. *"It's like the Meridian, but a million times bigger."*

My stomach twisted at the idea of being separated again. What if something happened? What if this was just like the last time?

But I knew he was right. "Go. Meet us there."

He kissed my forehead, and then Mom. She wouldn't let him go, and I would have been grossed out, but I was too worried that we might never see each other again. *Again.*

"Make us a path, Rat King," I said into our comms.

And then we were off. Mom and I moved as one with the stampede. The firemunk caught up to us, leaping onto my shoulder, the way Brixie usually did. The halls were full of hunters fighting off the muckers and trying to shove the magic beasts back in their cages. It was enough of a distraction to create a path through the crowded halls.

"How will I know which door?" I asked Iggy.

"Make a right. It should be—"

"Oh sugar," I said.

Mom glared at me, but let it slide.

The heart of the warehouse was still under construction. There was a huge metal arc, glinting gold, copper, and silver. On the platform, Uncle Raf was shouting at a bunch of hunters while Rome and Andie were hunched over a control panel.

We tucked ourselves behind a massive row of crates. Hunters zipped back and forth. Their focus was divided between the portal and the animals on the loose.

"Alpha One, what's your twenty?" I asked, crouching behind a rack of metal containers.

"I'm waving at you," she said.

Mom and I glanced back, but there was only a chunky red-striped bear cub with strange antennas ambling past. "What! An ursuline wasp! I—"

"Focus, querida," Mom said, rubbing my back.

I searched for where Lola could be hiding. She wasn't under the metal platform in front of the hunters' portal. She wasn't behind the crates. I snapped my gaze up. There, at the top of a tower scaffold, was Lola.

"What are you doing up there?" I hissed.

"I needed to get a condor's view. They have the egg up on the platform. I have a theory that Uncle Raf intends on using it as a bargaining chip against Saint Pakari. He's keeping it too close."

"Well, we can't let that happen," I said.

"Did you find—Dad?"

"Roger roger. He's on his way."

"Code Doom." A voice came over the loudspeakers. It was Uncle Rafael. *"I repeat, Code Doom. Initiating test sequence."*

"He's going to open the portal," Rome said.

"Who are you talking to?" Andie asked.

"Me!" I stepped out from behind the crates.

Andie's face contorted into anger. Rome grabbed the kaylorium core and dove off the platform. She tried to grab him, but Rome was fast. He landed on the metal ramp.

"Catch!" he shouted at me.

Leaping into the air, I caught the core. I'd never been much good at sports, but that move made me think I should join Little League or something. *Maybe.*

Uncle Rafael snapped his attention to us. He saw Lola climbing down the scaffold, then Mom and me. A vein on his forehead sprouted like a snake. "Your branch of the family is certainly like a weed that won't *die*. Revenge squadron, do you copy? I need ba—"

"Before you call for backup, Uncle Raf," I shouted loud enough that my voice echoed through the hanger. "Why don't you tell Andie the truth about Dad?"

Uncle Raf turned as green as the kaylorium in my fist.

Andie's bottom lip trembled as she faced our uncle. "What about Dad?"

We were silent, listening to the screams of the hunters and animals. I couldn't tell who was winning from the sound of it, but it was getting closer.

"What about Dad, Uncle Raf?" Andie yelled.

"Since he's too *cowardly* to tell you," I said. "Dad's alive."

Andie's face crumpled. She raised her stun gun at me. Her hands were shaking. "You're lying! It's a trick."

"Andie," Mom said, slowly stepping in front of me. "Querida. It's not a trick. We saw him. We freed him from—"

"He's *here*?" Andie cried, turning her stun gun at Uncle Raf. "My dad's been here the whole time?"

Uncle Raf gestured to the replica of the Meridian. "You know what we've been working for. You know there's always a means to an end."

"Is that what I am?" she asked, and she sounded so sad, I almost felt bad for her. "A means to an end."

The stun gun made a charging noise, and Uncle

Raf's hands trembled. "I can explain, Andie. Just let me explain!"

"I'd love to hear that explanation," Dad bellowed. He entered the room on the back of Sunku, the orü puma. Her teeth were bared, sharp fangs ready to shred through metal or bone. Her snake tail waved in the air and hissed. It was ready to strike.

"Daddy," Andie said. She took several steps back until she hit the railing of the platform. She held on and then lowered herself to the floor.

He nodded at us. I hated Uncle Raf for doing this to us. I hated that we couldn't celebrate our reunion because we were separated. Because he'd taken all Andie's anger and hurt and twisted it into something more painful. For the first time, I hated that we had to save the world. I just wanted us to be together.

Dad climbed off Sunku's back. He looked up at Lola. At Rome. At Andie and me and Mom. He stood taller, stronger. *We* made him stronger. "As you can see, Sunku and I are old friends. When I'd caught wind of her and we went on our mission to track her, Rafael was already there. He saw that opportunity and took us both."

"But the ear we found—" Andie said.

"That must have belonged to the unfortunate hunter trying to take Sunku's egg."

"None of you understand!" Uncle Raf said, fear making his voice shake. "The Order has plans. I had to follow them. That's all I've ever had to do, thanks to you."

"Thanks to me?" Dad took a step back.

Uncle Raf's face twisted into sharp lines and angry shadows. He punched his fist in the air in Dad's direction. "Of course because of you, Arturo! Someone had to be the good son. The one who made the family proud instead of bringing them shame and exile."

"You didn't have to hurt my family to do that," Dad said, anger darkening his features. "But it's over. The Order is not going to clean up your mess. Again."

Uncle Raf breathed quickly, gathering the egg like a shield. "Andie. Please. I trained you. I was there for you."

Andie wiped away her tears. She got up and leveled her stun gun. It whirled with neon-yellow electricity, ready to fire.

Then Dad stepped forward, climbing the platform. When he took another step, there was an audible crack. I didn't realize where it came from at first, but Uncle Raf cursed at the egg in his hold. A tiny paw punched through the scales, the little thing inside prying its way out until a golden orü puma stretched into the world.

Sunku growled and turned her attention to the hunter holding her young. Before I could blink, she charged at him, lashing out with her claws. Uncle Raf dropped the cub. I held my breath, but the little creature had the power of its wings, just barely. It fluttered to the ground, where its mother picked it up by the skin of its neck and carried it off to the corner.

For a moment, Uncle Raf looked relieved. But the orü puma wasn't the only creature Uncle Raf had hurt. The firemunk leapt from my shoulder and landed on the railing a few feet from Uncle Raf. It sniffed the air. It smoked from its nostrils, green slime bubbling.

"You haven't made a lot of friends, brother. You'd better run."

"This isn't over, Arturo," he warned.

"I think it is," Dad said as the firemunk spat a trail of flames.

The roaring stream chased Uncle Raf. But my uncle knew his way through the warehouse, and he vanished behind a hidden door.

"We shouldn't let him get away!" Andie said.

"That's not part of the plan," I said.

I picked up Uncle Raf's mic and broadcast a message. *"This your capitán speaking. I repeat, this is your capitán speaking. All units rendezvous to the*

343

control room for phase four. If you get lost, listen to Rat King lead the way."

"What's phase four, Capitán?" Dad asked me.

I took a deep breath, then opened up my fist to reveal the two kaylorium cores. "Home."

24

Even the Galactic Knight
Has a Vacation Home

When I stacked the kaylorium cores together and pressed them into the mechanism, it wasn't just a portal that opened. It wasn't a crack between the worlds. It wasn't Swiss cheese. It was a whole entire door.

A gateway.

Brilliant lights in every color spun and crackled to reveal the pink-and-purple sky of Finisterra. There was a moment when everyone held their breath. Andie and Mom. Rome and Lola. Dad. He stared at the landscape on the other side with a warm smile, like a memory he'd started to forget.

Me? I was still in charge, don't forget. Capitán, remember?

"The gateway is open," I announced, and then repeated it.

"Yeehaw!" came the hollering cries from Ozzy and Sarah Ellie's crew. They rode on the back of Erik the Red and a giant oozing ollifante with a trunk that spewed neon-purple slime. Behind them were dozens, hundreds of creatures. Most of them ran straight for the gateway and into Finisterra. Others kicked and brayed. I didn't understand. Why wouldn't they want to go back?

Before I could think too much on that, a familiar boy stepped forward. He was still dressed in his black tunic with rainbow embroidery. His staff clicked on the pulsing light at his feet. He didn't come into our realm, but he remained carefully on the threshold.

"My saint," Dad whispered. "You haven't aged a day."

Saint Pakari opened his arms and embraced my father. "It's good to see you, old friend. Though I wish the circumstances were better, eh?"

"Hi again," I said, coming up next to my dad. I held on to his hand. I couldn't have him going anywhere, could I?

"Again?" Dad asked.

"I'll—"

"Explain later," Dad finished. "It seems I have a lot of catching up to do with my family. I know I made a promise the last we met, but you're always welcome here for a change, Saint Pakari."

Saint Pakari shook his head. His pretty brown eyes flicked behind me where my siblings and my mom were gathered, and behind them the Cryptid Kids Alliance. I wondered if he wanted to come into our world, but he'd been gone for so long, maybe he didn't know where to start. Maybe even legends get scared. Maybe *everyone* was scared of change.

He tucked a loose strand of ink-black hair and gave a shake of his head. "I've got my own family to care for. Perhaps another time?"

"Family's always here, remember that." Dad embraced Saint Pakari once more.

A few skinny, horned llamas were slowly, painfully making their way across the gateway. Bringing up the rear was a guinea pig with lizard wings. It wobbled on stumpy little legs.

Saint Pakari laughed as the creature crossed the gateway. Then his whole face brightened as Sunku prowled forward, her cub dangling playfully between her teeth.

"There you are," he said. He picked up the cub like a puppy and pressed his nose to it. The little beastie make a yowling sound. "Let's get you home. There's someone there who misses you."

With a final wave, they were off.

"That's almost it," Sarah Ellie said.

"Almost?" Lola asked.

A handful of strays lingered. Erik the Red. The fire-munk. Brixie. A raptor-pig and a couple of unicorns. No matter how Ozzy and the Elwoods tried to lead them across the gateway, they wouldn't budge.

Brixie flew so close that for a moment I thought she was going to fly away without saying goodbye. She zipped forward and backward. She bit down on her pointy black talons.

"It's okay, Brix," I said, my voice cracking. "You can go home now."

Glistening sticky tears ran down her face. "But—but home is heres. Home is with my bestest friend, Val."

Dad squeezed my shoulder. He looked at me like he was seeing me for the first time. I guess, in a way, he was. I'd tried so hard to be the Before Times Valentina that I didn't realize I was the After Times Valentina. Or maybe I was a combination of both. I was Valentina Alexander Salazar, the one and only. Forever and always.

"That's right," Dad said. "Your home is with us."

"But, Dad—" Lola smiled and said it again. "Dad. What about the rules? Magical creatures and monsters must be sent home to Finisterra."

"Rules change, querida." He kissed Lola on the top of her head. "They have to."

"Brixie can stay!" the colibrix shouted. She flew so

fast she was nothing but a purple-and-blue blur across the giant warehouse.

"What about the others?" Rome asked.

"Don't you worry about that." The Elwoods stepped forward. Mr. Elwood's mustache was still singed on one corner. "We've got just the place."

After we powered down the gateway, Iggy and Ozzy shut down the Order's warehouse. They sent a computer virus through the whole server and crashed it. Joey had suggested burning the place down, but the other way was less conspicuous.

With the animals all cleared out, except those heading for a long spa day in Whispering Valley, we split up and checked every last room and cell. There would be time for celebrating, but the day wasn't over.

Dad led us to Uncle Raf's laboratory, where a room full of doctors and scientists were locked up. Among them was a face I'd only ever seen in pictures. Sequoia rushed through the crown and shouted, "Baze!"

Sebastian Thomas perked up at the sound of his sister's voice. He ran the short distance across the lab to hug her.

"The Order has been recruiting for far longer than I thought," Dad said behind me. He winced with every step of his left leg.

"I don't understand," I said. "Why would they do this?"

Sebastian looked up. One of the others, a young woman in a lab coat, shook her head. "We don't know. We were warned to do as we were told, or our families would be hurt."

"It's over now," Mom said.

But I had a strange feeling in my gut that it wasn't totally over. Not yet.

Maybe I was imagining it. After all, I'd helped save the day. Even if Uncle Raf and some of his hunters had gotten away, we'd found the Order's hostages. We'd rescued a ton of magical animals and monsters and gotten them home. We'd defeated the Order of Finisterra. We had my father back.

Together, we formed a caravan to a new rendezvous point. I can't tell you where it is, otherwise it wouldn't be a secret, would it? All I can tell you is that it was the perfect place to celebrate our victory. Protectors, muckers, Guardians of Skye. We were all together.

Ozzy turned his car into a DJ station, and Mr. Elwood put himself in charge of the grill. Brixie took it upon herself to house-train the firemunk and teach it not to set things on fire.

As for the rest of us, we had a lot of catching up to do. Dad washed up and changed into his old clothes.

They were big on him, but when he smiled, he was my same dad. Oh, he'd changed in some ways. We all had. But we were still family.

Dad took a seat in front of the fire. "Now. Tell me a story."

And I did. I had about eight months' worth of stories. Every case I'd searched for and hit a dead end on. Mom's discovery that he was still alive. Lola running off with Ozzy and the muckers (though he liked Ozzy's music a lot less after hearing that). He listened to every song Rome had discovered in Missing Mountain. And Andie—Andie hadn't spoken a word since we'd left the warehouse, but she remained by Dad's side.

She wasn't the only hunter kid left behind. Mariluz, Cali, Miguel, and a few others had been abandoned. The Elwoods offered a home and apprenticeship to those who wanted out of the Order, but only a few of them took the offer. The others ran off. Maybe they'd go back to the Order. Maybe they'd choose a different way. Mom said we couldn't decide for them.

"It'll be nice to see the old house," Dad said. He sipped on a cherry soda and ate his third burger. "Did I ever tell you that Aunt Hercilia was the one who took me in after I ran away?"

I sat up straight. "No! You never said that."

Dad chuckled. "I guess I have a few more stories left to tell."

"Wait," Rome said. "You *want* to go to Missing Mountain?"

Dad gazed at us. Rome, Lola, Andie, Mom, and me. He shut his eyes and twin tears rolled down his hollowed cheeks. "Would that be all right?"

"You want to leave the Scourge behind?" I asked.

Dad reached out and brushed my hair back. "Oh, querida. We'll always have the Scourge. That's our home. That's ours. But, do you remember in Episode Three—"

"The Queen's Final Song, duh," I finished for him.

"Well, even the Galactic Knight has a vacation home."

Andie snorted. "If you call the blue bogs of Planet Azulmir a *vacation*."

We stared at her, the fire crackling between us and Ozzy's catchy songs filling the night. And then we broke out into wild, loud laughter. Finally, finally, Andie hugged Mom and Dad. Honestly, I couldn't have asked for a better victory night.

You know how I said that sometimes memories get blurry because they're so intense and emotional? Well, sometimes, they're clear for the same reasons. Don't ask me. Memories are weird.

I just know that no matter how old I am, even if

I'm, like, thirty-five, I'm going to remember the cool desert night, the campfire, the alliance that helped rescue my dad and totally save the day.

In the morning, after everyone else went back to our homes and farms and bookstores, the Salazars hopped into the Scourge. Mom drove, and Dad took a long nap with me and Andie and Rome in the back. Lola navigated. Brixie ate Rome's snacks.

We stopped by Fontana, Florida, and left an envelope full of gold and gems we found that the Order of Finisterra had abandoned. It wasn't an orü puma egg, but I hoped it would help Peter Bereza take care of his family, the way I had to take care of mine.

There you have it. The real, true, honest-to–Saint Pakari truth. I know. Some of it is hard to believe. But that's the best part about believing. Sometimes, you just have to let your heart fill up with a million hopeful fireflies.

I guess the worst summer ever turned out to be the greatest after all.

Author's Note

Dear Reader,

I wanted to tell you a bit about my inspiration for helping Valentina Salazar tell her story.

I have an ancestor named Hercilia Salazar. I've always loved her name. It sounded so epic, I wanted to share this name with Valentina and her family. When I was a little girl growing up in Guayaquil, Ecuador, I loved listening to stories of creepy monsters that might come in the middle of the night and get me—especially if I behaved badly or didn't eat the (icky) rice soup my aunt Ne liked to make. Now that I'm a little older, I know there are so many monsters that are misunderstood. Like Valentina says, not all things that look scary are monsters, and so I wanted to write about a family that protects instead of hunts.

Like the Salazars, my family immigrated from Ecuador and made a new home in New York City. Still, the beautiful landscapes of the very real highlands in the Andes inspired the mythical hills of

Finisterra. The Elwoods' magical horse farm was inspired by my bestie's horse farm in North Carolina. The museum that the Salazars "borrow" from doesn't exist, but the stories of Anacaona, Francisco Pizarro, and Atahualpa are very real. There are a lot of stories about the past just waiting to be explored!

Thank you for going on this journey with the Salazars and the Scourge!

Love,
Zoraida♡

Acknowledgments

Valentina Salazar Is Not a Monster Hunter was written during the COVID-19 pandemic. In many ways, I needed this book to get through it. When we look back at this time, many of us will want to forget it. Many people can't. Because every word of this book was written and rewritten during a global crisis, it will always be tied to this period of my life. And yet, Valentina Salazar helped me through it. Her hope, drive, and honesty were the things I needed.

It wouldn't be possible without Mallory Kass, who patiently saw my vision grow with every draft. Thank you for going along with my chaotic monster kids and making this book better.

To the entire Scholastic family, especially David Levithan, Maya Marlette, Alex Kelleher-Nagorski, Keirsten Geise, and the production department. You all rock.

To Lissy Marlin for creating the epic cover illustration. The Salazars salute you!

To my Ecuadorian crew. I love you all.

To my friends, who are my constant source of inspiration: Danny, Natalie H., Sarah Y., Dhonielle, V, Natalie P., Tess, Mark, Alys, Danielle H., and Dharampaul. You all keep me going.

To my agent, Suzie Townsend, and the phenomenal team at New Leaf Literary.

And finally, to all aspiring monster protectors! Let's ride!

About the Author

Zoraida Córdova is the acclaimed author of more than a dozen novels and short stories, including the Brooklyn Brujas series, *Star Wars: Galaxy's Edge: A Crash of Fate*, and *The Inheritance of Orquídea Divina*. In addition to writing novels, she serves on the board of We Need Diverse Books and is the co-editor of the bestselling anthology *Vampires Never Get Old*, as well as the cohost of the writing podcast *Deadline City*. Zoraida was born in Guayaquil, Ecuador, and calls New York City home. When she's not busy writing, she's roaming the world in search of magical stories. For more information, visit her at zoraidacordova.com.